RIESE

KINGDOM FALLING

By **GREG COX**

Concept by **RYAN COPPLE**
and **KALEENA KIFF**

SIMON & SCHUSTER BFYR

New York London Toronto Sydney New Delhi

FIRST
EDITION

*For my parents, for driving me to all those bookstores,
libraries, comic book shops, science fiction conventions, and
monster movies . . . and encouraging all my weird interests*
—G. C.

ACKNOWLEDGMENTS

Over a year ago I took the bus to the New York Comic Book Convention to meet with the creators of this intriguing new Web series my agent had told me about. That was my introduction to the dark but fascinating world of *Riese: Kingdom Falling*, which I am now proud to have written so many pages about.

Many people helped make this possible. First of all I want to thank Ryan Copple and Kaleena Kiff for creating Riese in the first place and for generously making themselves available to answer my questions on all things Eleysian. And my editor, David Gale, for believing in me and making sure this book was everything it could be. And, of course, my agent, Russell Galen, for recommending me for the job and steering me through this project since day one. And let's not forget "Riese" herself, Christine Chatelain, who gave me her autograph at that convention way back when.

Outside Eleysia, I am astonishingly grateful to my family and friends back in Seattle, who rallied to deal with some serious challenges and crises while I was mostly pounding away at a keyboard three thousand miles away. I wish I could have been around more to help out.

Finally, as always, I could not have written this book without the help and support of my girlfriend, Karen Palinko, and our family of four-legged distractions: Churchill, Henry, Sophie, and Lyla. No wolves yet, but that's probably only a matter of time.

CHAPTER ONE

Now

A COLD WIND CHASED AFTER RIESE.

She drew her worn brown cloak, lined with faded remnants of imperial red, around her to keep out the chill. A pair of tinted brass goggles rested on her brow. She depended on her weathered leather tunic, wristbands, and trousers to protect her from the elements. The knife she kept strapped to her thigh provided protection of a different sort.

The wind blew her long dark hair across her dirty face. Years of hard living had not erased the somber beauty beneath the soot and grime, but few of her former admirers would have recognized the homeless wanderer she had become. Her slender frame was lean and taut, any unnecessary plumpness stripped away by privation. She couldn't remember the last time she'd had a decent meal, let alone a warm bath. It was only fall, but already the wind had a bite to it. She was not looking forward to another rough winter in the open.

She trod wearily through a bleak autumnal wilderness; her scuffed black boots were worn thin in places. She hiked beneath skeletal oaks and beeches that offered little in the way of cover or concealment. Fallen leaves crackled beneath her soles. The leaves were hidden by a clammy gray miasma that clung to the ground, while clotted black clouds obscured the sun. The air, which reeked of smoke and chemicals, stung her eyes. She lowered her goggles.

They helped a little.

The desolate terrain and acrid fumes depressed her. Geffion had once been a green and fertile realm, known throughout Eleysia for its thriving fields and farmlands, but that had been a long time ago. She paused atop a secluded rise to gaze down upon the remote valley below. Billowing black fumes belched from the smokestacks of ugly factories and sweatshops. Barren hillsides, stripped clean of timber, bore the scars of brutal mining operations. A handful of crude hovels clung stubbornly to the sides of the pillaged hills amidst squat wooden dormitories that had been erected to house the factories' impoverished laborers. A steam whistle announced the end of one shift and the beginning of another. Streams of downtrodden men, women, and children trudged joylessly past one another on their way to and from work. Some of the children looked like they were barely old enough to walk.

Riese watched from behind the trunk of a withered elm. A sooty film coated the bark, leaving it greasy to the touch. Despite the raw weather she was not at all tempted by the promise of shelter. Rather, she had gone out of her way to steer clear of the settlement below.

She had no desire to end up as forced labor.

A wolf growled nearby.

"Don't worry," she assured Fenrir. "We're not going anywhere near that pit."

The great gray wolf padded at her side, his head level with her hip. She scratched him between the ears, just the way he liked it. His dark ears and ruff were almost black compared to the rest of his fur. She took comfort from the wolf's presence. He had been her only companion for longer than she cared to remember.

A second growl, this time from her stomach, urged her to make camp for the night. She glanced to the west, where the sun was only beginning to sink below the horizon. Smog tainted the sunset, creating lurid purples and oranges. Night was falling earlier and earlier these days, but she judged that she still had light enough to travel by, at least for a little while longer. Perhaps she should put more distance between herself and the dismal factories.

Then again, she *was* cold and hungry. A warm fire and a bite to eat were tempting. She could always continue on in the morning. What did a few extra miles tonight matter anyway? It wasn't as though she had anyplace to go. . . .

"All right. That's enough for today."

She turned away from the rise and the oppressive vista it offered and gathered enough fallen branches and kindling to make a small campfire. With any luck the smoke from the blaze would be lost amidst the noxious effusions from the valley. She removed her goggles and tried to focus the fading sunlight through the lenses to light the kindling. Doing so would spare her flint, which was ground to a nub. At first she feared the polluted sky was too overcast, but then the clouds parted momentarily. She thanked her ancestors as she swiftly captured a feeble sunbeam and directed it onto a single crisp brown leaf, which blackened and smoked before igniting into a tiny orange spark. She blew gently on the spark, fanning the ember into a flame that spread quickly to the surrounding twigs and branches. Within moments a small fire glowed within a shallow pit. She warmed her palms over the blaze. Fenrir settled down beside her.

A brown leather belt was slung low about her waist. The pouches on the belt were not nearly as full as she would have liked. She fished through them to find only a few tough strips of smoked squirrel and a single stale biscuit she had bartered for several days ago. Her canteen was nearly empty too, which did not make chewing the dry, gristly jerky any easier. She would have killed for a cup of hot tea, or maybe even a skin of wine.

Wine . . .

Once, she had sipped the finest vintages from a crystal goblet. A servant would have refilled her cup before she even knew it was empty. Now she'd settle for the dregs of any old bottle.

A weary sigh escaped her lips, along with a muttered profanity. Fenrir could fend for himself, of course, and necessity had made her a skilled hunter as well, but there was no denying that her provisions were running low, as was her purse. She would probably have to risk visiting some small trading post soon, if only to get a new flint. Preferably some insignificant hamlet far beneath the Empire's notice, where she could come and go unnoticed.

She had spent years being no one. She hoped to keep it that way.

"Feel free to go bag yourself a plump hare," she told Fenrir. "You don't need to keep me company."

The wolf remained by the fire.

A girlish scream startled Riese. She sprang to her feet, her hand going instinctively to the hilt of her knife. Fenrir instantly went on alert as well. His hackles rose and his lips peeled back to expose his fangs.

Now what?

She heard racing footsteps pounding through the woods, growing louder by the moment. Riese threw dirt onto the fire, extinguishing it, and stomped out the embers with her boots. She drew the hood of her cloak over her head and retreated into the shadows of the surrounding trees. The lenses of her goggles had been finely crafted to amplify the dying light, allowing her to see in the dark. Fenrir stuck to her side.

The disturbance, whatever it was, grew nearer. She hesitated, torn between investigating and slipping away in the opposite direction. The latter was undoubtedly the smarter course of action, yet she could hardly ignore the naked fear and distress in that scream. Someone was obviously in trouble . . . and perhaps running for his or her life.

She knew the feeling.

"I'm going to regret this," she muttered before heading cautiously toward the commotion. Fenrir whined unhappily but did not attempt to steer her another way. They clung to the shadows as they stalked through the forest. Stealth was second nature to them both now. There was no point in showing themselves until they knew precisely what they were getting into. Perhaps they wouldn't need to get involved.

We should be so lucky, she thought wryly.

The footsteps seemed to be heading toward a small glade nestled between the surrounding woods. Riese and Fenrir crouched down behind a moss-covered log that offered a discreet view of the clearing. She kept her head down. "Quiet now," she hushed the wolf, probably unnecessarily. Fenrir knew when to be still.

They did not have long to wait. The source of the ruckus soon dashed into view—a young girl, ill dressed for the weather. Her dress of coarse brown wool looked stitched together from rags. A fraying shawl, on the verge of unraveling, clung to her shoulders, while her hair had been cut short so that only light blond stubble covered her scalp. She was breathing hard, and kept glancing back over her shoulder. She ran as though pursued by her worst nightmare. Her smudged, dirty face was a portrait in terror, as she watched anxiously for . . .

Them.

A trio of menacing figures pursued the girl. Their heavy overcoats of dark oil cloth provided far more protection than the threadbare garments worn by the pursuers' frantic prey. The men's faces were obscured by wide-brimmed hats and woolen mufflers. The men stomped through the bush and bracken, wearing gloves and heavy boots. They gripped cudgels, hatchets, and a net of knotted rope.

Fenrir bristled beside Riese. Her expression darkened as well. They both recognized the newcomers at once.

Huntsmen.

The ruthless mercenaries served the Sect, a fanatical religious order whose influence had transformed Eleysia into a place Riese barely recognized anymore. Her blood boiled at the sight of the Huntsmen. She had good reason to hate the Sect and all its minions.

"No!" the girl gasped as the Huntsmen closed in on her. Frantic to get away, she tripped over a root and fell onto the ground. She tried to scramble to her feet, but wasn't fast enough. The Huntsmen threw the net over her, entangling her. "No, please!" she shrieked. "Let me go! Don't take me back!"

The men ignored her pleas. Moving silently and efficiently, as though they had done this many times before, they drew the net tight. She flailed wildly but succeeded only in snaring herself further. She clawed at the ground, trying to find something to hold on to, to keep from being dragged away. But she could not dig her way to freedom.

"Let me go! I can't go back there! I can't!"

Riese could not turn away. The Huntsmen outnumbered her, and she knew better than most how dangerous they could be, but she had never been one to turn from a fight. The desperate fugitive reminded her of another girl, many years ago . . .

Despite the chill, Riese quietly shed her cloak. Experience had taught her that the cumbersome cape only got in the way in a fight. She tied back her hair and drew her knife. Its edge reflected the fading light.

It had tasted Huntsmen blood before.

Intent on their victim, the Huntsmen did not hear her approach until she seized the nearest mercenary from behind and yanked his head back, exposing his throat. She expertly drove her knife beneath his scarf and slashed across his jugular. Blood spurted from the wound. It steamed as it met the cold air.

The man died as wordlessly as he had stalked the girl. Only a muffled gurgle conveyed his final regrets, whatever they might have been. He stiffened in shock, then dropped limply to the ground. A studded metal club slipped from his fingers.

Riese kicked it away.

She did not mourn the Huntsman's passing. His kind had inflicted too much harm on her and hers, as well as the whole of Eleysia, to expect any mercy at her hands. No amount of retribution could ever balance the scales as far as she was concerned. Nor, she suspected, would anyone ever miss such a creature. Had there been time enough, she might have spit on his corpse. At the moment, however, there were still two more Huntsmen to deal with.

She had struck so swiftly and stealthily that her victim was cooling at her feet before his fellows even realized they were under attack. Startled by the sound of his body hitting the ground, they spun mutely around to confront her. No threats or angry curses escaped their scarf-swaddled lips. The one on the right gripped a hatchet, while his partner let go of the net and drew a small handheld scythe from his belt. The curved blade of the scythe resembled a crescent moon.

Riese stood over the lifeless body of their comrade, whose spilled blood glistened wetly on her knife. She beckoned them with her free hand, keeping their attention on her long enough for a sleek gray shadow to lunge from the woods. Fenrir slammed the Huntsman on the right to the ground. The wolf clamped his powerful jaws on the man's arm, and the hatchet flew from his fingers. The Huntsman thrashed beneath Fenrir, frantically trying to defend himself, even as the wolf snapped and snarled at him. Lupine fangs and claws tore through his heavy leather gear. His hat spilled from his head, revealing greasy black hair. Bloodshot eyes bulged in fear.

Good boy, Riese thought.

The remaining Huntsman attempted to come to the other's defense. Raising his scythe, he charged toward Fenrir, but Riese had other ideas. She snatched a rock from the ground and hurled it at the Huntsman, barely missing his head. The missile caught his attention, and she sprinted between him and Fenrir. She brandished her bloody dagger.

"Don't forget about me."

The Huntsman accepted her challenge. Abandoning his comrade for the moment, he turned his efforts to subduing their original attacker. They circled each other warily, looking for an advantage. She knew better than to underestimate his skill and experience. She had fought his ilk before.

Stay cool, she reminded herself. *Don't let anger make you careless.*

She did not bother taunting him or trying to negotiate a truce. Huntsmen were driven only by greed and a perverse pleasure in stalking human prey. Before the rise of the Empire, they had been the scum of the kingdom, mere cutthroats for hire. But now that the Sect had bought their loyalty, they had free rein throughout the land. There was no point in wasting words with these men. They would claim their bounty or die trying.

Works for me, she thought.

Hers was a stabbing weapon, while the Huntsman's

scythe was made for slicing. She kept a close eye on it while searching for an opening. His hard, flinty eyes offered little hint of his intentions, so she was almost caught off guard when he suddenly darted forward, swinging the scythe at her skull. She ducked beneath the blow, which whistled above her head, and drove the point of her knife into his gut.

Got him!

Tedious evenings spent honing the blade paid off as it sliced through the man's heavy clothing to the tender flesh beneath. She twisted the knife to inflict the most harm. A soft tearing sensation rewarded her efforts.

He grunted through his woolen muffler but did not immediately fall. He kneed her in the chin, and she tumbled backward onto the hard earth. Her knife came away with her, still clutched in her grip. The blow left her dazed and blurry. She tasted blood on her lips.

Where was Fenrir? Out of the corner of her eye, she glimpsed him a few yards away, still grappling with the second Huntsman, who was also proving stubbornly hard to kill. The wolf snarled furiously, no doubt scaring away every rabbit or deer for miles around. Fenrir had his own scores to settle with the Sect.

The wounded Huntsmen lurched toward her, clutching his stomach. Dark venous blood seeped through his fingers, while his other hand raised the scythe high. It swung down at her.

A warrior's reflexes came to her rescue. Shaking off her grogginess, she rolled out of the way of the descending crescent, which sank into the earth exactly where her head had been only heartbeats before. Lying on her back, she kicked out at her assailant, driving the heel of her boot into the very knee that had collided with her chin before. The Huntsman lost his balance and toppled backward, leaving the scythe wedged in the dirt.

He hit the ground hard and did not get back up.

Gasping, she climbed awkwardly to her feet. Chances were that the gutted Huntsman would not rise again, but she needed to be certain. She spat a mouthful of blood onto the forest floor and wrested the discarded scythe from the earth. The prospect of finishing off the Huntsman with his own weapon appealed to her. Why waste her own blade on the task?

She staggered toward the fallen man. With the light fading she couldn't tell if he was already dead or not. Maybe she wouldn't need to deliver a final blow.

"Watch out!" The girl's voice startled her. "Behind you!"

Riese spun around to see a *fourth* Huntsman charging out of the woods, bearing a hatchet. She hurled the scythe at the straggler. The crescent blade sank into his chest, eliciting an agonized grunt, but did not halt his momentum. He kept on coming, his axe held high. Riese readied her knife.

Fenrir spared her another duel to the death. The wolf pounced on the newcomer, who went down in a flurry of teeth and claws as Fenrir ripped the life from him.

Riese let out a sigh of relief. That had been a close call. She turned toward the girl, whose warning had come just in time. "Thanks for that."

Silence fell over the glade. She waited tensely to see if there were more foes to contend with, but it appeared the battle was over, at least for the moment. Huntsmen littered the ground. Riese checked to make sure they were all dead. Judging from the shredded remains of Fenrir's first victim, the wolf would not need to feed on a hare or squirrel tonight.

Confident that the men had joined their ignoble ancestors, Riese cut the girl free from the net and helped her to her feet. "Is that all?" she asked urgently. "Are there any more?"

"I don't know. . . . I'm not sure." Confused, she stared at Riese with wide blue eyes. "Who are you?"

"Later," Riese said curtly. She had questions of her own, but the three survivors needed to keep moving, just in case there were more stragglers. Taking a moment to catch her breath, she contemplated the gory scene. She and Fenrir had fared well against the Huntsmen, but she was not inclined to tempt fate. "Can you still run?"

The girl tested her limbs. "I think so."

"Good." Riese took the girl's arm. "You're going to need to."

So much for a quiet night by the fire. Along with Fenrir, she and the girl left the glade and the dead Huntsmen behind. The rush of battle still heated Riese's veins as they ran through the darkening forest. She wanted to get far away from here.

"I don't understand," the girl said. "Why are you helping me?"

Riese wasn't sure how to explain.

"I was your age once. . . ."

CHAPTER TWO

Ten years ago

"Princess, be careful!"

The wild boar was cornered and dangerous. Backed up against a hollow log, deep in the royal forest, he lowered his head to challenge his enemies. His piggy eyes glared balefully. Thick black bristles sprouted along his spine, while ivory tusks jutted from his lower jaw, which popped and foamed as he whet the tusks upon his stumpy upper chops, honing them to razor sharpness. Riese put his weight at two hundred pounds. Maybe more.

The young princess, only fifteen years of age, paid little heed to the gamekeeper's warning. They had been stalking the boar all morning, tracking it across the length of the forest, and she was eager to claim her prize.

"You be careful," she shot back. "That hog is mine!"

She sat astride a young white mare at the head of a small hunting party composed of herself, the gamekeeper, and a handful of attendants. Baying scent hounds, too valuable to waste in combat against the fierce razorback, strained at their leashes while their handlers fanned out on foot, blocking the boar's escape. The frenzied dogs raised a racket.

Riese leaned forward in her saddle. Her well-worn hunting leathers and boots were splattered with mud from the chase. A warm summer breeze rustled her wild unbound hair, and she breathed in the rich, earthy smells of the forest. Sunlight filtered through the leafy canopy overhead.

It was a beautiful morning for a hunt.

"I would not presume to deprive you of your prize," the gamekeeper assured her. The man, whose name was Tyr, rode up beside her. He and Riese were the only members of the party on horseback. Years of outdoor living had rendered his weathered face almost as leathery as the beast they were hunting. "But be wary. That boar will not be taken without a fight."

"I'm counting on it!"

She shrugged off his warnings. Tyr had been her father's gamekeeper, in charge of the royal hunts, for as long as she could remember. Clearly he had grown cautious with age.

Just as well, she thought. *I don't need any competition.*

Grinning wolfishly, she drew an arrow from her quiver and took aim at the boar. Her mount shifted restlessly beneath her, making it difficult to get a clean shot. Not that Riese blamed the horse for being nervous. The razorback's deadly tusks could rip through horseflesh like a butcher's knife.

"Easy now," she murmured to the mare. "Show me you're as brave as you are fast."

She let loose with the arrow, targeting a vulnerable spot behind the boar's ear. Alas, the snorting hog swung his head at the last minute, so that the arrow merely lodged in his shoulder instead, far from any vital organs. A crimson stream trickled down his side.

"Hel's spit!" Riese swore in a most unregal fashion.

Provoked by the arrow, the boar charged at the hunters like an armored war chariot. The attendants' hastily thrown javelins bounced off his tough hide as the dog handlers dived out of the way, lest they be gored by the boar's tusks or else trampled beneath its hooves. Before Riese knew it, the hog had barreled through her men and disappeared into the underbrush.

"After him!" she hollered. "Don't let him get away!"

She took only a moment to assure herself that none of the attendants had been grievously harmed, and then she tugged on the reins to wheel her courser around and dug her heels into its flanks. The horse took off after the boar, leaving the rest of the hunting party behind.

"Princess!" Tyr cried out in alarm. "Wait!"

Riese didn't even look back.

The gamekeeper's cries, and the frantic yapping of the dogs, receded behind her as she galloped headlong through the woods. Trampled bushes and traces of red upon the greenery marked the hog's boisterous flight if you knew where to look. Stray branches whipped against Riese's face while her heart pounded in exhilaration. The horse zigzagged around sturdy tree trunks and dense stands of foliage. Riese was impressed by its speed and agility.

"Faster!"

She heard splashing ahead, seconds before coming upon a shallow stream. Muddy tracks on the opposite shore betrayed which way the boar had gone. Spurred on by her rider, the horse vaulted over the stream. Riese let out a whoop; it felt like she was flying. The courser's pounding hooves touched down on the other side, throwing up mud. Riese thrilled at the jolt.

They plunged into the brush. Horns and baying dogs sounded behind her, trying to catch up, but Riese did not slow down. Instead she spurred the horse to go faster. She had already claimed first blood and had no intention of sharing this kill with anyone else, not even the hounds. The wild boar had been terrorizing the countryside for weeks now, uprooting crops and scaring livestock. Riese wanted to be the one to end its depredations.

If only her father could see her now!

Shiny red droplets, glistening upon moss and ferns, led her up a wooded slope, only to grow less frequent the higher she climbed. She scowled as she lost the trail. She slowed the horse to search for fresh evidence of the boar's passing. Had the beast gotten away from her?

The wind shifted. A familiar stench filled her lungs.

The horse whinnied nervously.

"Steady!"

Riese plucked a wooden spear from her saddle. The fire-hardened shaft was twice the length of her arm. An intricate copper band girded the spear about a foot below its tapered point.

The horse grew more agitated, despite Riese's efforts to calm it. It rolled its eyes and flared its nostrils. Riese struggled to hold on to both the spear and the reins.

"Behave!" she scolded her restive mount, which was proving more skittish than she had anticipated. "Or I'm not taking you on a hunt again!"

Seconds later the cause of the horse's fright revealed

itself. A rustle in the bushes less than ten yards away alerted her only a moment before the boar burst from a thicket. He charged at Riese, froth spraying from his jowls.

Wait, she thought. *Not so fast!*

With no time to aim properly, she flung the spear, which skidded harmlessly off the boar's padded shoulders before rolling downhill. The enraged hog kept on coming, his bloodshot eyes as red as fire. Panicked, the courser reared up, kicking out with its hooves to defend itself. Its lips were flecked with foam. A tusk gashed its foreleg.

"Whoa! Steady!"

Riese was thrown from her saddle. She landed flat on her back, the wind knocked out of her, even as the horse bolted down the slope, leaving her to face the furious boar on her own. Still dazed from the fall, she could barely lift her head. She desperately searched the hillside for the spear, only to spot it lying several feet away, maddeningly out of reach. A horn blared much too far behind her. Tyr was on his way, but not quickly enough.

On second thought, maybe she should have waited for the others.

The boar quickly abandoned his pursuit of the horse. He spun about on short, spindly legs and stampeded toward her like a battering ram with tusks. His vicious cutters threatened to rend her flesh. Sharp hooves would shred her to pieces. Riese roused her battered body into action and tried to scramble out of the way, but the boar was coming too fast. Death was only heartbeats away. It seemed she would not live to see her coronation ceremony, only a few months hence.

Farewell, she wished her family. *Don't let this break your hearts.*

She braced herself for the boar's tusks, hoping that her final moments wouldn't hurt too much, but just as she was about to join her legendary ancestors, a blur of gray fur leapt between her and her impending doom. Fangs flashed, and a savage growl startled the boar. He halted in his tracks.

Riese blinked in surprise. *What?*

Her rescuer was a young wolf cub, who looked to be no more than six months old. Riese recognized him from the palace. Wolves were sacred to her family and had served in the Eleysian Royal Guard since the founding of the kingdom countless generations ago. Riese knew the pack well. She had named this pup herself.

Fenrir.

The boar outweighed the cub many times over, but what Fenrir lacked in size and strength he made up for in ferocity. Heedless of the danger, he darted in and out of the boar's vicinity, snapping at its legs. The harried swine swung his head wildly from side to side, trying to catch Fenrir on his tusks, but the fearless young wolf managed to evade the jagged cutters.

But for how much longer?

Fenrir had bought Riese time; she would not waste it. Taking advantage of the distraction, she sprang to her feet and ran for the fallen spear, which had rolled farther downhill. She grabbed on to it with both hands, grateful to see that the fire-hardened ash shaft was still intact.

It was tempting to run away, but she had no intention of abandoning the hunt—or her newfound ally. She crouched upon the hillside and drove the butt of the spear securely into the rocky earth so that its point angled upward. She gripped the spear firmly, with one hand wrapped around its base and the other clutching the shaft as far up as she could reach. She checked one last time to make sure the spear was solidly in place. Her life depended on it.

She took a deep breath, then shouted at the top of her lungs, "Ho, you ugly slab of bacon!"

Fenrir seemed to know instinctively what she had in mind. As though reading her thoughts, he backed off to give Riese a chance to seize the boar's attention once more. He turned his blood-red eyes toward her voice. Her arrow was still lodged in the beast's leathery hide, which was stained with dried blood. *Better his than mine,* she thought.

"Remember me?" she taunted. "The one who shot you before!"

The beast clearly recognized her. Snorting angrily, he bore down on her again. His hooves thundered down the hill.

Riese gulped. She held the spear ready. Sunlight glinted off the copper ring near the top of the weapon. A metal button, molded in the image of a warrior's shield, caught her eye. Her heart skipped a beat.

She had almost forgotten the most important part!

She stabbed the switch with her finger, releasing a catch. A spring-loaded mechanism, devised by some ingenious artisan, caused a horizontal crosspiece to snap upward about a foot short of the spear's point. The metal bar locked into place with a reassuring click.

And none too soon!

Intent on mayhem, the crazed boar charged into the spear, impaling himself upon the shaft with his own weight and momentum. The spear sank deep into his chest until blocked by the crossbar which kept it from advancing any farther. Holding on to the spear with all her might, Riese silently thanked the nameless artisan. Without the crossbar, the skewered boar might well have forced himself all the way down the length of the spear to Riese's vulnerable flesh, goring her with its dying breath.

She shuddered at the thought.

The boar thrashed upon the spear as her straining muscles fought to hold back more than two hundred pounds of porcine fury. The shaft creaked ominously but, despite her fears, did not snap. The frothing boar gnashed its chops. Flailing hooves pawed at the empty air above her head while blood and froth splattered her dusty leathers. She felt its hot, sour breath upon her face . . . and then she didn't. The boar convulsed one last time before going limp. A mass of dead meat hung at the end of the pike.

Gasping, she rolled out from beneath the impaled carcass before it could crush her beneath its weight. She lay exhausted upon the hillside, her arms aching. Breathing hard, she hungrily sucked in air. It reeked of boar, but Riese didn't care.

She was still alive!

Heavy paws landed upon her chest. A wet tongue licked her face.

"Whoa there! It's all right! I'm fine!" Riese laughed out loud, Fenrir's eager attentions dispelling the fear and anxiety she had experienced only moments before. Sitting up, she clutched the squirming cub to her chest. "Aren't you the little terror?"

Gratitude flooded her heart. She knew the young wolf had saved her life.

"Your Highness!" Tyr came riding up the hill toward her, his anxious face drenched in sweat. His eyes widened at the sight of her squatting on the ground, playing with her new friend only paces away from the cooling carcass of the boar. The rest of the hunting party came crashing through the brush behind him. The baying of the hounds echoed off the hillside. "Are you well, Princess? Did the monster harm you?"

"Hardly!" She saw no need to admit that the kingdom had nearly lost an heir. She rose to her feet, wincing slightly, and wiped her bloody hands on her breeches. She was going to be black and blue tomorrow. "What took you so long?"

He dabbed the sweat from his brow. "Praise your honored ancestors for keeping you safe!" He sighed and shook his head. "You should not have chased after the beast on your own, Your Highness. You might have been killed."

Riese felt guilty for teasing him. He could not have been looking forward to telling his king and queen that their only daughter had been gutted by a boar. "It was all right." She petted Fenrir between his ears. "I had all the help I needed."

"So I see."

He gestured to the dog handlers to keep the hounds away from the wolf cub, then raised his horn to his lips. A single loud note signaled that the missing princess had been found. Riese flinched at the blast. It hurt her ears.

Why make such a fuss? She was still in one piece, wasn't she?

She drew a knife from her belt and approached the dead boar. Her men could field-dress the trophy for her later—that was what they were for, after all—but first she wanted to cut a choice portion for Fenrir. The young wolf had more than earned a treat.

But before she could make a single slice, she heard another set of hoofbeats coming up the slope. At first she thought it might be her errant mount, returning now that the danger was past, but, no, it was a courier instead, astride a sleek roan stallion that looked as though it had been ridden hard all the way from the palace. The rider appeared equally disheveled, although the fine cut of his riding gear would have betrayed his origins even if she hadn't recognized him from the castle. Riding past Tyr, he hurried toward her. He tipped his head in place of a bow.

"Your Highness!" he exclaimed. "At last I've found you!"

Riese didn't like the sound of that. "Yes, yes," she prompted. "What is it?"

"Your gracious mother, the queen, urgently desires your presence. I am to remind you that you are expected to pose for the royal portrait this afternoon."

"Oh, Helfrost," she groaned. "Was that today?"

"Indeed, Your Highness. The rest of your illustrious family awaits you."

Riese put away her knife. Given a choice, she would have preferred to face another raging boar. "I don't suppose you can pretend you didn't find me?"

The courier looked pained by the suggestion. "I would prefer not, Your Highness. The queen was most insistent."

"I'm certain she was," Riese said.

From the hillside, looking north, she could glimpse the royal palace of Asgard rising in the distance. Whitewashed stone walls shone like ivory in the sunlight. Its venerable turrets and battlements had stood proudly for centuries, long enough for its origins to blur into myth. It was more than just a fortress or palace; it was a timeless symbol of Eleysia's strength and stability. No invader had ever breached its ancient walls.

Riese called it home.

"Very well," she said grudgingly. She could have ordered the man away, as befit her higher station, but what was the point? Duty called, louder than any hunter's horn. "Master Tyr," she addressed the gamekeeper, "grant me your horse. I fear my own has gone missing."

"Of course, Your Highness." He dismounted quickly and handed her the reins. "Do not trouble yourself about your steed. We'll bring her home, and tend to your prize as well."

She expected nothing less, yet was grateful nonetheless.

"Many thanks."

She cast one last look at the skewered boar before reluctantly climbing up into the saddle. The palace loomed on the horizon, nestled in the foothills overlooking the city below. Towering mountains rose behind the castle. Riese scowled as she spurred the horse down the hill toward home.

So much for enjoying the rest of the afternoon!

Fenrir trotted beside her, keeping pace. If they hurried, she wouldn't be *too* late for the sitting. The wolf barked impatiently.

"I know, I know," she answered. "I'm a bad princess."

CHAPTER THREE

"RIESE! OH, MY BLESSED FOREBEARS. LOOK AT YOU!"

Queen Kara, monarch of the great and noble kingdom of Eleysia, gasped in dismay as her truant daughter rushed into the parlor, bloodied, breathless, and bedraggled. Riese tracked mud across the polished tile floor. Her dusty leathers were caked with dried blood and boar drool and her face was reddened by myriad small scrapes and scratches. Her hair was a fright.

Riese glanced down at her sorry state. "I'm sorry, Mother," she said sheepishly. "I'm afraid the sitting slipped my mind."

The rest of her family had already gathered in the parlor. Unlike Riese, her parents and younger brother were properly groomed and attired, ready to pose for a family portrait in honor of the queen's Silver Jubilee. The scruffy princess ill befit her elegant surroundings. Colorful tapestries depicting fabled battles and victories hung upon the paneled wooden walls. A picture window looked onto a lush green garden whose centerpiece was an antique marble sundial that had been there for centuries. A shadow moved across the face of the clock, marking the hour. Riese hoped she wasn't *too* late.

"But where have you been?" Kara asked. She was a handsome woman whose long brown ringlets had yet to turn gray. She wore a gleaming silver diadem upon her regal brow and a fur-lined robe draped over a velvet gown. The robe was held in place by an oval brooch. "And what on earth have you done to yourself?"

A young boy chuckled at the queen's dismay. Riese's brother was stretched out on a shaggy fur carpet, an open book in front of him. His sandy brown hair hung in bangs over bright, inquisitive eyes. His woolen tunic and trousers were in perfect condition. No more than seven years old, Arkin grinned at his big sister. "You look like you wrestled a bear!"

"A boar, to be exact." Riese couldn't resist bragging. "I killed it myself."

"A razorback?" Her father was instantly intrigued. The king leaned against the marble mantel above the hearth while whittling a wooden pipe. He wore an embroidered cloak and a fur cap girded by a silver band. His broad chest was adorned with medals and ribbons. Although his short, neatly trimmed beard now boasted strands of silver, he stood as tall and confident as ever. He beamed proudly at his daughter, the huntress. "How big was he?"

"Ulric!" his wife chastised him. "Do not encourage her." She circled Riese, clucking in disapproval. "Really, sweetheart, this just won't do." Her nose wrinkled. "Is this how a future queen is to be captured for posterity?"

"Nobody captures Riese," Arkin joked. "She wouldn't let them!"

Ulric laughed, which earned him a stern look from his wife. "That's enough, both of you. You're not helping." Clearly disappointed by her headstrong daughter, the queen took charge of the situation. She clapped her hands, and a small army of lady's maids scampered into the parlor. Kara nodded at Riese. "Believe it or not, girls, this unsightly ruffian is my daughter and heir, the princess Riese. Please make her more presentable, as briskly as humanly possible."

The maids rushed to their task. They hustled Riese into an adjoining antechamber, where an appropriate gown, shoes, and jewelry had already been laid out for her. The servants fell upon Riese with terrifying efficiency. Her filthy garments were stripped off and bundled away before she could even ask to hang on to her dagger. She caught a glimpse of her bare back in a mirror. The wolf's-head brand upon her shoulder marked her forever as a princess of Asgard. Riese scowled at the raised red emblem.

Sometimes she wished she could scrape the damn thing off.

The busy servants wrestled her into a heavy brocade gown that felt much less comfortable than her outdoor gear. She winced as they tugged on her hair with combs and brushes and dabbed at her face with a damp rag. She grunted in protest but found herself seriously outnumbered. Once, years ago, she had made the mistake of trying to feed a loaf of bread to a flock of hungry pigeons. Within seconds she had found herself under siege, surrounded on all sides by a mob of fluttering, insistent pests. She had barely been able to breathe.

Much like now.

"Easy now!" she ordered. "Not so rough! I'm your princess, not a mannequin!"

"Yes, Your Highness." The servant girls backed off, suitably chastised. Riese felt a little more in control, even if she still wished she were back in the forest. The servants went about their work with more deference. "If you please, Your Highness."

Faster than Riese would have thought possible, she was escorted back into the parlor, looking and feeling like a doll. The maids dutifully presented her to the queen before retreating back into the hall.

"Ah, that's a more becoming look for a princess," Kara said, her mood warming slightly. She came forward to inspect Riese more closely. She tried and failed to wipe away a scratch on Riese's cheek. "Your face still looks like you've been cuddling a porcupine, but I suppose the artist can leave the scratches out."

"Indeed, Your Majesty." The court portrait painter waited behind his easel. Harl of Gleipnir was a gnomish fellow with a bald pate and a waxed mustache, and he wore a rumpled linen smock. A rainbow of pigments was permanently embedded beneath his nails. He had a piece of charcoal tucked behind one ear. "You can count on me to present the princess at her best."

"Very well," the queen said. "It seems we are ready to proceed."

"Very good, Your Majesty." Harl gestured toward the hearth. "If you would all kindly take your places."

The family posed in front of the unlit fireplace. Kara and Ulric stood in the back, with their children before them.

Riese felt like a prize goat on display. As she understood it, Harl was simply doing some preliminary studies today, which meant that she was going to have to go through this all again sometime soon. She forced herself to smile.

"Perfect, perfect," the artist declared. He applied the charcoal to his canvas. "Stay just as you are."

Riese's stomach growled, reminding her that she had not eaten for hours.

Arkin giggled beside her. "Did somebody hear a bear?"

"Yes." She poked him with her elbow. "And it's hungry enough to eat a prince."

"Hush, children," Kara whispered. "Let Master Harl do his work."

Riese squirmed impatiently. Holding a single pose while smiling like a ninny proved infinitely harder and more exhausting than chasing a wild boar on horseback. "Is this going to last much longer?"

"If you had been here on time," her mother chided her sternly, "we might have been done already."

Riese groaned inwardly. She felt a lecture coming on.

"You aren't a child anymore, Riese," the queen said. "You need to take your responsibilities more seriously, especially with your coronation coming up."

"Don't remind me," Riese muttered.

By Eleysian tradition she was next in line for the throne. On her sixteenth birthday she would be formally coronated as crown princess and subjected to a ridiculously elaborate ritual that declared her of marrying age, with all the onerous duties and obligations that entailed. Riese was looking forward to the ceremony, and its consequences, as eagerly as she would having a tooth yanked out. She had no wish to be yoked forever to some boring prince or noble just for the sake of a convenient alliance. *I'm only fifteen. I haven't even kissed a boy yet!*

Not that being a princess made that very likely.

"Your mother is right," her father chimed in. "Like it or not, you will be queen one day. Our dynasty has brought peace and prosperity to the land. The people look to us for stability and reassurance. You are more than just our daughter. You are a symbol of Eleysia's future."

It felt like a sentence of life imprisonment. "But what if I don't want to be a symbol?"

"No frowning, please," the painter interrupted. "Smiles, everyone."

Easy for you to say, Riese thought. *Your future wasn't set the day you were born.*

"Excuse me, Your Majesties." A door swung open and an elderly gentleman entered the parlor. A renowned scholar, Mimir had tutored two generations of Eleysian royalty. Riese's parents still valued his counsel. He wore a dark blue robe over his portly form, while peering through a pair of thick glass spectacles. His lantern jaw was clean-shaven, and he wore his silvery mane long, perhaps to compensate for his receding hairline. He hobbled toward the family using a cane. "I apologize for intruding, but I'm afraid an urgent matter demands your attention."

The queen noted his somber tone. She and Ulric exchanged worried looks. "Does it . . . concern the matter we discussed before?" she asked.

"I fear so, Your Majesty."

Riese didn't like the sound of this. Mimir would not have interrupted unless this were serious.

Kara nodded gravely. She turned to the painter. "Master Harl, I'm afraid we will have to continue this session later. It seems there is business to attend to."

"Of course, Your Majesty," the painter assented readily. "I am at your disposal."

Although grateful for the interruption, Riese was worried as well. "What is it?" she asked. "What's happening?"

"Nothing you need worry about right now," Kara said unconvincingly. "Your father and I simply have some business to see to. You and your brother may attend to your studies."

Riese frowned. At her coronation she needed to be able to recite the entire genealogy of her line, stretching all the way back to antiquity, but the prospect of memorizing all those ancient names and unions struck her as unbearably tedious. She'd much rather be hunting and riding and sparring with the royal guards.

"We'll see you both at supper." Kara mustered a teasing smile. "And, Riese, try to avoid behaving like a berserker in the meantime."

"No promises," Riese said.

Her curiosity unsatisfied, she watched as her parents left the parlor in the company of Mimir. The painter began to gather up his tools and sketches, but Riese wasn't ready to let him go yet. "Excuse me, Master Harl, do you have any idea what that's all about?"

"Yes!" Arkin chimed in. "Why are Mother and Father worried?"

Riese wasn't surprised by her brother's curiosity. Despite his age, he had always taken a greater interest in affairs of state than she had. A shame the throne passed through the female line; he would have made a great king someday. He took more after their mother than Riese did.

"I'm sure it's not my place to speculate," the artist said hesitantly.

"Please," she asked. "Everyone knows how wise and worldly you are. You're so observant. You don't miss anything." She tugged on his sleeve. "You must have *some* idea of what's happening."

Her flattery worked wonders. "I suppose," he said, lowering his voice, "it probably has something to do with the Nixian situation."

Riese smiled. "Tell me about it."

"Well, as you've surely heard," he said, making a rash and unwarranted assumption, "Nixe has been stirring up trouble lately. No surprise there, considering their recent hardships."

Nixe was a minor kingdom to the north of Eleysia. Riese had never given it much thought before. "What troubles?"

"Fires and floods and everything!" Arkin said, jumping in. "I heard all about it! The generals took over the country and threw out the king and queen!"

"That's right, young prince," Harl confirmed. "The Nixians have suffered every sort of calamity over the last few years. Burst dams, wildfires, blighted crops, tainted wells, a military coup . . . It's almost as though they've been cursed. Your gracious parents have offered them assistance, of course, but it seems that wasn't enough. The Nixians have taken to raiding neighboring kingdoms. And they're moving toward us."

That seemed an amazingly foolhardy move on the Nixians' part. Desperate or not, they were playing with fire. Eleysia took its borders seriously.

"They haven't attacked us, have they?" Riese asked.

"Not yet," Harl said. "Although, there have been a few minor border skirmishes. But the Nixians are getting bolder, and the fighting is getting closer to our own borders." Worry showed beneath the paint speckling his features. "It could mean war."

Riese found that hard to believe. "Surely it won't come to that." Eleysia had not been forced to unleash its might for longer than anyone could remember. The great victories of the past were ancient history. "The Nixians wouldn't dare defy us."

"But what if they do?" Arkin asked anxiously. "Would Father have to go to war?"

His frightened tone made her regret bringing the subject up. Arkin was too young to have to fret about such things. They both were.

"Don't be silly." She deliberately made light of his worries. "You're just going to give yourself bad dreams again." She mussed his hair and drew him away from the painter. "That will be all, Master Harl. You may go."

"Yes, Your Highness."

The artist departed, but his ominous words seemed to linger in the air. "I'm scared," Arkin confessed. "I don't want there to be a war."

"I told you, it's all just talk," she said. "Forget all this boring grown-up stuff. Let me tell you all about the boar I killed."

That did the trick. Arkin's eyes widened in anticipation of all the gory details. "Was he huge?"

"Monstrous! And as fierce as a demon. . . ."

She hoped her story would make him forget all this crazy war talk. Their parents could handle the Nixians. They were the king and queen of Eleysia, after all. They knew what they were doing.

If only they could rule forever—so she wouldn't have to!

CHAPTER FOUR

Riese couldn't sleep.

She tossed and turned and kicked off the covers. Her bedroom was hot and stifling. Plastered white walls seemed to close in on her, suffocating her. Whenever she shut her eyes, those cursed genealogies paraded before her, a chain of hallowed ancestors binding her to the past—and defining her future. How was she supposed to sleep with an entire dynasty weighing down on her?

A doorway connected her chamber to Arkin's room next door. They often kept the door open. Arkin suffered from bad dreams, and it comforted him to know that his big sister was within earshot. She sometimes heard him crying out in the dark.

But not tonight.

At least one of us is sleeping well, she thought. She stared restlessly at the ceiling, before deciding she couldn't take being cooped up in the palace anymore. *I need to get out of here.*

Moving quietly, she slipped out of bed and tiptoed over to her wardrobe, where she changed into her riding gear, which had already been laundered by the palace's assiduous staff. She sniffed her tunic; it didn't smell like boar anymore. A hooded cloak and boots completed her ensemble. She retrieved a brass lantern from beneath her bed.

A stone fireplace occupied one wall. In the fall and winter it housed a crackling blaze that kept the bedchamber warm and toasty, but in the summer it often sat empty. No logs or coals were stacked within the hearth, which was fine with Riese.

She had found another use for the fireplace.

She crept over to the hearth, and then knelt and reached up into the chimney. A brass lever was hidden out of sight there. She yanked on it and heard a familiar click. Ancient gears creaked behind the fireplace, and the glazed back wall of the hearth slid away, revealing a secret passageway. Darkness hid what lay beyond.

Riese silently thanked her brother for stumbling onto the fireplace's secret while delving through the palace library. The castle had a venerable history, dating back to less civilized days when it had been more fortress than palace. Riese suspected that the hidden exit had been built to allow the fortress's inhabitants to escape in the event of a siege. Who knew? Perhaps it had also been employed over the years by illicit lovers conducting secret trysts. In any event the passage had been her and Arkin's secret for some time now. She doubted that even Mimir or her parents knew about it.

Without hesitation she crawled into the pitch-black cavity. The hidden doorway clicked shut behind her. A spiral stairway led several stories down, and a dank smell wafted upward from somewhere far beneath the castle, below even the cellars and dungeons. She lit the lantern and held it aloft. A flickering light cast dancing shadows upon the bare stone walls. She watched her step as she descended the stairs. Cobwebs hung upon the walls. Mice scurried out of her way.

The forgotten steps led to an underground cistern, built to store drinking water, for use in the event of a siege. Rain was channeled into the vast reservoir, whose vaulted ceiling was supported by sturdy granite columns. Ceramic tiles and mortar kept the water from draining into the earth. Bats, already returned from their nightly hunting, hung from the ceiling. Mold coated the walls. Stagnant air smelled of mildew, while the rippling water reflected the glow of her lantern. The water looked to be only knee-deep, but a paved walkway along the edge of the reservoir spared her from having to wade through it. The damp stones were slippery, forcing her to walk carefully until she reached a shorter series of steps that ascended to a drainage tunnel leading out of the castle. Riese assumed the tunnel was there to keep the cistern from overfilling. She glimpsed moonlight at the other end.

It was a tight squeeze, but Riese crawled through the tunnel on her hands and knees. She emerged from a cleft in a hillside beyond the outer walls of the palace. She found a bundle of supplies hidden just inside the cave, where she had left them before. She claimed a foot-long metal baton for protection. Eleysia was a peaceful kingdom, but it wasn't paradise. There were still bandits and other unsavory individuals lurking in the shadows sometimes. She needed to be able to defend herself if necessary.

Pine-covered mountains rose behind the palace, defending it from sneak attacks. The pipe emptied into a ravine shielded from the view of the sentries above. She doused her lamp and made her way by moonlight up the ravine until she reached a wooded trail leading farther up into the hills. Fallen leaves and needles littered the path. An owl hooted in the branches, and a wolf howled in the distance. She was not frightened by the latter. Legend had it that the founder of her dynasty had been suckled by a she-wolf many centuries ago. Wolves were family.

Riese took a deep breath of the fresh night air, which tasted wonderful after the dank odor of the cistern and the stifling atmosphere of the palace. *That's more like it,* she thought. Let her parents rule Eleysia, just as they always had. *I'd rather enjoy my freedom while I can.*

There was a special place, not far from here, that Riese knew very well. She hiked briskly up the path, eager to reach her destination. Although the moon provided plenty of illumination, she probably could have navigated the route with her eyes closed. The way was that familiar to her.

She heard the roar of the falls before they came into view. Ahead of her the path opened up onto a ledge overlooking a steep cliff face. A waterfall flowed over the cliff to a moonlit lake at least fifty feet below. The water came from a stream trickling down a rocky slope behind the ledge, but that was hardly the most striking aspect of the scene.

Standing stones, erected by some bygone race, formed a semicircle atop the ledge. Upright slabs of weathered granite, they stood twice as high as the tallest man. Although a few of the stones tilted precariously, only a single monolith had fallen, forming a bench of sorts beside the others. Time and the elements had all but erased the runes inscribed on the stones, leaving their origins and purpose lost to history. Had this place once been a temple to some forgotten god, or perhaps a memorial to a legendary birth or battle? Riese had no idea, but she could only imagine the effort it had taken to haul the stones to the top of the cliff and set them standing for all eternity. Clearly the ancients had regarded this place as sacred. She knew how they felt. The secluded location had always been a sanctuary of sorts, where she could go to escape the suffocating rigors of her royal duties.

But tonight her sanctuary had been violated.

To her dismay she heard a stranger humming up ahead, beneath the stones. She ducked behind a bush and peered at the intruder, who turned out to be a wiry, sandy-haired youth perhaps only a few years older than she. He perched on the edge of the cliff, sketching in a notebook. A worn leather vest complemented his simple tunic and trousers. His clothes appeared humble but in good condition, so that he looked like a commoner, not a beggar. A pair of tinted goggles rested on his brow. He gazed out over the falls at the rear of the palace.

Riese scowled. How she was supposed to be alone with her thoughts with this stranger hanging about? This was her personal refuge. He had no right to invade it. Who did he think he was? He was trespassing upon royal land. By rights she could have him jailed, although that seemed a bit excessive. Still, she hadn't crawled through that slimy tunnel just to turn back now, and she had no intention of sharing her spot with this interloper. Maybe there was some way to scare him away?

She glanced down at the baton in her hand, which reminded her of her earlier concerns about bandits. She smiled mischievously. Pulling her hood over her head, she pressed a metal stud along the side of the rod. A spring-loaded mechanism caused the baton to double in length, turning it into a full-size staff. Just the sort of weapon a genuine cutthroat might carry.

"Ho, lambkin!" Without pausing to consider her actions, Riese sprang from the bushes. She made her voice sound as gruff and menacing as possible, while whirling the staff above her head. "Say your prayers, dead man! This hill is mine!"

She expected him to run for his life, so that she could have the ledge to herself again, but instead he hastily stuck his sketchbook beneath his vest and snatched up a long wooden staff of his own, which she had failed to notice lying by his side. He jumped to his feet and charged her. His staff came swinging at her head.

What in Hel's name? She parried the blow only seconds before it connected with her skull. To her surprise she suddenly found herself in the middle of a heated battle. The nameless youth fought in earnest, no doubt believing his life to be in jeopardy. Their staffs cracked against each other in a spirited exchange of attacks and blocks. Riese tightened her grip on her stave, lest it be knocked from her hands.

"Fool!" she grunted, still clinging to her disguise. "You should've run when you had the chance!"

"I don't know," he fired back. His defiant green eyes met hers. "Looks to me like you chose the wrong victim."

Not too bright, she decided, *but I can't fault his courage.*

Caught up in the fight, she refused to give ground. Her father's soldiers had trained her well, so she was no novice here. She gripped the staff with both hands, being careful to keep her fingers out of the way of her opponent's attacks, and blocked his blows with the middle of the rod, while deftly jabbing at him with both ends of her weapon. Steel clanged against wood as the falls rumbled in the background. White water crashed down onto the jagged rocks below.

They battled fiercely at the brink of the cliff. The youth knew what he was doing, she gave him that. Seeing through what she thought was a clever feint, he blocked her real attack and followed through with a sideways swing at her ribs, which she dodged just in time. Her heart pounded in excitement. Her trainers always went easy on her. This was a real fight—against a worthy foe.

She'd have to remember to thank him afterward.

When in doubt, fight dirty, she thought. Spinning her staff about, she launched an overhead attack on his head and shoulders. He brought his own staff up to meet hers and while his eyes and weapon were focused elsewhere, she jumped forward and kicked him hard in the stomach. Her heel slammed into his gut.

"Oof!" He staggered backward, the wind knocked out of him.

She lunged ahead, intending to knock his legs out from under him. After that? Well, she wasn't quite sure what she had in mind. Maybe give him another chance to run away?

But before she could deliver the decisive blow, the ground itself betrayed her. A patch of loose mud and gravel slid out from beneath her foot, and she lost her balance. One minute she was on the verge of victory, and the next she found herself going over the edge of the cliff. Frantic, she let go of her staff and grabbed on to a slippery root. Hanging on by her fingertips, she dangled over the brink. Gravity tugged at her legs. Dislodged pebbles and clumps of dirt preceded her onto the rocks below. The root began to tear loose. A high-pitched scream completely spoiled her attempt to pose as a ruthless bandit.

"Hold on!" A strong hand closed on her wrist. "I've got you!"

Taking care not to follow her over the edge, he pulled her to safety. She helped by wriggling forward once she managed to get elbows up onto the ledge. Her hood fell back, exposing her face.

His eyes widened. "Huh? What kind of bandit are you?"

"I'm no brigand," she confessed. "I just wanted to scare you."

Exhausted, she plopped down next to him, a safe distance from the edge. Their discarded staffs lay atop each other a few paces away.

"A risky prank," he observed. "I could have killed you."

She snorted. "Don't flatter yourself."

He looked her over. "You always this reckless?"

"Look who's talking. Why didn't you just run away like you were supposed to?"

"Why should I? I can take care of myself." He shrugged. "Besides, I like the view."

"The view?" she echoed. "You fought a murderous bandit for the view?"

"Er, when you put it that way . . ." He grinned sheepishly. "I guess we were both being a bit reckless."

Fair enough, she thought. "Good thing we didn't kill each other, then."

"Well, the night is young . . ."

Riese laughed. Whoever he was, he was growing on her. *At least he doesn't treat me like a princess,* she thought, *and he did save my life.* Plus, to be honest, he was actually somewhat pleasant to look at. Wavy brown hair sprouted above the straps of his goggles, which were raised high enough to give her a good luck at those emerald eyes. She liked his smile, too.

Maybe they could share this spot, after all.

He held out his hand. "My name's Micah, by the way. What's yours?"

Riese hesitated. She didn't want to ruin things by revealing her exalted status. "Valka." She took his hand. "You can call me Valka."

The name, which had just popped into her head, came from one of the ancient chronicles she'd been forced to study. It had belonged to a rebellious princess who was said to have fled an arranged marriage by becoming a wanderer in far-off realms. She had rather liked that story.

"Pleased to meet you." He released her hand and leaned back against one of the standing stones. "You come here often?"

"Sometimes," she admitted. "When I want to think."

"About what?"

Riese frowned. Maybe he was a little too inquisitive?

"Nothing in particular." She quickly changed the subject. "What about you? How is it that you're abroad at this late hour?"

"I'm an apprentice to a local apothecary," he volunteered. "Often this means prowling the hills in search of the odd root or herb. After dark is best, especially for the night bloomers. Besides, it gets me out from under the old tyrant's thumb for a while."

She could sympathize. Daytime brought too many demands on her as well. "I understand perfectly."

"Really?" He eyed her curiously. "What do you do?"

Riese thought fast. "I'm just a serving girl . . . at the palace."

"The palace?" He sounded both impressed and interested. "That must be exciting. Have you met the royals?"

"A few times," she hedged. This was not a discussion she wanted to encourage, so she latched on to another topic. "What was that book you were scribbling in before?"

"You saw that?" His hand went to his vest pocket. "I just like to sketch the plants and flowers I find, that's all." He tried to shrug the whole matter away. "Nothing very interesting."

"I don't know about that." As artists went, he was much more appealing than hunched old Harl back at the palace. "Can I see?"

He shook his head. "Sorry." An apologetic smile softened his response. "Nothing personal. I'm just not comfortable showing other people my sketches yet. Maybe later, when I'm better."

She found his shyness about his art endearing. "So you don't mind dueling with bandits, but you're afraid to let people see your drawings?"

43

"Something like that."

"All right." She didn't press him. After all, it wasn't as though she were revealing everything to him either. Beneath her leather tunic her royal brand itched.

She fought the urge to scratch it.

They sat in silence after that, simply enjoying the night. The ivory walls of the castle, although visible from atop the ledge, seemed comfortably far away. The city itself lay beyond the castle, at the base of the mountains. Distant streetlights glowed like stars far below Riese and her new acquaintance. He was right, she decided. The view was worth fighting for.

Perhaps even more so when you had someone to share it with.

The sky was just beginning to lighten when he finally rose to his feet. "Long day ahead. I suppose I should get a few hours' sleep." He reached down to help her up. "Perhaps we'll meet here again sometime?"

She was sorry to see him go, despite having done her best to brain him earlier.

"I'd like that," she admitted.

CHAPTER FIVE

"Riese, wake up."

An eager hand shook her, rousing her from an unplanned nap. She woke up on a couch in the parlor, where she'd been unhappily studying for her coronation ceremony. A heavy tome upon her lap lay open to an illuminated family tree with far too many branches and roots. She must have dozed off reading it.

Small wonder, she thought. The dreary history was enough to put anyone to sleep, even if she hadn't been out all night meeting a strange boy at the falls. Riese had crept unnoticed back into the castle shortly before dawn. She wondered if Micah was just as drowsy today.

"Come on!" Arkin nudged her again. He was annoyingly bright-eyed and alert. "Now is no time to sleep the day away."

She yawned and rubbed her eyes. Her simple burgundy dress was rumpled. She put the boring tome aside. "What is it?"

"The Nixian ambassador is here." He was practically bouncing with excitement. "Mother and Father are meeting with him now."

"Nixian?" She recalled the border skirmishes that had called her parents away from the portrait sitting the day before. "Has he come to apologize?"

If the Nixians promised to stop raiding their neighbors and offered restitution, she was sure Eleysia would pardon their recent transgressions. Her parents could be quite forgiving, as she knew better than most.

"I don't know," Arkin answered. "Let's go see."

The throne room was on the ground floor of the castle, a few stories down from the family's private chambers. Riese and Arkin took the stairs two at a time, then hurried through the palace's bustling corridors, which were filled with courtiers, guards, scribes, and servants going about their business. Riese hoped the meeting hadn't started without her. She seldom paid much attention to state affairs, which she usually found unbearably tedious, but this was different. If there was actually a chance, however remote, of war breaking out, she didn't want to miss it.

Grim-faced guards wearing steel helmets and chain mail were posted outside the main entrance to the throne. A pair of heavy oak doors, wide enough to allow a team of horses through, barred their way.

"Hel's spit," Riese cursed.

"The meeting is supposed to be private," Arkin explained. "But I know how we can listen in."

Taking her hand, he guided her away. They bypassed the sealed entrance to approach the chamber from behind. A narrow archway led them to a musty passage, scarcely larger than a closet. Hanging drapes blocked their view, but she heard muffled voices on the other side of the heavy fabric. Arkin raised a finger to his lips, signaling her to silence, before drawing the drapes open just a crack. She peered over his shoulder as they spied on the meeting.

The throne room was the grandest chamber in the palace. Tapestries adorned the wall, and chandeliers hung from the high vaulted ceiling. The king and queen reigned from matching wooden thrones atop an elevated stone dais at the back of the chamber. The polished oak arms of the thrones were carved in the likenesses of wolf paws. The spacious room was large enough to hold several dozen people, although only a handful of guards and advisers, Mimir among them, were presently in attendance. The somber men and women watched warily as a stranger faced the sovereigns. A small contingent of aides flanked the ambassador.

"Welcome to our court," Queen Kara greeted him. Riese gathered that the usual introductions and formalities were just concluding. "We appreciate your prompt response to our summons. It is our wish that any present difficulties can be settled in a manner satisfactory to all."

"Of course, Your Majesty." The Nixian ambassador wore a blood-red military uniform bedecked with medals and decorations. The creases of his uniform looked sharp enough to draw blood. His dark hair met in a widow's peak upon his brow. "But to what 'difficulties' do you refer?" he asked with a crisp Nixian accent.

Riese bristled. Was it just her imagination, or was there a hint of mockery in his tone? King Ulric stiffened on his throne as well, but said nothing. Queen Kara was the diplomat in the family. He tended to defer to her except in military matters. As in a wolf pack, the queen and king ruled equally but according to their strengths.

"It has come to our attention that Nixe has recently imposed on its neighbors in a manner that threatens the general peace. And that your unprovoked campaign of conquest approaches our borders. This concerns us greatly."

The ambassador did not seem bothered by this. "With all due respect, Your Majesty, I fail to see what business that is of Eleysia's. If our neighbors lack the strength to oppose our will, then they must yield to a superior force."

Ulric's expression darkened. A vein pulsed upon his temple while the cords in his neck stood out. Riese recognized the clear warning signs of a kingly storm. Kara placed a restraining hand upon his arm.

"Ambassador Borgos," she said patiently, "let us not be at odds. We are aware of the many trials your nation has endured of late. We knew and respected your former monarchs but wish to have a fruitful relationship with your new military government. Know that Eleysia is more than willing to provide whatever assistance you may require, provided you leave your neighbors in peace."

"We do not need your charity," the ambassador said haughtily, all but sneering at the queen's generous offer. "Nixe is no longer content to live in Eleysia's shadow."

Riese was appalled by the man's blatant disrespect. Unable to keep silent any longer, she burst from hiding. "Watch your tongue, you insolent cur! That is the Queen of Eleysia you are talking to! And my mother!"

"Riese!" Kara exclaimed, startled by her daughter's sudden appearance and outburst. "Control yourself!"

"Hush, Daughter!" her father echoed. "This is not how a princess behaves!"

Riese blushed, embarrassed to be rebuked by her parents before the court. She knew she had acted rashly, but she couldn't help it. The Nixian blackguard had insulted her parents. He'd had it coming!

"Forgive my daughter's immaturity," Ulric said. Despite his stern admonitions, however, he appeared to share her sentiments. "The girl spoke out of turn, but she was not wrong to remind you to whom you are speaking." He rose to his feet. "Hear me now, Ambassador. Do not tempt Eleysia's wrath, now or in the days to come. We do not want war, but we will defend our borders, no matter the cost."

"That may be more than you reckon," the ambassador warned. "Others may cower before Eleysia's vaunted might, but when was the last time that might was tested?"

Despite herself, and her pride in her kingdom, Riese had to wonder if the ambassador had a point. Eleysia had known nothing but peace for generations. Centuries had passed since they had fought an actual war.

The queen rose to stand by her husband, presenting a united front. "The king speaks bluntly, but you would be foolish to disregard his words." She took Ulric's hand. "Call off your acts of aggression and do not venture any closer to Eleysia. Should you dare to cross our borders in force, Nixe will suffer the consequences." She gazed sternly at the ambassador. "Do we make ourselves clear?"

"Perfectly, Your Majesties." He gave them a perfunctory bow. "Now, then, if there is nothing more to be said . . ."

"You are dismissed," the queen said frostily. "And take

our warnings back to your kingdom, where I hope they will fall upon wiser ears."

"We shall see, Your Majesties."

Riese watched as the Nixian delegation marched out of the throne room. The footsteps echoed in the hushed silence they left behind. Riese could not believe what she had just witnessed. Never before had a foreign envoy dared to defy her parents to their faces, let alone risk provoking the fabled power of Eleysia. Glancing over at the drapes, she spotted Arkin peering out from behind the curtains. No longer excited, he looked scared enough to worry Riese as well. Could it be that dark times really did lie ahead?

Don't be ridiculous, she scolded herself. Shaking her head clear of such doubts, she took comfort in the sight of her regal parents standing strong and sure, just as they always had. They were the king and queen, after all; their combined wisdom and valor were enough to keep Eleysia safe no matter what. The Nixians had merely been blustering to save face, that was all. They wouldn't dare challenge Eleysia.

Would they?

CHAPTER SIX

Now

"Please," the girl gasped. "I can't go on."

Night had fallen entirely, cloaking the forest in darkness. Only a sliver of moonlight made it possible to traverse the woods at all. Riese halted their urgent flight long enough to take stock of their situation. They had been running through the forest for at least half an hour; in theory they had left the corpse-littered glade some distance behind them. She glanced back the way they had come and listened intently for any sounds of pursuit, but all she heard was the usual nocturnal chorus. Owls hooted overhead. Small animals rustled in the underbrush. If there were more Huntsmen behind them, they were concealing their presence well.

"Fenrir?"

The wolf's senses were keener than her own. Better suited to nighttime prowling, he had been leading the way. She looked to him for counsel. Had they truly eluded the girl's pursuers? Was it safe to pause for a rest?

Fenrir circled back to join her. His tufted ears were raised and alert, but his hackles lay flat against his back. His tail was lowered. She judged that they were not in immediate danger.

"All right." Riese kept her voice low, just in case. "We can stop running . . . for the moment."

In truth she could use a break herself. The rush of combat had faded, leaving her drained and weary. She sagged against a sturdy tree trunk, grateful for its support. She and Fenrir had already put in a long day traveling before they'd come to the girl's defense. The fierce battle against the Huntsmen had exhausted the last of her reserves. She needed rest.

And answers.

The girl flinched at Fenrir's approach. She hid behind Riese, who recalled that the girl had only lately seen the wolf tear apart two men with its fangs. Nor did it help, Riese imagined, that the Sect had been demonizing wolves for more than a decade now. No doubt the girl had grown up hearing that wolves were nothing but vile beasts fit only for extermination. The Empire had hunted Fenrir's kin to near extinction. Chances were, the girl had never actually laid eyes on a wolf before. Riese couldn't blame her for being apprehensive.

"Don't worry about him." She petted Fenrir behind the ears. "He won't bite . . . unless you deserve it."

"Really?" The girl sounded unconvinced. She kept her hands tucked behind her back, out of snapping range. She watched the wolf warily. "Is he yours?

"He's my friend, not my property," Riese explained. "But what about you?" She looked the girl over. Freckles dotted her cheeks, and her shorn hair made her look like an escaped convict. She looked cold and tired. Riese took off her cloak and draped it over the girl's trembling shoulders. "Who are you? And why were those . . . creatures chasing you?"

She did not dignify the Huntsmen by thinking of them as people. They had sacrificed that privilege when they'd sold their allegiance to the Sect for gold. In a better world they would be the ones being hunted.

"My name is Usla," the girl divulged. Her accent suggested that she had been born and raised not far from here. She hesitated, as though uncertain how much she could trust Riese. "I . . . ran away."

"From whom?" Riese prompted. "The Sect?"

The girl nodded. "They took me from my family. Said I had been 'called' to serve the Sect. I wasn't the only one either. They came to our town and took about half the girls my age. Me, my friends . . . They rounded us up like cattle."

"What about your families?" Riese asked. "Didn't they fight back?"

"A few tried." An anguished expression hinted at past horrors. She choked back a sob. "But you know how it is. You can't fight the Sect. They're too powerful. If you even try to defy them . . ." She trailed off, unable to finish the sentence. "It's not my parents' fault. They didn't have any choice. None of us did."

That's no excuse, Riese thought. She knew firsthand just how ruthless the Sect could be, yet she still found it hard to believe that people would willingly surrender their own children to the cultists. The very thought sickened her. What had become of Eleysia? Was no one else willing to resist the Sect's tyranny?

"And yet you ran away," she reminded Usla. "From where?"

"They called it a 'convent.'" She practically spat the word. "But they just wanted to use us as breeding stock. We were to bear children for the Sect, children who would be taken from us when they were born." Anger twisted her features. Her voice took on a defiant edge. "I wasn't going to turn my baby over to those monsters, no matter how much they preached at me all day long, so I slipped over the fence when I thought no one was looking."

Riese was appalled but not surprised by the girl's story. She had heard rumors about such "convents," as well as so-called schools and seminaries where stolen children were forcibly indoctrinated in the Sect's teachings. There were even whispers about obscene medical experiments performed upon such children in order to "purify" them in the eyes of the cult's enigmatic goddess. Riese had no way of knowing if such rumors were true, but she was not inclined to dismiss them out of hand. She had learned the hard way never to underestimate the Sect's capacity for cruelty.

"That was very brave of you." She inspected the girl, who seemed scarcely more than a child herself. She did not appear to be showing, and yet . . . "Forgive me, but I have to ask." She glanced pointedly at Usla's midsection. "Are you . . ."

A blush betrayed the girl's shame, but she gazed back at Riese with her chin high. She placed her hand over her belly. "It's my baby and no one else's. It belongs with me and my family, not those prophecy-spewing pieces of puke."

Riese admired her spirit. If only more Eleysians were

so willing to defy the Sect. She spotted a tattoo on Usla's right wrist. A black circle pierced by a crossed bar was inked indelibly on the girl's fair skin. Riese recognized the symbol, which combined the signs of both male and female, as the mark of the Sect. Usla would bear the mark for as long as she lived.

"I understand," Riese said. "But this isn't over."

More Huntsmen would be dispatched to find Usla. The Sect could not tolerate any challenge to their authority. Usla had defied them by escaping the convent with her unborn child. They needed to make an example of her.

Usla stared anxiously into the woods behind them. "What do you mean?"

"We need to keep moving," Riese said. "There will be more coming soon."

The girl did not dispute the point. No doubt she had suffered under the Sect long enough to know how relentless they could be. Instead she examined her mysterious rescuer.

"Who are you?" she asked. "What's your name?"

That was a secret too dangerous to share with anyone.

"No one," she said. "Not anymore."

CHAPTER SEVEN

Then

"So what are the royals like anyway?" Micah asked. "Do they mingle with the servants, or are they surrounded by guards all the time?"

Riese groaned inside. She already regretted telling Micah that Valka worked in the palace. At first it had seemed close enough to the truth that it wouldn't trip her up, but he was asking too many questions as they sat side by side atop the falls. Moonlight shone down on them and on the castle far below. She had been glad to find Micah back at the falls tonight. It was nice to have somebody to talk to, especially after all the tension back at the castle.

"Not *all* the time," she hedged, before changing the subject. "Tell me about yourself. I don't know anything about you."

He shrugged. "Not much to tell. Like I told you before, I'm just an apprentice."

"Not good enough." She reached over and lifted the goggles from his brow. He didn't protest the theft. "What are these for?"

"They help me see in the dark," he explained, "when I'm out prowling for roots and herbs."

She held the goggles up to her own eyes. Micah had not been exaggerating. The finely cut lenses amplified the moonlight, allowing her to peer into the murkiest shadows. Riese was envious; she could use these goggles to navigate the tunnels under the castle. "Very nice. Where did you get them?"

"They belonged to my father." Sorrow crept into his voice. "He was a miner."

"Was?"

"He died in a cave-in when I was very young." He took back the goggles. "This is all he left me."

"I'm sorry." Riese couldn't imagine losing her father—or any of her family. "What about the rest of your kin? Do you have anyone else?"

"A sister," he divulged. "Our mother passed away some time ago. It's just the two of us now."

She could tell that he cared deeply for his sister. *Should I mention my brother,* she wondered, *or would that give too much away?*

"Does she live with you?"

He shook his head. "No. She's . . . being taken care of by others. Far from here."

It was clearly a painful subject. Riese felt bad about bringing it up. "I'm sure she knows you love her."

"I hope so." He placed the goggles aside and sprang to his feet, as though eager to escape the past. "Enough talking. This is too beautiful a night to waste gabbing." He shot her a devilish grin. "How do you feel about a midnight swim?"

A swim? There was a lake at the bottom of the falls, but

that was a long hike down. She was comfortable where she was. "Are you serious?"

"Why not? The night is warm enough."

Before she could raise an objection, he stripped off his tunic and vest, revealing a tanned and sinewy chest. His bare skin caught the moonlight. Old scars hinted at an orphan's hard life. A second later his boots, trousers, and unmentionables joined his goggles and upper garments in a heap by a stone pillar. Blushing, Riese tried not to gape. She had never seen a naked boy before.

Not that she intended to admit that.

Doing her best to maintain her composure, as though his lack of attire was scarcely worth mentioning, she arched a skeptical eyebrow. "And do you intend to walk all the way down to the pool like that?"

He grinned back at her. "Who said anything about walking?"

To her surprise he ran straight for the edge of the falls.

"Micah!" she cried out. "Don't!"

What on earth had possessed him? Had he gone mad?

"See you at the bottom!"

She gasped in horror as, right before her eyes, he threw himself over the edge and plummeted from sight.

"Micah!"

Her heart pounding, she raced to the ledge and peered over the brink, dreading the sight of his bloody body shattered upon the rocks dozens of feet below. Frantic eyes searched for him, but all she saw was the surging foam, crashing against the base of the falls. "Micah!" she called out desperately. "MICAH!"

Please, she prayed, *don't let him have perished!*

Endless seconds later, just as she despaired of ever seeing him again, his head and shoulders erupted from beneath the surface of the pool. Soaked brown hair was plastered to his scalp. A gigantic smile stretched across his face. He appeared to be very much alive.

But how had he survived?

Looking more closely, she spotted an open gap between two spray-slick boulders, where the water must have been deep enough to dive into. You just had to know where to jump, she realized, and hope you didn't miss.

Had he done this before?

"Come on!" he shouted to her over the rumble of the falls. His grinning visage bobbed up and down in the spray. "Don't be afraid!"

Did she dare? Riese peeked over the edge. The steep drop looked more than a little risky. What if she missed and hit the rocks instead? Her guardians back at the palace would be horrified that she was even contemplating such a reckless stunt, which just made it all the more tempting.

Why not? she thought. *I haven't been crowned yet. I can do what I want.*

"Well?" He splashed around in the pool. "Are you coming or not?"

Suddenly she couldn't wait to join him. If he could do it, why couldn't she?

"Just stay out of my way!"

Moving quickly, before she could change her mind, she peeled off her own clothing until she was wearing only a fine linen shift. For a daring moment she considered shedding that as well, only to remember the telltale brand upon her shoulder. Even in the dark it wouldn't do to let Micah get too good a look at it, not if she wanted to continue posing as Valka.

The rocky ledge felt cool beneath her bare feet. Her loose hair blew in the breeze. Keeping the exact location of the open gap fixed in her mind, she backed up to get a running start. Second thoughts threatened to hold her back. Did she really want to do this?

"Hurry up!" Micah shouted. "What are you waiting for?"

His challenge emboldened her. "Not a thing!" she yelled back. "Watch out below!"

She tossed her fears to the wind, and the rest of her followed shortly. Racing over the brink, she dived headfirst toward the churning foam. Wind and spray pelted her face as the roiling water seemed to surge up at her with breathtaking speed. Jagged rocks loomed murderously to both sides. Whooping like a berserker, she barely remembered to hold her breath before slicing into the water like a human spear.

Despite everything, she half-expected to crash onto a submerged boulder, but instead she plunged deep beneath the froth. The sudden immersion in the cool water jolted her; it was almost as exhilarating as the dive itself.

Why had she never done this before?

Moonlight rippled above her. Reversing course underwater, she kicked toward the surface. Her head burst into the warm night air. She gasped it down, filling her lungs. Blinking eyes gazed up at the high cliff towering above her; she found it hard to believe that she had actually dived from all the way up there—and that she already wanted to do it again. An exuberant laugh exploded from her chest.

"There you are!" Micah swam toward her, strong strokes carrying him swiftly through the water. He grinned at her. "I was starting to think you didn't have the nerve."

"Then, you don't know me very well." She splashed him in the face. "And that's for scaring me half to death!"

He sputtered and wiped the water from his eyes. "What do you care? You barely know me."

"That doesn't mean I want to see you splattered all over the rocks." They paddled circles around each other. "It would have completely spoiled the view!"

He laughed and swam closer, until they were less than a foot apart. Those striking green eyes put her in mind of a seductive merman. Water sluiced from his hair onto his shoulders. A triumphant smile revealed even white teeth. "But it was fun, wasn't it?

"More than fun," she confessed. "It was astounding!" She groped for the right words to convey just how thrilling it had been. "Better than . . ."

Killing a wild boar?

"Than what?" he prompted.

"Er, I'm not sure." She doubted that many serving girls went boar hunting on their own. "I can't think of anything more exciting."

"I can."

With a single kick he closed the distance between them. His lips surprised hers.

By the Fates! she reacted, almost sinking. *Is this really happening?*

The kiss was as warm as the water was cool. Curious, she allowed it for a moment before paddling backward. She eyed him warily.

"And what was that?"

"I thought that was obvious." He kept his distance, but looked quite pleased with himself. "Didn't you like it?"

In truth she had little to compare it with. As a princess of the realm, she'd led a sheltered life where boys were concerned. For all she knew, his kissing her constituted high treason . . . at least as far as her father was concerned.

"I don't know," she admitted. "I'm not in the habit of letting cocky apprentices take liberties."

"Fine talk for a servant girl," he teased her. "I thought you were bolder than that."

"I'm as bold as I want to be. And no more."

But how much was that? Diving off a cliff was one thing, but this was almost scarier . . . and more thrilling.

"Don't get me wrong," he insisted. "I like servant girls. One in particular."

Riese gulped. Nobody had ever flirted with her like this before. She hid her face beneath the water so he wouldn't see her blushing.

Nothing can come of this, she thought. She'd known all her life that there was an arranged marriage in her future, to cement an alliance to some stuffy crowned head or another. Once she was crowned, only a few short months from now, those negotiations would surely begin in earnest. But for now she couldn't help enjoying the illusion that she was just an ordinary girl enjoying a midnight rendezvous with a boy.

"Flatterer."

"Can you blame me?" He brushed wet bangs away from his eyes. "How often do I meet a girl who can beat me at quarterstaves—and jumps off cliffs in her shift?"

The soggy garment clung to her. She checked to make sure it was still in place, covering the wolf's-head brand. The last thing she wanted was for him to start treating her like some lofty, unapproachable princess. Or for him to find out that she had been lying to him ever since they met.

"Not too often, I hope." She nodded at the waterfall, then kicked toward the shore rapidly, leaving him behind. "Let's do it again!"

He swam after her. "Wait! What about another kiss?"

"Maybe later." She waded up onto the rocky shore. Water streamed from her soaked hair and skin. Barefoot, she made her way toward the steep trail leading back to the top of the falls. A misty spray christened her. "After you put some clothes on!"

She heard him splashing behind her.

"Race you to the top!" she said.

CHAPTER EIGHT

THE CEMETERY LAY BEYOND THE CITY WALLS, surrounded by a spiked iron fence. Micah wondered if it was supposed to keep the living out or the dead in. He shivered despite the warm summer night. His hair was still damp from the falls. At the moment, he wished he was anywhere else, like maybe back at the standing stones with Valka.

A bell tolled in the distance. More than an hour had passed since he'd kissed her good-bye. The memory warmed him, bringing a smile to his lips. The taste of her lingered. She was an amazing girl, funny and fearless and a match for him in every way.

If only he could tell her the truth about himself . . .

He crept silently toward the gate. The woods surrounding the cemetery appeared to be deserted, but he was taking no chances. His goggles allowed him to make his way through the darkness without need of torch or lantern. He silently thanked his father for leaving them to him, although he wasn't sure his dad would have approved of the use to which he was now putting them. His father had been an honest miner. He had never needed to slink through the night like a thief . . . or a spy.

It's not like I have a choice, Micah thought, frowning. *I'm just doing what I have to do.*

He heard footsteps approaching. The glow of a lantern fell beyond the southwest corner of the fence, warning of someone coming. Micah ducked behind a tree, his heart pounding. He cautiously peered around the tree trunk.

A watchman rounded the corner. He wore a light cloak over leather armor. His meaty hand held up a lantern, and a short sword was sheathed at his waist. A large black wolf patrolled at his side, its massive paws padding upon the ground. The wolf paused and sniffed the air.

Micah held his breath. He prayed the wind wouldn't shift.

"What is it, boy?" the guard asked. "You smell something?"

The wolf growled softly. He peered into the shadows with his yellow eyes. He snuffled at the ground.

"Enough of that," the watchman grumbled. "My breakfast is waiting." He snorted. "There's nobody to be bothered here but the dead anyway. Waste of time to guard this boneyard if you ask me. Who'd want to visit this haunted place after dark?"

He made to continue his rounds, but the wolf balked. Tail half erect, he turned his nose toward the woods where Micah was hiding. He began to trot forward.

"C'mon, you mangy cur." The guard swatted the wolf on the butt. "You can chase rabbits on your time. Hurry along now, and I'll give you a bit of my stew."

The wolf glanced once more toward the woods, then relented. He loped after the watchman.

Micah waited until they were out of sight before sighing

in relief. Thank the Fates for the hungry guard's impatience. Not that he blamed the man for wanting to hurry through his rounds; talk about a thankless job.

Wonder who he ticked off to get this shift?

The guard's footsteps receded into the night. Micah counted to fifty just to be safe, then emerged from hiding. He stared up at the wrought-iron fence. Chances were, the guard had locked the gate before heading for his stew.

No problem, Micah thought.

As agile as a monkey, he clambered over the fence, taking care not to catch himself upon the spikes. He glanced around to make sure no one was looking, then dropped nimbly onto the grounds of the cemetery.

He took a second to survey his surroundings. Thanks to his goggles, he could see the cemetery almost as clearly as though it were day. Despite its age, the graveyard had been well maintained out of respect for those buried there. Granite monuments, inscribed with runes, rose from the grass in neatly ordered rows. Marble statues immortalized the honored dead. Imposing stone mausoleums housed the bones of families far more prosperous than his own. His mother's body, he recalled bitterly, had been consigned to a pauper's grave, like so many Nixians in recent years. Even in death the Eleysians were far more comfortable than anyone else. Perhaps they deserved what was coming to them.

Even Valka?

Guilt pricked his conscience. He shook it off in order to focus on the task at hand. Now was no time to brood over the past, or worry about whether he was doing the right thing. He had business to attend to.

Making his way through the cemetery, he prowled the grounds until he found the mausoleum he was looking for. Marble columns rose before it. Chiseled sword maidens stood guard over the entrance. The mausoleum sat silently amidst the other death houses. Micah appeared to be the only living soul around.

But appearances could be deceiving.

He stepped up to the entrance and glanced around furtively. He rapped three times upon the door.

A knock answered him from inside the tomb. The door slid open without any of the noisy scrapes or creaks you might expect from such a place. Every hinge had been carefully oiled in advance. Silence was imperative in such matters.

A pale face glared at him from within. Vulpine features gave the man a crafty look. An eye patch covered what was said to be an empty socket. A receding hairline exposed a furrowed brow. Worry lines were etched deep into his face. His nose was sharp enough to poke someone's eye out.

"You're late," Graz grumbled. A dark overcoat hung upon his bony frame. He poked his head out the door to make sure Micah had not been followed. He stepped aside to let Micah pass. "Get in here. Hurry."

Micah slipped past him into the tomb. The door slid shut behind him.

The interior of the mausoleum had been converted into a makeshift office. Niches filled with dried-out skeletons lined the walls. Books and papers had been stuck in among the bones, turning the niches into bookshelves as well. A huge marble sarcophagus occupied the center of the vault. Graz was using it as a table. A lantern rested atop the sarcophagus, along with a bottle of ale and a plate of cold meats. A knife lay next to the plate.

Micah shivered. He had been here before, but the morbid setting never failed to chill him. Why couldn't they meet in a cozy attic or basement instead?

"Sit down." Graz gestured at a stool at one end of the "table." He took a seat at the other end, nearest the food. The sliced meat made Micah's mouth water, but Graz didn't offer him a bite. Instead he helped himself. "What took you so long?"

"I'm sorry." Micah sat down. His stomach grumbled. "I had to avoid the guards. There seemed to be more patrols than usual outside the city."

"Get used to it. Once the war breaks out, the Eleysians will be sure to tighten the security around the capital." He smirked at Micah. "But you can handle that, can't you, thief? You're good at sneaking around where you don't belong."

"I suppose. If you say so."

Micah gazed longingly at the ale. His mouth felt as dry as the fabled Sands of Eostre. He couldn't help it. Graz made him nervous. The man had come to power along with the new regime that had seized control of Nixe during the recent turmoil, when the people had turned against the monarchy that had failed to protect them from plagues and famine. Rumor had it that Graz had personally overseen the burial of the old king and queen, whose bones were said to be hidden away where none could find them. The cunning spymaster knew too many secrets, but Micah didn't even know if Graz was his real name.

Probably not, he guessed.

"Don't just sit there," Graz said. "Report."

"Yes, sir." Micah fished his sketchbook from beneath

his vest. "I've been keeping the castle under observation as ordered." He handed the notebook over to Graz, who leafed through the pages while nibbling on a slice of ham. "As you see, I've recorded the rotations of the sentries and the locations of every visible gate. Just as you instructed."

Graz studied the notes and sketches. "Any signs that the palace is preparing for a long siege? Are they expanding the garrison or reinforcing the hoardings? What about their stores? Do they appear to be stocking up on extra arms and food?"

"No," Micah said. "Not that I've noticed."

"Any other changes in their routines?"

Micah shook his head.

"Typical." Graz sneered at the notes before him. "That's sheer Eleysian arrogance for you. They've been unchallenged for so long that it would never even occur to them to prepare for a siege. They've forgotten that their pretty palace used to be a fortress, and that the world can still be a dangerous place." He smirked at Micah again. "But you haven't forgotten that, have you?"

Hardly, Micah thought. *How could I?*

He knew too well how hard the world could be. He had known it practically his entire life, ever since his parents had died and he and his little sister had been cast out onto the streets. Orphaned and alone, with nobody but each other to rely on, he and Aliza had survived by begging and stealing and grubbing for food. Getting by on the streets was hard enough in the best of times, but the last few years had made life in Nixe a constant losing battle for almost everyone. Despite the promises of the new regime, times remained precarious. Poverty, disease, and famine had driven ever more people to the edge, increasing the competition for whatever scraps remained. Charity had become a luxury Nixe could no longer afford, along with decency, security, and hope. Desperation was a way of life.

Ugly memories intruded into the present. He and Aliza begging on street corners, only to be spat upon by wretches scarcely better off than they were. Being chased through grimy alleys by gangs of feral children. Digging through trash for moldy crusts and half-rotted vegetables. Squatting in abandoned hovels and temples. Breaking into shops and houses, then running like mad before the constables arrived. Hiding from pimps and procurers. Shivering in the cold, terrified of catching a fever like the one that had stolen their mother. Ducking the army's brutal press-gangs. Picking pockets and snatching purses. . . .

Until the police caught Aliza.

"How is my sister?" he asked. "Is she well?"

"She is being looked after," Graz assured him. "You need not concern yourself with her, as long as you continue to make yourself useful."

The Nixian secret police had seen potential in Micah. Rather than execute Aliza or throw her into some filthy pit, they had offered Micah a chance to earn her freedom and perhaps a pardon for both of them. Provided he spied on Eleysia for them.

"When can I see her?"

"In time," the spymaster said. "For now you need to concentrate on your assignment." He ripped the latest pages from the notebook and tucked them beneath his coat before handing the book back to Micah. "Have you anything else to report?"

Micah hesitated, unsure if he should mention Valka.

As shrewd as he was devious, Graz immediately picked up that Micah was holding something back. His single eye narrowed.

"What is it?" he demanded. "Speak up."

Micah realized that he had best come clean. "Well, there's this girl . . ."

Graz frowned. He fingered his knife in a way that made Micah uneasy. "We recruited you to spy on Asgard, not chase after trollops."

"No, it's not like that," Micah insisted. "She works in the palace as a serving girl. I'm getting to know her . . . to find out more about what goes on there."

That was only partly the truth, but Graz didn't need to know that.

"Is that so?" the spymaster said suspiciously. Even with only one eye he seemed to see right through Micah. "Careful, my resourceful young thief. Don't get too attached to this girl." He put down his knife, but not too far from his fingers. "Never forget where your true loyalties lie. That girl is the enemy."

"I know," Micah said. "She'd expose me in a heartbeat if she knew the truth."

But did he really believe that? Valka was an Eleysian, true, but despite what he needed to tell Graz, she didn't feel like an enemy to him. He hated lying to her, but what else was he supposed to do? His sister was depending on him.

I'm sorry, Valka, he thought. *I pray that you can forgive me someday.*

After Nixe conquered Eleysia.

CHAPTER NINE

"WELCOME, COUSIN. IT IS GOOD TO SEE YOU AGAIN."

The queen extended her greeting in the privacy of the castle parlor. Later on tonight there would be a formal dinner in their guest's honor, but Kara had wanted a more intimate family reunion first. She held out her arms.

Her cousin, Amara, rushed to embrace her. "Kara, my queen! It has been too long."

Riese observed the tender scene from the sofa, where she and Arkin sat side by side, both of them groomed and attired within an inch of their lives. Their father occupied a comfy wingback chair across from them. A platter of berries and sweetmeats had been laid upon a low maple table. The wolf cub, Fenrir, was curled up at Riese's feet. She snuck him a tasty morsel.

"I trust your journey was pleasant?" Kara asked.

"Longer than I would have preferred," Amara stated, "but well worth it to see you all again."

The queen's cousin was just a few years older than Riese. Auburn hair, elegantly coifed, complemented her dark eyes. Eye shadow and lipstick enhanced her aristocratic good looks. A tight-fitting sable gown flattered her striking figure. A gleaming silver pendant and earrings relieved the severity of the dark gown, which she wore in mourning of her husband, the late Baron of Hariasa. Amara had only recently assumed the throne of that northern port state, following the baron's unexpected demise. Widowhood appeared to agree with her.

Kara and Amara broke apart. Amara glanced around the parlor, openly admiring the sumptuous furnishings. She ran her hand over the polished marble mantel over the hearth. A ruby ring glittered upon one finger. "What a lovely home you have," she complimented them. "I had almost forgotten how gorgeous the palace is."

"Thank you," Kara replied. "It's kind of you to say so." She guided Amara toward the couch. "But of course our true treasures are our children." She beckoned her offspring. "Riese, Arkin. Say hello to our guest."

Riese and Arkin rose dutifully to their feet. "Welcome, Cousin Amara," they recited in unison.

"Oh, my ancestors!" Amara exclaimed. "Is that little Riese, all grown up? Look at you! You're practically a woman now."

Riese braced herself for the obligatory hug and peck on the cheek, but before Amara could get too close, Fenrir growled softly. His hackles rose.

"Fenrir!" Riese chided the cub. "Hush! Amara is family."

The wolf reluctantly settled down. Riese slipped him another treat to keep him quiet.

Amara backed away slightly. "Your pet doesn't seem to like me."

"I'm sure he's just being protective," Kara said, attempting to smooth the waters. "Riese, perhaps your bold little friend would be happier elsewhere?"

"Yes, Mother." Riese took hold of the ruff at the back of Fenrir's neck and escorted him toward the door. The wolf dragged his feet, but Riese shooed him into the hall. "Come on, killer. Out you go!"

She shut the door to keep him from running back in. He whined unhappily on the other side.

Riese was puzzled by the cub's behavior. *What was that all about?*

Meanwhile their guest had turned her attentions to Arkin. "And you!" she cooed while Arkin squirmed uncomfortably in her embrace. "The last time I saw you, you were just a baby. And now you're a handsome young prince with your whole future in front of you."

"Thank you, Cousin Amara," Arkin said politely before extricating himself from her grasp. "I hope you enjoy your visit."

"I'm certain I shall." She helped herself to a honeyed treat from the dessert platter. "After all, I could hardly overlook your mother's Silver Jubilee." She sighed. "A pity my own mother did not live to see this day."

"Indeed," Kara said. She had been very close to her late aunt, who had passed away some years before. "I miss her still. But it gladdens my heart to have you with us. I can see her in your face."

"You flatter me," Amara said, "but it pleases me to hear you say it. My mother would want me to be here. Nothing was more important to her than family."

"She was a wise and noble woman," Ulric agreed. "And a trusted adviser to the throne."

"I only hope I can live up to her example." Amara approached the king, who rose to meet her. "Ulric! You're looking well."

"As are you." He took her hand. "My condolences once again upon the tragic passing of your esteemed husband. He also was a loyal subject—and a good friend."

Riese eyed Amara. The late baron, who had been *much* older than Amara, had supposedly passed away in his sleep, but there had been talk that his death might not have been entirely natural. Just scurrilous gossip and rumors, probably, of the sort that the queen would never allow to be bruited about in her presence. Riese scolded herself for doing Amara an injustice. The stories were just rumors, after all.

"Thank you." She dabbed at her eyes. "He often spoke highly of you as well."

"I hope the demands of the province are not weighing too heavily on you?"

Amara sighed again. "In these uncertain times, how can they not?" She placed a hand upon the king's arm. Her expression grew more serious. "Indeed, we should talk."

Something about her tone got Riese's attention. Did Amara have more on her mind than just the queen's Jubilee?

"About what?" Kara asked.

"The coming war, of course." She addressed her remarks to both the king and queen. "There are urgent matters to be discussed."

"I see." Kara's manner became less familiar and more regal. Riese recognized her mother's business face. The

75

queen glanced at Riese and Arkin. "Perhaps, then, the children should be excused."

"No, Mother," Riese protested. "I think I should stay. As you often remind me, I am not a child any longer—and will be named crown princess soon. I need to pay more attention to the affairs of the kingdom."

Kara thought it over. She cast a questioning look at Ulric.

"She has a point," he said. "We can't shelter her from the world forever."

Amara frowned. "I'm not sure this is for such delicate ears."

Delicate? Riese resisted an urge to snort indignantly. *Dead husband or not, you're not that much older than I am.*

"No," the queen decided. "Riese is right. It is time she takes part in our deliberations." She smiled proudly at her daughter. "Arkin, please excuse us."

"But, Mother!" Arkin was in no hurry to leave. "Do I have to go? I want to hear this too!"

"Maybe in a few years," his mother promised. "Right now the adults need to talk. Why don't you go play with Fenrir?"

"But it's not fair!" Arkin objected. "I always get left out."

"You heard your mother," Ulric said sternly. "Leave us."

Riese winked at her brother. *Don't worry,* she told him silently. *I'll tell you all about it later.*

Only slightly placated, he trudged toward the door. "It's still not fair," he muttered under his breath. "This is my kingdom too."

Not really, Riese thought. She was next in line for the

throne. Chances were that Arkin would eventually be married off to the queen of some neighboring kingdom, cementing that realm's loyalty to Eleysia. Assuming he didn't devote himself to scholarly pursuits instead.

The adults and Riese waited until Arkin had grudgingly departed. "Very well," Kara said after checking to make sure he wasn't listening on the other side of the door. She sounded saddened that affairs of state had intruded on their carefree reunion. "What concerns you, Cousin?"

Amara sat down on the couch beside Riese, who scooted over to make room. She caught a whiff of expensive perfume. "My apologies, my queen. But I thought that we might enjoy our time together more if we dispensed with less sentimental matters first."

"Such as?" Kara prompted.

"At your command Hariasa's armories are working around the clock in anticipation of the coming hostilities. My people are busily engaged in forging the finest in arms and armor for Eleysia's defense."

Riese gulped. This was the first she had heard of such preparations. Although, now that she thought of it, it made perfect sense. Hariasa was known throughout the kingdom for the skill of its artisans. And her mother, as Riese well knew, was always well prepared for any eventuality.

But did this mean her parents were seriously anticipating war?

"Your people's industry is greatly appreciated," Kara said, "especially at this crucial juncture. But is there a difficulty?"

"Perhaps," Amara said. "Such industry does not come

cheap, nor do the supplies and material needed to produce weapons in sufficient quantities. I fear such increased production has placed an undue strain upon my treasury."

Ulric scowled. "We have already provided you with a goodly sum."

"And your royal generosity honors me, truly it does," Amara insisted, "but my expenses continue to mount." She paused, as though hesitant to impose. "Perhaps, for the sake of Eleysia, you could see fit to provide more gold for the war effort?"

"You fret about gold at a time like this?" Ulric's face darkened. "What of your duty to Eleysia and the throne?"

"That is my only concern, I assure you!" Amara's hand went to her heart. "And it deeply pains me to raise such a vulgar matter on so festive an occasion. But such is the way of the world. Swords and armor do not grow on trees."

Ulric struggled visibly to control his temper. An angry vein pulsed at his temple. "Perhaps you would prefer to see the Nixians overrun the kingdom? I'm sure they would consider Hariasa a tempting prize."

"Please, let us not argue." Kara stepped between Ulric and Amara. She held up her hand to forestall any further acrimony. "We hear your concerns, Amara, and do not wish Hariasa to bear an unfair burden. I know that you want only what is best for Eleysia, just as your mother did. But what you ask is difficult. This war could be a costly affair, for all of us, and our armies must be clothed and fed, and the victims of the war provided for as well. We must husband our resources, and, as was said, you have already been generously compensated for your troubles."

"And do not think that I am not grateful! But perhaps you should raise taxes," Amara suggested. "If I may be so bold."

Riese was appalled. Hariasa was a rich and prosperous province; she doubted that Amara was hurting that badly. Yet the widowed baroness almost seemed intent on profiting from the unrest in the land. Or was Riese misjudging her?

Kara saw her daughter frowning. "What do you think, Riese?"

Riese thought of Micah, who couldn't even afford to look after his sister by himself. "I think we should think twice before asking our people to make hard sacrifices for the sake of our own treasuries. We have so much, and many of them so little."

Amara smiled sadly. "A lovely sentiment, darling. I wish I had the luxury of being so blithe about the hard realities of the throne. But ultimately the people must contribute to their own protection. It is in their own best interests, after all."

So they must choose between want or being conquered? Riese thought. *That hardly seems fair.*

She was tempted to suggest that Amara sell off some of her shiny jewelry, but held her tongue for her mother's sake. Riese needed to prove that she could be diplomatic when she had to be. Plus, Amara *was* family.

"We will take your petition under advisement," Kara assured Amara. "But for now let us simply enjoy one another's company while we can." Her regal persona melted and she was a loving mother once more. "Riese, will you please fetch your brother? I'm certain Cousin Amara is missing him already."

"You know me too well," Amara agreed, flashing a brilliant smile. "And I apologize again for spoiling the moment with talk of war and finances. Let us speak no more of it for the time being. Just being here with all of you is treasure enough at the moment."

"Just so," Ulric agreed, sounding somewhat mollified. "We must not let the challenges of these days turn us against one another, or place undue strain upon the sacred bonds of kinship. We share the same noble ancestors. That is what keeps us strong."

"Well said," Amara said. "I could not have put it better." She patted Riese's hand. "Don't you agree, little cousin?"

"Of course," Riese said. She resolved to give Amara the benefit of the doubt.

She heard Fenrir scratching at the door outside.

I suppose I should keep him outside, she thought. *For Amara's sake.*

CHAPTER TEN

HER PARENTS' FEARS PROVED WELL FOUNDED. WAR WAS AT HAND.

Only days after Amara's arrival, Riese found herself bidding farewell to her father on the Queen's Road outside the palace. A train of horse-drawn carriages and wagons waited to carry the king and his army to the front. The cavalry, resplendent in their uniforms and plumed helmets, sat atop their steeds. Infantrymen and -women stood in formation. The king's armored war chariot, which was large enough to carry three men into battle, was hitched to a wagon, while his personal coach bore the embossed wolf's-head seal of the royal family. Additional wagons were crammed with troops and arms. The royal family stood upon a low platform decorated with flags and bunting. A marching band loudly played a patriotic anthem. The sky was somber and overcast.

A bad omen, Riese thought.

The family maintained a brave face for the crowd before stepping into the king's coach to make their final farewells in private. The interior was richly appointed, with wood-paneled walls, polished oak seats, and velvet cushions. The drapes over the windows were drawn.

"Must you go, Father?" Arkin clung desperately to Ulric as the family huddled together, prolonging their good-byes for as long as possible. A sob caught in the young prince's throat. "I don't want you to leave!"

"I fear I have no choice," Ulric told him once more. "The Nixians have forced my hand."

Riese understood. No longer content to raid and retreat, the Nixians were advancing toward Eleysia. Indeed, their troops were reported to be massing just across the border from Geffion, an agricultural province north of Asgard, known for its rolling fields and abundant crops. No doubt the hungry Nixians intended to reap its harvest, provided they were not driven back to their own blighted homeland.

News had already reached Asgard of what the Nixians had done to other kingdoms. Shaken couriers had spoken of how the Nixians had devoured all before them. It was said that they cut venerable stands of timber to the ground, using the raw lumber for their own purposes. Their steam-powered extractors, armed with iron scoops and drills, tore open the rolling hills, wresting vital minerals and ores from the earth. The invaders ransacked green fields and pastures, the captured crops and livestock going to feed their hungry hordes. What little the armies did not consume was shipped back to Nixe. The armies seemed less interested in occupying others' lands than in pillaging them and stealing their resources.

And now they aimed to do the same to Eleysia.

Ulric shook his head at the enemy's audacity. "As king it is my duty to personally command our forces—and defend our home."

"Let me come with you!" Riese blurted. "And fight at your side!"

Ulric laughed and hugged her tightly. "Spoken like a true princess of Asgard!" He affectionately tousled her hair. "Your spirit does you honor, Daughter, but I will fight better knowing that you and your brother are safe at home." He bent to pet Fenrir, who had accompanied Riese. The cub was on his best behavior. "Besides, someone has to defend the palace in my absence!"

He was just humoring her, Riese knew, but she didn't want to argue with him. Not now. Who knew when she would see him again?

"Do not fear for your family, Ulric," Amara assured him. She stood beside Kara, her arm draped over the queen. "They are in good hands."

The baroness had volunteered to prolong her visit to help out in Ulric's absence.

"Thank you, Cousin." Kara was clearly grateful for her cousin's support. "It is good of you to stand by us in these trying times."

"That's what family is for," Amara insisted. "My mother would have done no less. You can count on me to render whatever service and counsel you may require . . . while the king is sadly away."

Ulric grunted in response. Unlike the queen, he appeared to merely tolerate her presence. Riese guessed that he had not entirely forgotten her efforts to wheedle more money from the treasury. Only slightly acknowledging Amara, he drew Riese closer to him.

"I will not be gone long," he promised. "The Nixians are nothing but glorified brigands. When they behold our might, they will surely flee back to Nixe with their tails between their legs. I will be back before you have time to miss me."

"We will hold you to that promise, my love." Kara pulled away from Amara. Tossing royal decorum aside, she embraced her husband and gave him a passionate kiss. "Take care," she whispered, loud enough for Riese to hear. "And stay safe until you return to us."

"Do not waste a moment worrying about me," he insisted. "It is the upstart Nixians who need fear for their safety—and beg the spirits of their unworthy ancestors for mercy."

His confidence encouraged Riese, and gave her the strength to let go of him after one last hug. She, Arkin, and Amara exited the coach to give their parents a few final moments together. Kara emerged at last from the carriage. Her eyes were moist.

A trumpet sounded and the procession got under way. Standing together on the platform, the royal family watched the coaches, horses, wagons, and infantry set out for the north. The ground trembled beneath the army's tread. Riese's throat tightened. Despite her father's comforting words, she found herself plagued by doubts.

Would this war truly be as short as her father predicted? What if the Nixians proved more dangerous than expected?

Fenrir whimpered at her side.

"The emissaries are here to see you, Your Majesty."

Despite the king's departure and the Nixian threat, life at the palace did not come to a halt. Sitting beside an empty throne, the queen presided over the throne room. Courtiers and advisers lined the great hall, conferring quietly among themselves. Riese and Arkin occupied smaller thrones of their own one level below their mother, as did

Amara, who had been granted a seat by virtue of her noble blood. Although bored by court business, Riese felt obliged to keep her mother company while they waited for news from the front. Fenrir rested at Riese's feet. The wolf cub was a frequent companion these days.

"Thank you, Mimir," the queen replied. "Please show them in."

The elderly counselor nodded at the guards. The pair of high oak doors swung open to admit two curious visitors. Riese's eyes widened. Fenrir growled.

The emissaries were strange and somewhat unsettling in appearance. Leather masks, dark green in color, concealed the upper halves of their faces. Gleaming copper gears were affixed to their garb, and perhaps even their bodies, so that they almost resembled clockwork automata more than creatures of flesh and blood. Their bizarre attire struck Riese as better suited to a masquerade or a pageant than an audience with a queen. Oiled cogwheels whirred and clicked as they approached the throne.

Arkin let out a gasp. She couldn't blame him. The strangers looked like something out of the nightmares that often plagued him. She took her brother's hand to comfort him.

It was trembling.

"Hail, Great Queen." The older of the two emissaries spoke. Tinted goggles hid his eyes. A silver symbol, unfamiliar to Riese, was embossed upon his brow. His cowl exposed a strong chin. He looked tall and fit beneath his dark green garb. His voice was cool but dignified. "I bring you greetings from Cacilia, high priestess of the Sect."

Little was known of the mysterious cult, which had

originated in a distant province. Riese had heard of the Sect but had never actually encountered any of its followers before. She straightened up in her seat. Perhaps this afternoon was not going to be so dull, after all?

"Your priestess is most kind," Kara declared. "And you are?"

"I am called Herrick, Your Majesty. Long a magister of the Sect." He gestured toward his companion. "And this my acolyte, Randolf."

The younger man bowed his head. He appeared somewhat less imposing than his superior. Cropped brown hair showed above his mask, which also exposed clear walnut-colored eyes. Fewer gears, screws, and sprockets clung to his frame.

"Your Majesty," he said stiffly.

The queen leaned forward on her throne. "Why do you conceal your faces in my presence?"

"No disrespect is intended," Herrick stated. "We merely honor the tenets of our faith, which call upon us to renounce our former identities when we dedicate ourselves to the Goddess. I assure you, we have nothing to hide."

"I will take you on your word for that," Kara replied. "Nor will I ask you to compromise your beliefs, no matter how strange and unfamiliar they may be."

Riese wondered what sort of Goddess the Sect worshiped. Most Eleysians were content to merely honor the spirits of their ancestors and perhaps a totem animal as well. The concept of devoting one's life to the service of some heavenly deity was alien to her. You would think that a goddess would have bigger things to worry about than the affairs of mortals!

"Your Majesty is most understanding," Herrick said. "As all the world knows."

"Eleysia has no quarrel with those who practice different customs, provided they respect our laws and our citizens." The queen settled back upon her throne. "Perhaps now you can tell me why your priestess requested this audience."

"To properly introduce the Sect to Your Majesty, so that you might know you can count on our friendship."

He showed far more respect to the throne than the Nixian ambassador had, Riese gave him that. Too bad he struck her as cold as ice as well.

"With your permission, may I present you and your regal family with a few humble gifts on behalf of our Goddess?"

Kara nodded. "You may proceed."

Randolf went to the door. He beckoned to those waiting outside.

A procession of masked acolytes entered the throne room, bearing silver-wrapped packages that ranged in size from two small boxes to a larger bundle that required four men to carry it. The acolytes silently deposited the objects before the throne, then departed.

"How intriguing!" Amara cooed. "I adore gifts."

Riese had to admit she was curious as well.

The largest of the tributes was tall and rectangular and stood upright like a cabinet or wardrobe. A shiny silver sheet was draped over it. Herrick took hold of the sheet and yanked it off with a flourish. Oohs and aahs greeted the unveiling of an ornate mechanical clock, housed in an elegant cabinet of polished brass and crystal. A clock dial faced out from each of the cabinet's four sides. Its moving hands ticked off the passage of hours. A glass door revealed a gleaming steel pendulum swinging inside the clock. A horizontal metal ring, like an elevated walkway outside a watchtower, orbited the cabinet just below the clock faces.

Riese wondered what purpose the ring served.

"This modern clock," Herrick declared, "represents the finest in Sect craftsmanship and ingenuity. It is impervious to the elements and can be counted on to keep far better time than the sundials and hourglasses of old. It is also intended to amuse . . . as so."

He reached out and moved a clock hand so that the hour tolled. The clock chimed, and small metal doors opened in the cabinet. A pair of small mechanical figures, cast in the image of a hunter and a snarling wolf, emerged from hiding. The hunter chased the wolf around the circular track beneath the clock dials. Or was the wolf chasing the hunter? The tiny brass automata circled the clock once before disappearing back into the cabinet. Applause and laughter arose from the audience.

"Delightful!" Amara said, clapping loudly. She glanced up at the queen. "It would look exquisite in the garden outside the parlor, don't you think?"

"Perhaps." Kara smiled at Herrick. "A lovely gift, Magister. Many thanks."

"We present it to you with our hope that it will toll many glorious hours for Eleysia." He stepped away from the clock. He turned his gaze toward Riese and Arkin. "And, naturally, we have gifts for the prince and princess as well."

Randolf came forward and handed Herrick a gift-wrapped box. The magister approached Riese. At her feet

Fenrir growled and bared his teeth. His hackles rose.

"Shush," she ordered. "Behave."

The cub lowered himself unhappily to the floor.

Herrick ignored the wolf. Close up the man smelled of machine oil, which probably explained the pup's reaction. He brushed his gloved fingers against Riese's as he offered her the box. Her skin crawled at his touch, but she did her best to conceal her distaste. The man was a guest, after all.

"For you, Your Highness."

She unwrapped the package to find a polished ebony music box with brass trim. A tinny melody played when she opened the lid. She did not recognize the tune, which had an odd atonal quality. Something about it sent a chill down her spine.

"It's enchanting," she lied. "Thank you."

"You are most welcome, Princess."

Randolf presented Herrick with another package. The magister turned toward Arkin. "And now for you, young prince." He knelt to look Arkin in the face. "Do not think that we have forgotten you."

His icy voice robbed his words of whatever soothing quality might have been intended, so that they sounded almost more like a threat than a promise. Arkin recoiled from Herrick. A frightened whimper escaped him.

"Don't mind my brother, Magister," Riese said quickly. "He's a little shy today." She squeezed her brother's hand. "It's all right, Arkin. He just wants to give you a present. Isn't that exciting?"

Rather than push the gift on Arkin, Herrick unwrapped it himself. He revealed a windup toy soldier complete with a miniature saber. A horned helmet capped the toy's head. Chain mail was painted onto his trunk. The toy reminded Riese of the valiant warriors who had gone off to fight beside her father.

"A loyal soldier for your army," Herrick explained. After winding the key in the toy's back, he set the soldier down before Arkin to demonstrate how it worked. The tin soldier marched across the dais, then stopped and raised its saber in salute. "To defend your land and conquer your enemies."

Riese suspected that her brother would have preferred a book instead. Still, she picked up the toy and gave it to Arkin. He accepted it from her without complaint.

"Thank you again, Magister," Riese said on Arkin's behalf. "We can never have too many soldiers."

"Indeed, Your Highness. Nor too many allies."

Herrick withdrew from the dais. Riese found herself distinctly relieved to have a little more distance between them.

"Is that all?" Amara asked, pouting slightly.

"My apologies, Baroness," Herrick said. "We did not think to bring you a tribute as well. Rest assured that we will remedy this unfortunate omission in due time."

"I will hold you to that promise," Amara said teasingly. "Don't think that I won't."

"Regardless," the queen declared, "the Sect's generosity is duly noted. I only regret that my noble husband is not present to extend his thanks as well. Alas, he was called away to defend the peace."

Herrick nodded. "We are aware of the menace posed by Nixe and its recent incursions. Know that the Sect stands ready to offer whatever assistance we can render."

"Eleysia is quite capable of defending its borders on its own," the queen said confidently.

"No doubt," Herrick agreed. "Your nation's might is famed throughout the world. Yet even the strongest of kingdoms can benefit from the right alliances. That, in part, is how they remain strong in the face of unexpected challenges."

"This is so," she conceded, "and we value your kind offer." She paused to give the matter further thought. "Although, I would ask what the Sect desires in return."

"Merely the throne's blessing to spread the word of the Goddess throughout this fair land," Herrick replied evenly. "And perhaps establish a monastery or two."

"That seems harmless enough," Amara opined. "And perhaps advantageous too. As you said, Magister Herrick, one can never have too many allies in these turbulent times."

Not so fast, Riese thought. *What do we really know about the Sect?*

Her mother also seemed in no hurry to commit herself. "You may tell your high priestess that Eleysia is pleased to make the Sect's acquaintance. We look forward to learning more of your faith in times to come."

"That is all we ask," Herrick assured her. "Many thanks again for receiving us."

Fenrir growled at the newcomers as they departed. He clearly didn't like the way they smelled.

Riese had her doubts as well.

CHAPTER ELEVEN

THE WOODEN STAFF CAME SWINGING AT HER HEAD.

"Very good, Princess," her fighting instructor praised Riese as she parried the blow with her own staff, feeling the jarring impact all the way down her bare arms. She shoved against the strike, then jumped backward out of range. He grinned in approval. "You're getting better."

"I would hope so." She jabbed the lower end of her staff at his foot. Their staves collided again. "Especially now that we may be at war."

They were sparring in a lush green garden behind the palace. She inhaled the scent of the fragrant rosebushes. Neatly trimmed hedges gave the two of them a degree of privacy, although it was possible people were watching from the rear windows overlooking the garden. They fought atop a carpet of thick green grass that waited to cushion any falls. The sky was clear, with no hint of war clouds on the horizon, and the day was warm enough that she could wear only a light sleeveless tunic, linen trousers, and boots. Her hair was tied back behind her.

"I wouldn't fret about that, Your Highness." Hund was

a retired army sergeant who had earned his scars keeping Asgard's roads clear of highwaymen. "The king will send those Nixian swine packing soon enough."

She hoped he was right. Only days had passed since her father and his troops had marched north to Geffion, but she already missed him. Advance reports were that the Nixians were continuing to mass along the border. These could not be mere maneuvers or saber rattling. A full-scale invasion seemed imminent, unless the Nixians came to their senses and withdrew back to their own domain. Eleysian forces were already being diverted from elsewhere to provide reinforcements if necessary. Riese could not remember the last time her father's army had gathered in such numbers, let alone faced anything more than bandits or minor insurrections.

The staccato click of staff against staff punctuated the afternoon. If nothing else, the sparring helped take her mind off her father's absence—and whatever danger he might be facing soon. Would the Nixians truly dare to invade Eleysia itself?

"Not that you're not ready to kick some Nixian rear," Hund assured her. He beamed at her proudly even as he tried unsuccessfully to batter her to the ground. "I pity any rogue who tries to fight you for real."

She smiled to herself, wishing she could tell him about her bout with Micah and how she had bested him. But nobody could know about her clandestine trysts with the handsome young apprentice. That was her own special secret. A warm glow came over her. She couldn't wait to meet with Micah at the falls again.

Maybe tonight?

Daydreaming, she almost missed an overhead swing at her skull. A hasty parry halted the strike only inches from her nose.

"Careful, young cousin!" A cheerful voice, accompanied by a brittle laugh, distracted Riese. "You need to keep your wits about you, or you could lose your pretty head."

She turned to see Amara entering the garden. Riese was slightly annoyed by the interruption, but smiled back at their guest for manner's sake. She lowered her staff.

"Hello, Amara."

Hund tipped his head in respect. "Baroness."

Amara barely acknowledged his presence. A rich purple tunic was belted at her waist. Tight silk leggings were tucked into a pair of knee-high black boots. Auburn hair fell in waves past her shoulders. Riese caught some of the sentries discreetly admiring the attractive widow. She wondered if Micah would do the same.

Amara glanced around the garden. "Is your pet about?"

"Fenrir is in the kennel," Riese told her. "Taking a nap with the other cubs."

"Probably just as well," Amara said. "I fear he still hasn't warmed to me." She shook her head. "I understand that you have your traditions, but, really, I'm not sure why you put up with those beasts. They belong in a cage, not a palace."

The same reason we welcome you, Riese thought. *They're family.*

"They make excellent guards," Riese volunteered instead. "Fenrir would never let any harm come to me."

"It looks to me like you can take care of yourself." Amara

smirked at Riese's staff. She stepped forward and claimed Hund's stave from the surprised veteran. "Or am I mistaken?"

Was Amara challenging her? Riese hadn't expected that. "You can use a staff?"

"Naturally." Amara twirled the borrowed stave around her body in a blur of motion. She showed off a few more moves before assuming an offensive posture opposite Riese. "A true royal must always be prepared to defend one's position—or risk losing it."

"I hadn't thought of it that way," Riese admitted.

Amara smirked again. "You should."

Not waiting for Riese to accept her challenge, she lunged forward, thrusting the right end of the staff directly at Riese's heart. Caught off guard, the princess barely got her own stave up in time to block the blow. The force of the attack almost knocked the staff from her fingers. The match, it seemed, was under way.

All right, Riese thought. She tightened her grip upon her staff. *Let's see if you can do more than tricks.*

The two women circled each other, testing each other with tentative feints and lunges. Riese quickly realized that Amara knew was she doing. Her staff came at Riese with speed and precision, forcing Riese to respond in kind. The crack of wood against wood, colliding time and again in an intricate dance, disturbed the tranquil serenity of the garden. Riese found herself working up a sweat, even as Amara rose in her estimation.

She can fight, Riese conceded. *I'll give her that.*

"Excellent form and technique," Amara observed. She

seemed to be enjoying herself. "You're clearly your father's daughter."

"And my mother's," Riese insisted. Just because the queen excelled at diplomacy and statecraft didn't mean that Kara did not have the heart of a she-wolf. People underestimated her at their peril. *If only she could be queen forever.*

"Of course." Amara momentarily retreated. "I didn't mean to imply otherwise."

A small audience of guards and gardeners gathered to watch the duel. Curious heads leaned out of palace windows. Riese overheard wagers being made on the outcome, and was gratified to note that she was the favorite. Not too surprising in Asgard, perhaps. She wondered if the odds would be different in Hariasa.

Possibly.

"You must be looking forward to your coronation," Amara cooed, making conversation while throwing a roundhouse kick at Riese's chin. She chuckled as Riese ducked beneath the kick. "How exciting for you!"

Riese shrugged. "I suppose."

"But to be so close to the throne!" Amara sounded puzzled by Riese's lack of enthusiasm. She shifted her grip on the shaft and swept the lower end at Riese's knees. "Only one step from becoming queen!"

Riese jumped above the swing so that it passed harmlessly beneath the soles of her boots. "My mother is queen. I'm in no hurry to take her place."

"You make it sound like a burden!" Amara scowled, visibly annoyed by Riese's words. Her affectionate manner slipped somewhat. "There are many who would kill to be in your place." She launched a furious attack on Riese, driving the younger woman back toward the high stone walls of the palace with a rapid barrage of blows. Riese felt spittle against her face. "Eleysia deserves to be ruled by someone who truly desires its throne—and is not afraid to wield its power."

Amara's emotions made her careless. She raised her staff high above her head, like an executioner about to behead a prisoner, and brought it down in an arc. The staff whistled through the air, but Riese deftly sidestepped the blow, then spun and swept Amara's legs out from under her. The uprooted baroness landed flat on her back upon the grass. A chorus of laughter and applause erupted from the onlookers. Money exchanged hands.

"I don't know about power." Riese stood over her fallen opponent. She gently pressed the blunt end of her staff against the base of Amara's throat. "But I think I can wield a staff."

"So it appears," Amara said sourly. She obviously didn't like losing. Her staff slipped from her fingers. "I yield, little cousin."

Riese withdrew her own weapon. Her parents had always taught her to be gracious in victory, so she extended a hand to help Amara up. "Thanks for the bout. You put up a good fight."

"Not good enough." Amara quickly let go of Riese's hand. A stern glance silenced their audience, who quickly dispersed. "You won this time, Cousin." She brushed the grass from her clothes, then managed a slightly forced smile. "Perhaps we will test each other again someday."

"Perhaps." Riese accepted a skin of water from Hund. The cool refreshment tasted delicious after the hot, sweaty fight. She offered a sip to Amara, who shook her head. Riese shrugged. "Someday."

As invigorating as the bout had been, Riese didn't need a rematch anytime soon, not if it meant spending more time with Amara. Blood kin or not, something about the woman got on Riese's nerves. Amara always said the right thing, and fell over herself to be part of the family, but at times she reminded Riese of a greedy hyena coveting a wolf pack's kill. Like she was really only looking out for herself.

Or maybe it was just that the baroness didn't like wolves.

In any event, Riese hoped Amara would be leaving soon.

Maybe after her father got back from the war?

"Tell me about your sister," she asked. "If you don't mind."

"Aliza?" Micah asked. "Why?"

"No reason," she lied. "I'm just curious."

Riese rested her head against Micah's shoulder as they reclined against the standing stones, gazing out over the falls. A blanket, smuggled from the palace, was stretched out beneath them. A picnic basket held a flagon of fresh cider and a couple of apples that she had filched from the kitchen. She kicked off her boots. Her cloak was draped over the fallen monolith a few paces away. It was warm enough that she didn't need it.

In truth she wanted to get to know him better. Sparring and swimming and cuddling were all good enough, but she felt a desire to get closer to him. Or at least as close as she could while pretending to be someone else.

"You don't have to if you don't want to," she added hastily, hoping she hadn't gone too far. He had spoken briefly of his sister earlier, before his thrilling dive over the falls, and it had been clear that this was a painful subject for him. "I don't mean to pry."

"No, it's all right," he assured her. "You'd like her, actually. She's a lot like you—tough, stubborn, reckless . . . and not afraid to smack me about the head when she feels like it. She's younger than me by a few years, about your age, but does she listen to me because I'm older? Of course not." He chuckled at the memory. "Ever since our parents died, we've had only each other to depend on. It's been the two of us against the world."

Riese nodded. It meant a lot that he was sharing this with her. She felt closer to him already.

"Do you miss her?" she asked.

"More than you can imagine," he admitted. "I just have to hope that we'll be together again someday . . . after I've finished my apprenticeship, that is." He turned toward her. "How about you? What's your family like?"

Riese swallowed hard. *I guess I asked for this,* she realized. She would have to be careful what she said, but she could hardly ask him to open up and not reciprocate in kind. Perhaps if she just spoke in general and left out the royal trappings?

"They're just a normal family, I suppose. It sounds like my brother is a bit younger than Aliza. He's incredibly bright for his age . . . and a much better student than I am."

"What about your parents?" Micah asked. "Do you get along with them?"

"I used to," she confessed. "But lately . . . I don't know. It seems like I'm always disappointing them, Mother particularly. We used to be close, but now it's like she wants me to be somebody completely different from who I am. Sometimes I think she'd be happier with a different daughter. Somebody like my cousin, perhaps."

"Cousin?"

"Well, she's my mother's cousin, technically, which makes her . . . what? My cousin once removed?" Genealogy had always bored Riese. "Anyway, she's been staying with us while my father is away, and she's just so helpful and polite and well behaved that she makes me look even less like the person my mother wants me to be. I'm the bad daughter, you see."

Her throat tightened. This was more than she had planned to divulge, but once she'd started, she couldn't stop. It felt good to finally share these feelings with someone.

Especially Micah.

"I'm sure that's not true," he said forcefully, like he wanted to make sure she heard him. "You're an amazing girl. I can't imagine any mother or father not being proud of you."

Riese blushed and felt warm all over. She saw nothing but admiration in his eyes, which was just what she craved right now.

"I don't know about that," she quipped, trying to hide the depth of her emotions. "I am here with you, after all."

"And what's wrong with that?"

He leaned in to kiss her, and she did not back away.

Her troubles melted away for a time and she stopped being Riese, reluctant heir to a kingdom on the verge of war, and was just Valka, a girl enjoying a romantic night with a boy. When they finally came apart, she felt like somebody at least liked her just the way she was. She was glad she had brought up his sister.

"Yes," she sighed. "This is just what I needed."

"Glad to hear it," he said. "Any reason in particular? Besides the obvious, I mean."

"A break from the palace," she answered honestly. "And everything going on there."

"Is it really that bad? Even for the servants?" He eyed her curiously. "I would have thought that you would be spared any royal intrigues or war talk."

Careful, she cautioned herself. *Don't give yourself away.*

"You'd be surprised. Everyone is waiting anxiously for news from Geffion. The king has issued an ultimatum to the Nixians, warning them to withdraw their troops from the border by noon two days hence. They say the fighting could start at any moment." She hesitated. "My father is away at the war . . . with the king."

She shuddered at the thought of her father riding into battle. Despite the pleasant weather, she snuggled closer to Micah. Although she had known him for little more than a week, she looked forward all day to their clandestine evenings together. They were her only escape from the gloom of the palace—and the future bearing down on her like a war chariot. With Micah she could be herself.

Sort of.

"Do you really think there will be a battle?" he asked.

"Is Eleysia prepared to go to war if the Nixians defy the ulti-matum?"

"Why wouldn't we be? Eleysia has kept the peace for centuries."

"True," he granted. "But what if the Nixians are stron-ger than expected? Does Eleysia have any allies it can call upon?"

Riese thought of the unsettling emissaries who had visited the court days before. The Sect had offered their assistance against Nixe, she recalled, although she doubted Eleysia would need it. Surely her father could drive back the raiders without any help from Herrick and his ilk!

Or so she hoped.

"Let's not talk about the war," she insisted. "I hear enough of that back at the castle." Her royal brand itched beneath her tunic. "Can't we just enjoy the night together?"

She had brought a candle as well, to create an even more romantic atmosphere, but Micah had wisely talked her out of lighting it. With the palace on a war footing, now was no time for the sentries below to spot a mysterious light in the hills. Somebody might think that a spy was signaling the enemy!

"Fair enough." He draped an arm over her shoulder. "Although I'm afraid I'm going to have to disappoint you tomorrow night."

Riese was sorry to hear it. "Why?"

"I'll be away for a day or two," he explained. "I'm leav-ing in the morning to deliver healing herbs, potions, and powders to the army."

She sat up straight, her eyes alight with excitement. "You're going to the front?"

"In the morning." He sighed at the prospect of the long trip. "Hopefully I'll be back in a day or so, after I've dropped off the supplies."

Riese couldn't believe her luck. She couldn't stand being cooped up in the palace while her father was risking his life to defend Eleysia. This was too good an opportunity to miss.

"Perfect," she exclaimed. "When do we leave?"

Micah blinked in surprise. "We?"

CHAPTER TWELVE

"I STILL CAN'T BELIEVE YOU TALKED ME INTO THIS."

Micah guided the horse-drawn cart down a lonely country road. Riese sat beside him at the front of the cart, behind a plodding gray nag. Their crates of healing herbs and powders were stacked in the back of the cart, which they had secured at a nearby village after traveling by carriage all day and all night to get here. By now someone had surely found the note she'd left behind at the palace, explaining that she had gone to see her father. She felt a twinge of guilt.

Her mother would be upset, Riese knew. A responsible heir and daughter would not run off like this, leaving her mother to worry. But Riese couldn't help it. She couldn't just sit at home and wait like a good little princess while her father marched into battle without her. That wasn't who she was, at least not yet. There would be time enough to do the sensible thing later, when they stuck a crown on her head. *Besides,* she thought, *what's the good of being a princess if you can't do what you want?*

"Thanks again for letting me come with you." She gave Micah a grateful kiss on the cheek. "I've been so worried about my father. Do you think we'll get there in time for the battle?"

A starry night sky stretched above them as the cart rolled past sleeping fields, pastures, barns, and farmhouses. She guessed that it was well past midnight. Dawn was still hours away.

"We should." He consulted a map by lamplight. His goggles rested atop his brow. "We're almost there."

"Good." Riese almost hoped that the enemy would defy her father's ultimatum. "I want to see those Nixian devils get what's coming to them."

Micah gave her a funny look. "You really hate them that much?"

"Why shouldn't I? Everything was fine until they started stirring up trouble." She recalled how that preening ambassador had openly disrespected her parents in their own court. "Eleysia offered Nixe help and friendship, but they chose to behave like rabid dogs instead. Because of their greed and arrogance, innocent people are in danger."

Like her father.

"Maybe they have their reasons," Micah suggested. "Things aren't always black and white." He kept his eyes on the road, avoiding hers. "Perhaps they've been driven to their deeds, by troubles not of their making."

His attitude puzzled her. She stared at him in confusion. "Why are you defending them? Don't tell me you condone their barbaric behavior?"

"No, no. Of course not," he added hastily. "I was just saying that sometimes good people have no choice but to do bad things." He made a transparent attempt to change the subject. "Aren't they going to miss you at the palace?"

"No," she said. "The princess was very understanding."

"What's she like?"

"Nice enough, I guess." Riese preferred to talk about the war. "Although I'm sure she's worried about her father."

"Who wouldn't be?"

Riese appreciated his sympathy, even if he didn't know he was talking about her. He had already lost his own parents, she recalled. She couldn't even imagine that.

"Look," he announced, with a trace of relief in his voice. "We're here."

Praise the Fates, she thought.

Coming over a rise, they spied the Eleysian army camped out in a sprawling meadow below them. Campfires and hanging lanterns lit up the camp. Armed sentries stood guard while the rest of the soldiers tried to get some sleep before the coming battle. Cavalry horses were penned near the rear of the camp. Canvas tents housed the officers and nobles, while the infantrymen and -women slept out in the open. Riese spotted her father's standard blowing above the largest and most richly trimmed tent. His chariot waited outside the tent, its armored plates gleaming in the starlight. An expectant hush hung over the camp.

Who knew what the morning might bring?

"Whoa," Micah said, slowing the cart.

They paused atop the hill to take in the view. Riese wanted to race straight to her father's tent, but forced herself to hold back. She could not go running to the king and still maintain the fiction that she was just a humble servant girl named Valka. Besides, she didn't want her father to have to worry about her safety on the eve of battle; he surely had more important matters on his mind. She needed to keep her distance, no matter how hard that was. It would have to be enough just to be here, which was better than sitting home waiting for news.

"Do you want to look for your father?" Micah asked.

"Maybe later," she hedged. "I don't want to get him in trouble with his commander. Maybe I just want to see what happens." She searched the horizon. "Where is the enemy?"

"Over there, beyond the woods." Micah pointed to the dense forest that began at the far end of an open expanse of meadow. The leafy barricade blocked their view of the enemy camp. He reached beneath the seat and handed her a spyglass. "If you look carefully, you can see the smoke from their fires."

Riese peered through the glass. True enough, white tendrils rose like ghosts in the distance on the other side of the woodlands. A chill ran down her spine. All at once the Nixian threat, which had been merely an abstraction before, felt all too real. Despite her earlier hopes of seeing the Nixians get what was coming to them, she now prayed that the enemy soldiers would retreat before the might of Eleysia. Perhaps this war could be nipped in the bud before any more lives were lost?

"I suppose we should find the surgeon's tent," Micah said solemnly. He glanced back over his shoulder at the crates piled in the back of the wagon. "They may need these supplies."

The cart ambled forward, but before they could head downhill, a blinding white light fell over the meadow, miraculously transforming night into day. Down in the camp startled warriors sprang to their feet and grabbed their weapons. Riese blinked against the glare. She didn't understand what was happening.

"Hel's spit!" she blurted. "What sorcery is this?"

She had never believed in such things before, but how else to explain the dazzling light?

"Not sorcery," Micah said grimly. "Lamps of some sort." He pointed at the woods. "Look. Up in the trees!"

The glare came from powerful glass lights mounted in the treetops. They flooded the meadow and Eleysian camp with an unholy white radiance that burned far brighter than any flame or candle. Riese marveled at the strange lights, which were like nothing she had ever seen before; it was as if the Nixians had bottled lightning somehow. The enemy must have placed the lamps in the trees without anyone noticing, Riese realized, but to what end?

The answer came quickly. Fireballs came arcing over the meadow, crashing down into the camp. Tents and corrals burst into flame. Frantic soldiers ran from the fiery barrage. It was as though the heavens themselves were throwing comets at the Eleysians.

"This isn't possible!" Riese gasped. "How are they doing this?"

"Catapults," Micah said. "They're using catapults."

She stared at him in disbelief. "At this range? That's not possible."

Catapults were crude devices, good for throwing small missiles short distances. They had some small use in siege warfare, where they could be used to pound away at an enemy fortress, but in the field they were no match for a charging cavalry. Most soldiers disdained them. A true warrior met his foe face-to-face.

"Looks like they've gotten better," Micah said. "A traveler spoke to me of this once. It's said that the armies of the Far East have been building better, stronger catapults."

Riese had never heard of any such innovations. She had studied warcraft, of course, but her lessons had always centered on the great battles and tactics of the past. Her glorious ancestors had never needed machines to win their wars. Theirs was a hallowed tradition of cunning and courage that had served Eleysia well for countless generations. Riese had always thought that would be enough.

Until tonight. None of her lessons had prepared her for this moment. All that mattered now was the havoc the blazing missiles were inflicting on her father's army. Riese watched in horror as the fireballs rained down upon the camp. Burning bodies now lay among the wreckage.

"This isn't fair! They're cheating!" She was appalled at the Nixians' treacherous nighttime attack. "Battles are supposed to start at sunrise!"

That was the way it was done, according to the codes of honorable combat. The rules of war had been laid down long ago. The Nixians *had* to know them. They were breaking all the rules!

But dawn had come early, bringing with it death and terror. Caught sleeping, the army responded with admirable speed and valor. Brave men and women snatched up their spears, swords, and battle-axes. The cavalry hurried to mount their warhorses, even as the fireballs kept plunging from the sky. Flames leapt from tent to tent, consuming everything in their path. Screaming people ran for cover. Smoke added to the confusion. Riese could smell it all the way up the hill. Her father's tent was not on fire yet, but it was one of the few that weren't. The camp was already under attack and the Nixians had yet to show their faces.

Cowards! Cheats!

The fireballs were just the beginning. Glass spheres crashed down from on high, shattering on impact and releasing clouds of sickly yellow gas. The sulfurous fumes spread quickly through the camp, mingling with the smoke from the fires. Stricken soldiers choked on the gas. They doubled over, vomiting and clawing at their eyes. Broken glass and writhing figures littered the ground.

"Poison!" Riese realized. "The fireballs were not enough? Now they're using poison, too?"

Was there no limit to their perfidy?

The gray nag whinnied in fear. Micah fought to keep the horse under control. He shot a worried look at Riese. "Do you want to get out of here?"

"No!" This was her fight too.

He nodded, not disagreeing with her. "Neither do I."

She claimed the spyglass again. Peering anxiously through the glass, she saw her father burst from his tent dressed for battle. He wore a shirt of the finest chain mail over his broad torso. A steel helmet, crafted in the likeness of a snarling wolf's face, crowned his head. A fur cloak was draped over his brawny shoulders. His face flushed with anger. He clutched a broadsword in one hand as he shouted furiously to his troops. Riese could not make out what he was saying, but she knew he must be rallying his forces. Her heart swelled with pride—and fear for his life.

Horns sounded. Well trained, the army fell into formation with lightning speed. Ulric boarded his chariot, which was hitched to four black warhorses. The wheeled basket, made of reinforced wood and metal, was large enough to carry a driver and shield-bearer as well. The king rode swiftly to the front of the army and raised his sword high so that all could see. Cheers rose from the ranks of the Eleysian war-riors. He swept his sword down.

The battle was on!

Bellowing like berserkers, the pride of Eleysia charged toward the enemy. The cavalry led the way, followed by waves of infantry. Valiant men and women brandished their weapons. The king rode amidst the foot soldiers, who doubtless took heart from his presence. Riese had never been more proud of him.

Now the Nixians would pay for their treachery!

Missiles shot from the woods. Whistling through the air, they resembled arrows but were the size of pikes. The huge bolts struck the charging cavalry head-on, spearing horses and riders alike. Impaled destriers crashed to earth, their riders flung onto the soft green grass, which quickly grew soaked in gore. Unseated riders were crushed beneath their own mounts.

Riese couldn't believe her eyes. "What? Where are those coming from?"

"Ballistae," Micah said. "Giant crossbows."

That didn't help. "What are crossbows?"

Bravely the cavalry continued their charge, even as their ranks were thinned by the lethal bolts. Forced to vault over fallen comrades and horses, they galloped forward, deter-mined to root the craven Nixians from their hiding places. Pounding hooves tore up the meadow.

"Ride on!" Riese cheered them. "For Eleysia!"

The enemy finally showed their faces. They burst from the woods like wild boars. Through the spyglass she caught her first glimpse of the invaders.

Unlike the Eleysians, who wore furs, leather, and armor

into battle, the Nixians flaunted wool uniforms dyed an identical shade of crimson. Leather caps with visors protected their skulls. Bandanas covered their mouths and noses, possibly to shield them from the fumes and smoke wafting from the camp. In all, they looked less like proper warriors than a swarm of angry red ants. Riese hated them on sight.

Their weapons were also new and strange. While some of the invaders bore ordinary swords and axes, others wielded odd weapons the likes of which she had never seen before. A handheld wooden contraption fired metal bolts the size of arrows, much smaller than the ones that had impaled the horses before. Riese guessed these were the crossbows Micah had spoken of. She saw at once that they were both deadly and accurate.

Larger ballistae rolled into view behind the first wave of Nixians. The massive war machines stood taller than a man and seemed to be operated by taut ropes and levers. Nixian soldiers reloaded the ballistae with terrifying efficiency. Metal pikes fired over the heads of the Nixians into the oncoming Eleysians. Valiant men and women were cut down where they ran.

Even stranger were the Nixians sporting riveted copper tanks upon their backs. Each of these men held a hose attached to his tank and aimed a metal nozzle at the oncoming Eleysians. Streams of fire sprayed from the nozzles.

"I don't believe it!" Riese gasped. "They're throwing fire!"

Micah reached for the spyglass. "Let me see!"

She refused to surrender the spyglass, holding on to it

with all her strength. What she was seeing was like a night-mare, but she couldn't look away.

What sort of battle was this? The Nixians were not fighting fair!

A line of fire throwers met the cavalry's charge. Alarmed by the crackling flames, the warhorses balked and reared up in fright. They whinnied and backed away while their riders tugged on their reins. Whips of fire lashed the air between the two armies. Gas bombs crashed into the midst of the infantry, who halted and looked anxiously to their king.

Ulric did not falter. Waving his sword high, he urged his chariot on as though he intended to personally trample the enemy beneath thundering hooves and wheels. Cross-bow bolts bounced off the chariot's iron plates. The king's shield-bearer defended him while the driver cracked a whip above the heads of the horses. For a second Riese allowed herself to hope that her father could turn the tide of battle through sheer will and courage alone.

Then the ballistae fired again. A lucky shot impaled the chariot's lead horse, which tumbled to the ground, drag-ging the rest of the team behind it. The chariot struck the downed horses and flipped forward. The shield-bearer was flung from the basket. The chariot crashed down onto Ulric.

"No!" Riese shrieked.

The attack on the king ripped the heart from the over-whelmed troops. Terrified men and women broke ranks and fled from the meadow. Riese could scarcely blame them. This was no glorious battle, pitting sword against sword, such as they had always fought before. It was a slaughter.

The Nixians had changed the rules.

A heroic charge turned into a rout. Entire divisions abandoned the battlefield and the burning camp. Not just soldiers ran, but cooks and medics and smiths as well. No horn sounded the retreat, which, in truth, was nothing more than a panicked, disorderly flight. The screams of the dying and wounded added to the pandemonium. The wind shifted, carrying the smell of smoke and worse. Whiffs of vapor caused Riese's eyes to water. Her throat burned. Micah coughed beside her.

It was too much for the agitated dray horse. The nag wheeled the cart around, dragging its passengers with it. "Whoa! Whoa!" Micah shouted at the beast, but he wasting his breath. He tugged futilely on the reins. "Whoa there, you stupid horse!"

"Stop her!" Riese shouted. She stared back over her shoulder at the battlefield, where her father lay wounded, dead, or dying. Smoke and gas, as well as hordes of stampeding deserters, blocked her view. She couldn't see her father. "Stop! We're going the wrong way!"

"I'm trying!" He yanked on the reins. "I can't get her under control!"

She felt the cart carrying her away from her father. The frightened nag was not going to listen to them, and who could blame her? Riese realized there was only one thing left to do.

"I'm sorry!" She snatched Micah's goggles from his head. "I have to do this!"

With no time to explain or even say good-bye, she jumped from the cart. Her body hit the ground and rolled across the bumpy dirt road.

"Valka!"

Looking up from where she'd landed, she caught only a glimpse of his shocked expression before the bolting horse carried him away. Cart, horse, and Micah sped back down the road, shrinking into the distance.

"Take care," she whispered. She assumed he would be safe, provided he stayed ahead of the enemy, but she couldn't worry about that now. She needed to get to her father.

She climbed to her feet, ignoring the bruises the fall had brought her. After brushing herself off, she put on the goggles; with any luck they would help protect her eyes from the fumes. She tied a handkerchief over her nose and mouth. Her baton hung upon her belt. She unclasped it and pressed the hidden stud. It snapped out to its full length.

Armed and ready, she ran downhill into the madness. Screams and smoke surrounded her. The fumes stung her eyes but not enough to blind her. The former camp was now a shambles. Pennants and standards lay discarded upon the ground, trampled beneath the feet of the deserters. A mob rushed past her, buffeting her, so that she felt like a salmon fighting its way upstream against a raging current. She lashed out with her staff to keep from being carried back the way she had come. Whirling blows cleared a path through a flood of fear-crazed bodies. If not for her staff, she surely would have been trampled as well.

"Stop! Come back!" she hollered, trying to rally the fleeing soldiers. "Your king needs you!"

Her voice was lost in the tumult, her face unrecognized behind the goggles and handkerchief. She was just a girl in a cloak, running the wrong way into danger. Nobody paid any attention to her. A panicked infantryman, bleeding from a shoulder wound and almost twice her size, charged toward her. She knocked him aside with a swing of her staff.

"Sorry about that."

More bodies impeded her progress. At this rate she'd never get to the battlefield in time. Frustrated, she glanced around for some way to get past the deserters.

Her gaze fell upon a frightened white courser tethered to a tree. Forgotten in the confusion, the horse pulled at its reins. The scorched body of an army courier lay nearby. Riese guessed that the woman had been meaning to carry word to the palace before being killed by a fireball.

There was no time to mourn her. "Easy now!" Riese told the horse as she scrambled onto its back. She cut it loose with a swipe of her dagger. "Let's go find our king!"

The courser was of sterner stuff than the dray horse. It took only a firm hand and a confident voice to turn it toward the battlefield.

"That's it!" Riese said. "Ride!"

They galloped across the blood-soaked meadow, through the fleeing troops. Riese's brown cloak flapped behind her. Holding on to the reins with one hand, she wielded her staff against anyone who got in her way. Peering through goggles, she searched the battlefield for her father's overturned chariot. Where exactly had she seen it last?

"Faster!" she urged the courser. "We need to find him!"

The once peaceful meadow had become a hellish limbo. The bright lights blinded her. Corpses were strewn upon the grass. Fallen horses posed obstacles to be hurdled over. The heavy gas clung to the ground like fog. She choked on the fumes even through the cloth over her mouth. The goggles seemed to help, though. She would have to thank Micah for them later.

If she ever saw him again.

Up ahead, far too close for comfort, she spotted the enemy forces advancing toward her. Slowly, methodically, they made their way across the meadow. Fire throwers cleared the way with a bright orange wall of flame. Crossbow bolts struck Eleysia's defenders in the front and back, depending on which way they were running. Catapults and ballistae had been wheeled out from beneath the cover of the woods. Riese gaped at the huge wooden machines. Who had devised these terrible weapons of destruction?

The breathless ride felt like it took forever, but it was only minutes before she reached the upside-down chariot. To her relief a small cadre of loyal guards had formed a defensive circle around the site of the crash. Eleysian archers fired back at the Nixians with their longbows while their comrades strained to rescue the king from beneath the chariot, whose wheels had stopped spinning. Riese spotted the body of the shield-bearer lying on the grass nearby, his neck obviously broken. The remaining horses had already been put down so that their frantic struggles would not drag the chariot over the men underneath. The stench of blood and sweat filled the air. Riese gagged behind her handkerchief.

Just as she arrived, a crushed body was dragged out from beneath the chariot. Riese braced herself for the worst, until the body was turned over and she saw that it was the driver and not her father. Even still, the sight of the woman's crumpled remains filled Riese with dread. Was her father in the same awful state—or worse?

A groan from beneath the basket made her heart jump.

"He's alive!" she cried out, riding up to the scene. "Do you hear that? Help him!"

A soldier recognized her voice. His jaw dropped. "Princess?"

Riese knew him to be a member of her father's personal guard. What was his name again? Geir? She lifted her goggles to reveal her face. It was probably just as well, she reflected, that Micah was not here to witness this encounter, not that she really cared about that now. Saving her father was more important than hiding her true identity from a boy she barely knew.

"See to my father!" she commanded. "The enemy approaches!"

The guard remained transfixed by her unexpected arrival. Sweat and soot could not conceal his confusion. "But . . . Your Highness, what are you doing here?"

"Never mind that." She threw him her staff. "Try this!"

The soldiers put their backs and shoulders to the task. Using Riese's staff as a lever, they managed to lift the chariot high enough for the other guards to pull the king free.

Father! Riese thought. *Please don't die!*

They laid him gently upon the ground. She saw at once that he was still alive, but injured. The crash had dislodged his helmet, and his gray hair was awash with red from a bloody head wound. He groaned pitifully but refused to let go of his sword. Dazed eyes found her upon her horse. His brow furrowed in bewilderment.

"Riese?"

His eyelids drooped. He slipped into unconsciousness.

"Father?"

She glanced up at the advancing Nixians. They were getting closer. Crossbow bolts steadily cut down the king's defenders. The smoke from the fire throwers had a harsh chemical smell.

"You need to leave this place!" Geir insisted. "Both of you!" At his direction the other guards lifted Ulric from the ground and draped him over the back of the white courser. Straps cut from the dead horses' harnesses tied him in place securely. "Go!" the guard urged her. "We'll hold the bastards off for as long as—"

A metal bolt struck him in the back. His life gurgled from his lips and he dropped to the ground. The other guards fired back at the Nixians, but they were fighting a losing battle. Riese could already feel the heat of the fire throwers upon her face. The Nixians jeered and shouted as they approached.

"Go to your ancestors," Riese whispered to the lifeless body at her feet. Geir had given his life for his king. She did not intend to waste it. "Go!" She wheeled the horse around and dug her heels into its sides. "Run for Eleysia! Run for our lives!"

The horse galloped away from the chariot and its doomed guardians. Riese could hear the Nixians marching behind her.

She did not look back.

At least Micah is safe, she thought. I hope.

CHAPTER THIRTEEN

A PAIR OF GUARDS ESCORTED RIESE INTO THE ROYAL LIBRARY. They were under strict orders to see her safely back to the palace, regardless of what the princess herself thought of that plan.

"Riese!" Her mother looked up from behind her desk, which was buried beneath heaps of maps, scrolls, and other documents. The busy queen rose to her feet. She did not appear happy. "What were you thinking?"

Riese braced herself for her mother's wrath. She had been expecting this.

"Yes," Amara chimed in. The baroness reclined upon a nearby divan, idly flipping through some dusty tome. She did not get up. "We've all been worried sick." She shook her head sadly. "That was very thoughtless of you."

The baroness seemed in no hurry to go home. She claimed it was because she wanted to be there for their family while the king was away, but Riese suspected that Amara just liked being so close to the throne and was using the crisis to push her way into the middle of things. She had already taken to supervising minor household affairs, so that the queen could concentrate on larger matters. Riese was starting to think Amara was overstepping her bounds, but Kara seemed grateful for Amara's support—and perhaps a trifle blind to her ambition. Riese was tempted to say something, but now was probably not the time. If anything, Amara was making her look bad by comparison.

"I'm sorry, Mother," she apologized. "I just wanted to be with Father."

"But you could have been killed." Kara came out from behind her desk. The strain of the last few weeks showed upon her careworn features. She looked like she had not been sleeping well. "As if I don't have enough to worry about these days!"

Guilt stabbed Riese. But how was she to know that the war would go so badly? The Nixians were supposed to have been the ones who fled in disarray. Her father had said so.

"I left a note," she said sheepishly.

"And you think that excuses you?" Kara shook her head in disbelief. "A note?"

Riese didn't know what else to say. She stoically awaited whatever punishment her mother had in store. *Let me have it,* she thought.

But the queen could not stay angry at her reckless daughter. Relief overcame her ire, and she rushed forward to embrace Riese. "Thank the Fates you're safe!"

"Yes," Amara echoed dutifully. "Thank the Fates."

She rose to welcome Riese, who grudgingly accepted her embrace as well. Amara could be a bit much sometimes, but she was still family and a fellow Eleysian. Now was no time to let petty squabbles divide them. So what if Amara was maybe a little too eager to trade on their family ties?

They needed to stand together against the Nixian menace.

"And your father?" Kara wrung her hands anxiously. "They say he was hurt."

"He is well," Riese assured her. Thankfully Ulric's injuries had proved less grievous than they had first appeared. He would likely have a scar on his brow, and might walk with a limp for a time, but he had been back on his feet when last Riese had seen him. Their reunion had been painfully brief; he had insisted on staying behind with what remained of his army, which was now fighting a rearguard action against the advancing Nixians. "But many others are not."

The queen nodded. "So we understand." No doubt she had already received many dire reports of the defeat in Geffion. "And is the enemy truly as fearsome as they say?"

Riese slumped, weighed down by the horrors she had witnessed. "You cannot imagine."

The rout in the meadow had been only the beginning. Before her father's guards had put her on the first carriage back to Asgard, she had watched from afar as the voracious Nixians had begun to pillage the lands they had overrun. Farming families, who had nurtured their lands for generations, were forced to abandon their homes, joining a growing stream of refugees and deserters flowing out of Geffion. Most appeared to be flocking toward Asgard and the capital. Riese wondered if her mother had any idea of the misery marching toward them at this very minute.

"It was horrible, Mother. They're like locusts, consuming everything in their path."

"Take heart," Kara said, trying to reassure her. "We have lost only a solitary battle. Eleysia shall prevail, as we always have before. Your father and I will soon find the means to repel these invaders."

Riese wished she shared her mother's confidence. Memories of the Nixians' dreadful new weapons haunted her. *She hasn't seen what I saw.*

"Riese!" Arkin came running into the library. "You're back!"

"Hey there, little one!" Riese held out her arms, choking up at the sight of her brother. Although she had been gone for only a few days, her eyes grew moist nonetheless. She hugged him tightly, while struggling to hide her emotions. "I'm sorry I didn't get you anything."

"That's okay." Something sharp and metallic jabbed her in the ribs as he hugged her. She endured it until he finally let go and stepped back. She saw then that he was holding the windup toy soldier the Sect had given him. "I've been playing war." He held out the tin warrior for her inspection. Its pointy metal sword was raised high. "We've been killing Nixians!"

Riese smiled wryly. *If only it were that easy!* A pity the Nixians' new "toys" were far more lethal.

"Did you see Father?" he asked.

"Yes. And he sends his love."

Arkin pouted. "You should have taken me with you."

"Maybe next time."

"Don't even think of it," Kara said sternly. She gazed sadly at her children, clearly grateful to have them both where she could see them. "Please, Riese, you mustn't run away like that again. Promise you won't."

Riese hesitated. She didn't want to bind herself to the

palace from now on, not with everything that was happening. "I promise," she said finally, just to give her mother some peace of mind. She crossed her fingers behind her back. *I suppose I can try to keep this promise . . . for a while at least.*

"I still don't understand," Amara said. "How did you get to the front in the first place?" She eyed Riese suspiciously. "Did someone help you?"

"No," Riese lied. She had no intention of implicating Micah, least of all to Amara or her mother. "I simply hitched a ride on a supply wagon, all by myself."

She tried not to let her anxiety show. In truth she had not seen Micah since they had lost each other during the battle. She could only hope that he had gotten away safely as well, although she would not truly rest easy until she saw him again.

Wait for me at the falls, she willed him silently. *I'll be there as soon as I can.*

"At least you're back home again." Kara sighed. "That's the important thing."

But was Micah safe? Or her father?

Were any of them really?

"No! Let me go! Don't hurt me!"

Her brother's cries roused Riese from slumber. She heard him through the open doorway connecting their rooms.

"Arkin?"

She stumbled out of bed and raced into his room. Moonlight, coming through an open window, guided her steps. Arkin thrashed beneath his sheets, obviously in the grip of a nightmare. Riese was alarmed by the sheer panic on his face. He had suffered bad dreams before but never like this. He looked like he was being tormented by a demon.

"It's here," he whimpered. "Ragnarok . . . "

"Arkin! Wake up." She nudged his shoulder. "You're having a bad dream."

She failed to rouse him at first. He flailed at her with his fists, and she had to hold his arms down to avoid being pummeled. She shook him harder.

"Arkin! It's me, Riese!"

She finally snapped him out of it. His eyes flickered open, and his frantic contortions quieted. He stopped straining against her. Groggy, he gazed up at her in confusion. "Riese?"

"It's all right." She stroked his brow, gently brushing his bangs away from his eyes. He felt slightly feverish. "It was only a dream."

He sat up, shivering. "But it seemed so real."

"That's just how dreams are sometimes." She climbed into bed with him and held him close. He trembled against her. His nightclothes were soaked with sweat. "But it's over now."

"Are you sure?"

She wondered if he needed to talk about it. "What were you dreaming about?"

"Ragnarok," he spoke in a hush, as though afraid to say the word out loud. "The end of the world." He shuddered and squeezed his eyes shut. "There were flames and blood and screams. Bad people were coming for me. I couldn't get away . . ."

Poor baby, Riese thought. *He's been listening to too much war talk.*

"It's just a border dispute, Arkin. Not the end of the world."

"But this is just the beginning," he said, not sounding comforted at all. "The final battle is coming, between the Goddess and her evil brother, who corrupted the world. Magister Herrick says only the purified will survive . . ."

"Herrick?" She recalled the Sect's austere emissary. "He's been here again?"

Arkin nodded. "He's been meeting with Mother and Cousin Amara."

Her blood boiled. How dare those odd clockwork cultists scare her little brother like this? Funny that they didn't mention this Ragnarok business while talking to Mother.

"And he's been filling your head with his nonsense?"

"My soldier broke, but his helper fixed it for me." The windup toy sat on a table by Arkin's bed. "Herrick says that Lune—that's the Goddess's brother—is jealous of her and wants to destroy all that she created. The whole world and all the people and animals."

"That's just silly," she assured him. She tapped down her anger for the time being, the better to soothe Arkin's fears. "You're my brother, aren't you? And you would never hurt me."

"No," he admitted. "I don't want to."

"Of course not." She hugged him tightly. "I don't care what Herrick told you. Brothers and sisters take care of each other. They don't go to war."

"Not even if they're gods?"

"Especially not." She gently eased his head back down onto his pillow and slipped out of the bed. "Now try to get back to sleep. It's late."

"I'll try." He drew his covers up to his chin. "Can I have my soldier?"

"All right," she said, trying not to frown. At the moment she wasn't favorably disposed toward anything having to do with the Sect. "If it will make you feel better."

He clutched the tin warrior close to him as she tucked him in. Despite her efforts to comfort him, he still looked worried.

"Riese? We'll never be enemies, will we? Like the Goddess and her brother?"

"Never." She kissed him on the forehead. "Don't be ridiculous."

She stood by the bed, watching over him, until he finally drifted back to sleep. He tossed fitfully in his bed but did not cry out. She could only pray his dreams were less troubling than before.

Her anger at Herrick returned. He had no right to frighten her brother with his scary teachings. Making her way back to her own room, she spied the ebony music box resting upon a shelf. Another of the Sect's unwanted gifts.

Her face hardened. Only the fact that Arkin was sound asleep kept her from snatching the music box and hurling it against a wall.

Just wait until she saw Herrick again!

CHAPTER FOURTEEN

Now

THE SUN WAS ALREADY LOW IN THE SKY BY THE TIME THEY reached the small township Usla had once called home. A timber stockade defended the town, which a simple wooden sign identified as Valgard. Riese had never heard of it before. If only it had been able to escape the Sect's notice as well.

Fenrir trotted at the women's side. "This is as far as you go," Riese told him. "Wait for me outside the village."

He whined unhappily but knew better than to accompany her into Valgard. Even back in the old days, one could hardly expect to walk a wolf through a town without attracting attention. Now, with a bounty posted on his entire breed, they would all be safer if Fenrir stayed behind. Riese watched the wolf disappear into the woods. She knew she wouldn't truly relax until they were together again.

Don't worry about him, she told herself. *He can take care of himself.*

Unlike Riese, Usla looked relieved by the wolf's departure. One night spent camping out in the woods, and a full day's hike across country, had not been enough to dispel the girl's discomfort around the beast. Riese couldn't blame her. Fenrir was a formidable adversary—as those Huntsmen had learned last night.

Riese felt much less safe without him.

"Thank you again for bringing me home," Usla said. Riese's wool cloak was draped over the girl's shoulders. The hood shrouded her face. She quickened her pace as they approached the stockade. "I can't wait to see my parents again."

Riese frowned. "I'm still not sure this is a good idea. The Sect will expect you to go home. This is the first place they'll look for you."

"But you killed the Huntsmen chasing me!"

"There will be others," Riese reminded her. "And they'll be coming here."

"Please," Usla begged. "Just a short visit! I have to see them!"

Riese didn't like it, but she knew how the girl felt. If there were even a chance that Arkin or her parents were still alive, she'd risk any odds to see them again. How could she deny Usla the same?

"All right," she said. "But we have to be quick about this. We can't stay for long."

"Thank you so much!" Usla exclaimed. "You don't know how much this means to me."

Yes, Riese thought, *I do.*

She hoped the girl would not be disappointed, but wondered silently what sort of reception was waiting for them. Usla's family and neighbors had let her be carried off by the Sect, after all. Would they be willing to harbor the fugitive now?

"I'm sure they'll be happy to see you, too," Riese lied.

Even if the girl's parents welcomed her back with open arms, the entire family would have to flee Valgard soon, before the Huntsmen caught up with them. One way or another this homecoming would be short-lived. "Let's go find them."

A solitary guard, wearing a gray leather cap, was posted at the town gate. His ill-fitting overcoat was frayed at the edges; it looked like it should have been replaced years ago. A metal pike leaned against the stockade. He snatched it up as the women approached.

"Hold! Who goes there?"

His tone was gruff. The business end of the pike pointed at the women. Riese guessed that Valgard didn't get many visitors.

The girl threw back her hood. "It's me. Usla."

The guard squinted at her. He had a grizzled face and gray whiskers. "Usla?"

"Yes, Olav. Truly." She clearly knew the guard of old. From the look of him, he had likely been manning his post since before she was born. "I've come home."

"Is that so?" The tip of his pike dipped slightly, but he did not lower it altogether. He cast a suspicious look at Riese. "Who's your friend?"

"Just a traveler," Riese answered. She felt uncomfortably exposed without her hood, although it was doubtful that anyone in these parts would recognize her, especially after so many years. "I met Usla on the road. She spoke highly of your town's hospitality."

"Did she now?" He scowled and kept the pike aimed in her direction. "It may be that things have changed."

"I won't be staying long," Riese promised. She wondered what she would do if the guard permitted only Usla to pass. Was she comfortable abandoning the girl at this juncture?

She might have no choice in the matter.

"Please, Olav!" Usla begged. "I just want to see my mother and father again." Moist eyes implored the guard. "How are they faring? Are they well?"

He looked away, unwilling to meet her gaze. Riese saw a muscle twitch in his cheek. "Best you see for yourself." He finally lowered the pike and stepped aside. "Go on." He gestured brusquely toward the open gate. "Curfew is at sunset. Don't you be forgetting that."

The guard's evasive manner troubled Riese, but they hurried past him before he could change his mind. Once they were inside, Olav closed the gate and bolted it from the inside, cutting them off from the outside world. The sound of the bolt sliding into place sent a chill down Riese's spine. She resisted the temptation to turn around and ask Olav to let her out again. Fenrir would be waiting for her.

No, she thought. *Don't think like that.*

She had resolved to deliver Usla back to her family. She meant to see that through, despite her growing uneasiness. Perhaps the cranky old guard was simply leery of strangers? Who wouldn't be in these benighted times?

Usla was too excited to be home to notice the guard's reticence. "I don't believe it," she said, choking up. "I never thought I'd see these streets again."

Beyond the stockade Valgard resembled any number of small towns Riese had visited both before and after the rise of the Empire. A dirt courtyard led to a warren of narrow streets lined with shops and stables. To make the most of the constricted space, the upper stories of the buildings jutted out over the cobblestone avenues. Typically these would be people's private quarters; most townsfolk lived above their businesses. Pitched roofs crowned the wooden structures, which were rarely more than two or three stories tall, although Riese glimpsed the top of a high domed tower deeper within the town. Carved signs hung in front of the shop's various entrances, advertising what sort of trade was practiced within. An oversize wooden shoe identified a cobbler's shop. A hanging wooden key spoke of a locksmith. According to Usla her parents ran a bakery. Riese kept her eye out for a sign shaped like a pastry or perhaps a loaf of bread.

Like the rest of Eleysia, Valgard had seen better days. Weeds sprouted between the paving stones, while broken windows were patched with paper or rags. Peeling paint and missing roof tiles suggested that the inhabitants no longer had the means to look after their homes, or perhaps had simply lost the will to care. Riese saw only the flicker of candles and lanterns, even though electric lights, powered by household generators, could now be found in many parts of Eleysia. Horse droppings rotted in the streets. Rats scurried through murky alleyways, which were clotted with broken-down junk and refuse. Many homes and businesses had obviously been abandoned, their gaping doors and windows dark. A feral cat hissed at Riese from the threshold of a deserted butcher's shop.

"I don't understand." Usla looked about in confusion. "Where is everyone?"

The townsfolk took the curfew seriously, it seemed. Although twilight had yet to fully surrender to night, the streets were largely empty. The few people still out quickly retreated into their homes at the sight of Riese and Usla. Metal shutters were pulled down over shop windows to protect whatever meager wares were on display. Doors slammed shut, ratty window curtains were hurriedly drawn, and locks clicked into place.

"What's wrong?" Usla asked aloud. This was not the homecoming she had expected. "What are they so afraid of?"

Us, Riese realized. *And what your return might bring.*

Usla spotted another familiar face. Her face lighted up at the sight of an older woman, gray-haired and stooped, trying to shoo a scrawny slow-moving hound into a run-down general store. Like the rest of the town, the dog appeared poorly looked after. Its coat was matted. Its nails needed trimming. Riese could see its ribs.

"Gudrun!" The girl rushed toward the old woman, her arms outstretched. "It's me! Usla!"

The crone blanched. She kicked the hound in the ribs, spurring it through the door, and disappeared inside without even acknowledging Usla's greeting. By the time the girl reached the stoop, the door had swung shut. The dog barked at her from the other side of the door. It was not a friendly bark.

Usla stepped away from the door, obviously shaken by the rebuff. "This is insane," she protested. "Gudrun's known me my entire life. She was like a second mother to me!" She ran a hand over her shorn scalp. Little of her blond hair remained. "Maybe she didn't recognize me?"

"Perhaps not," Riese said, although she privately doubted that was the case. She glimpsed the Sect tattoo upon Usla's wrist. As the guard had tried to warn them, things had changed. "Forget her. Where do your parents live?"

Usla seized on the prospect of seeing her family again. "This way." Turning away from the store, she guided Riese through the empty streets, which she clearly knew by heart. "Follow me."

They encountered no one else, but Riese was aware of furtive eyes peering out from behind tattered window curtains. She could practically feel the entire town tracking their progress as they made their way along the winding avenues. Too many eyes were watching them; Riese didn't like it. Her hand rested on the hilt of her knife.

This may have been a mistake, she thought.

"Hurry!" Usla urged her. "We're almost there!" Her earlier excitement returned, and she broke into a run. "Wait until you taste my father's pies. They're the best in Eleysia!"

Riese wasn't really thinking about pies. She just wanted to get off the street—and away from the eyes.

"This way!" Usla was sprinting now. Riese had to run to keep up with her. "It's just around the corner!"

She eagerly rounded the turn, then froze in shock. Her family home sat before them, at the end of a small cul-de-sac, but it was clearly not as she had left it. The one-time bakery was a ruin. Every window was shattered, and the front door had been smashed in. The sign—a cherry tart, as it turned out—dangled askew from a single link above the stoop. Broken glass littered the pavement in front of the vandalized building, which showed every sign of having been looted. The windows and doorway were dark; there was no evidence of life or light inside. No smoke rose from the chimney. And, most ominous of all, the mark of the Sect was painted in sinister black strokes upon the outer wall of the bakery.

Like a warning.

An anguished wail tore itself from Usla's lungs. "Momma! Poppa!" She rushed toward the breached doorway, heedless of the noise she was making. Glass fragments crunched beneath the soles of her shoes. "MOMMA!"

"Wait!" Riese called out, but Usla wasn't listening. The girl dashed into the building before Riese could stop her. Riese heard her shouting frantically inside. She hurried after Usla, cursing under her breath. Given the condition of the bakery, and Riese's own history with the Sect, she shuddered to think what the girl might find.

I was afraid of this.

The front door had been knocked off its hinges. Riese trod upon it as she entered the bakery. Little light entered the shop from the outside; it took her eyes a moment to adjust to the gloom. She saw at once that the bakery was just as ruined inside as out. The front of the shop, where the customers had once gathered, had been ransacked. Overturned stools and tables were smashed to pieces. Axe marks gouged the walls. The wounds looked fresh, suggesting that the bakery had been attacked only within the last few days. Plaster had been peeled from the walls, the front counter hacked apart. Pans, rolling pins, and shattered crockery were strewn across the floor. Spilled flour dusted everything.

Rats fought over crumbs and moldy crusts of bread. They squeaked defiantly at her, refusing to abandon their prizes.

"Vermin!" Their boldness disgusted Riese. She snatched a dented tin pan from the floor and hurled it at the rats. "Scram!"

The pan clattered against the floor, scattering the rats. Riese looked for Usla but didn't see her. "Usla? Where did you go?"

A stairway led to the family's private quarters one story up. The banister had broken off. Dried brown puddles stained the steps. Riese grimaced.

Whose blood had been spilled?

"Usla?"

She started up the stairs but had gone only a few steps before she heard a strangled cry from the rear of the bakery. Riese rushed back down to the ground floor and vaulted over what remained of the counter. She followed the sobs into a kitchen in the back. As one might have expected, the kitchen counters and oven took up much of the first floor.

"What is it? What's wrong?"

She found Usla crouched on the floor in front of a generously sized oven whose iron doors had been left open, exposing its cavernous interior. No coals burned inside the oven, whose fires were extinguished. Once, not so long ago, Riese assumed, the oven had baked all manner of tempting treats. The mouthwatering aroma of freshly baked bread and pastries had doubtless wafted throughout the premises and perhaps even into the street outside.

But no more.

Two charred human skeletons were half buried within the ashes filling the oven. The blackened bones were those of a grown man and woman; Riese had become far too familiar with mortal remains over the last decade. Bits of metal and cheap jewelry were fused to the bones—a belt buckle, a copper broach, a few charred clay beads. Mercifully the fleshless skulls could no longer convey the horror of the couple's final moments. Empty sockets gazed back at the two women. There was no way of telling if the bodies had been fed to the oven before or after they had been slaughtered.

Riese didn't want to know.

"Your parents?" she asked, although she already knew the answer. She placed her hand on Usla's shoulder. The girl flinched at her touch but did not pull away.

Usla nodded. "It's them. It has to be." She trembled as though caught in an ice storm. Her face had gone as white as the flour blanketing the floor. "But why?" she asked hoarsely. "Who would do such a thing?"

"You know who," Riese said.

Usla could not have missed the Sect's mark on the wall outside, the same as the one on her wrist. The girl's family had been punished for her heresy, as a lesson to anyone else who might consider defying the Sect.

No wonder the rest of the townsfolk wanted nothing to do with her!

"It's not fair," Usla sobbed. "My father . . . he wanted to fight them when they came for me. My mother, too. They weren't going to let them take me." Tears flooded her cheeks. Her nose ran. "But I begged them not to. I didn't want the Sect to hurt them. It wasn't worth their lives."

Her words dissolved into wrenching sobs. Riese's own

heart ached. She knew exactly what Usla was going through right now. She had lost her own family to the Sect many years ago.

A palace in flames. Burning tapestries falling from ageless stone walls. Swords clashing in the corridors. Screams and angry curses. Wolves howling. A torn coronation dress, splattered with blood. A family portrait consumed by fire . . .

Riese shook her head. Now was no time to wallow in her own jumbled memories. Usla had fled the convent only a few days ago, which meant that this atrocity was a fresh one. The Sect had already been here, and might still be nearby.

"We need to go," Riese said firmly. "Now."

Usla was too overwhelmed with sorrow to realize the danger. "But we can't just leave them here, not like this." She wiped her nose, struggling to pull her thoughts together. "We need to bury them, arrange for a funeral—"

"That's not going to happen." Riese wished she could give Usla time enough to mourn, but that wasn't safe for either of them. She tugged on the girl's arm, pulling her to her feet. "Don't you understand. The Sect beat us here."

She dragged the stricken girl out of the kitchen and toward the front door. Thankfully Usla was too overcome by grief to put up much of a fight. Riese hoped the girl was still capable of guiding them back to the town gate. If they hurried, perhaps they could convince Olav to let them leave Valgard immediately.

"Wait!" Usla tried to pull away. "Where are we going?"

"Away." Riese tightened her grip on the girl's arm. "I know how hard this must be, truly, but you can mourn them later. We can't stay here. This isn't your home anymore."

That much was obvious. The girl nodded numbly. She lowered her gaze, not wanting to see the desolate ruin the bakery had become. Her family, her home . . . She had just lost everything she had ever known. Riese wondered if Usla could ever truly recover from such a blow.

Have I?

The fallen door wobbled beneath their feet as they emerged from the bakery, only to discover that they were no longer alone. A trio of Huntsmen waited in the court-yard in front of the building, their weapons drawn. Their other hands held aloft burning torches. Scythes and hatch-ets glinted in the torchlight.

Damn it, Riese thought. *They found us.*

Had the Huntsmen been lying in wait all this time, wait-ing for Usla to return? Or had one of the townspeople alerted the mercenaries? Perhaps Olav the guard? Or Gudrun?

It didn't matter, Riese realized.

I should never have let Usla come back here.

"You!" Fury jolted Usla back to life. "You killed my family!"

She lunged toward the Huntsmen, but Riese grabbed on to her, holding her back. Usla twisted in her grip, trying to break free. The blood rushed back into her face. Hot tears released her anger. She shook her fists at the newcomers.

"Why? How could you?"

"You brought this reckoning upon them," a harsh voice answered her. "By forsaking your duty to the Sect."

The Huntsmen were not alone. A grotesque, sinister figure stepped forward, his imposing form encased in a stiff olive-green uniform ornamented with burnished bronze gears, sprockets, and other clockwork mechanisms. These were holy relics of the Sect, proclaiming the degree to which he had Purified himself in the eyes of his Goddess. A leather mask covered his entire head, hiding his face entirely. Opaque glass lenses, mounted in copper frames, had replaced his eyes. Breathing tubes coiled at the back of his hood. Every inch of his body was covered by metal or fabric. No bit of flesh or humanity showed through.

For a moment Riese thought the figure was Herrick, whom she now regarded as her personal nemesis. In the years since she had first met him, he had grown progressively more inhuman, so that he now looked much like the figure before her. A closer look, however, revealed that this was another of the Sect's creatures. He was shorter and stouter than Herrick, with what appeared to be an entirely prosthetic right hand. Although muffled by his mask, the man's voice was different too, and held a native accent not unlike Usla's. Riese assumed he was a local as well. Perhaps the regional magister?

"Give us the heretic," he demanded.

Riese did not bother replying. Instead she dragged Usla back into the shadow of the doorway and pulled down her goggles to obscure her identity. As far as the world knew, the Princess Riese had perished years ago, along with her entire family, but it was best not to take chances. Who knew whether the Sect truly believed her dead?

"We have no quarrel with you, traveler," the magister stated, "unless you choose to join the heretic in her apostasy." His Huntsmen spread out, blocking their escape. "Turn over the girl. She belongs to us . . . as does the child she carries."

Never, Riese thought.

"Is there a back door?" she whispered to Usla.

The girl nodded.

"Show me."

She released Usla, who turned and fled back into the bakery. Riese chased after her, even as the nameless magister called out to his minions. "Stop them! Don't let them get away!"

The Huntsmen pursued them.

CHAPTER FIFTEEN

RIESE AND USLA RACED THROUGH WHAT WAS LEFT OF THE BAKERY. Riese averted her eyes from the charred skeletons in the oven. A doorway at the rear of the kitchen led to a storeroom. Empty shelves and broken barrels indicated that the bakery's stores had been pillaged during the earlier raid. A crude wooden door, less elegant than the one that had once greeted customers, blocked their escape. Usla hastily unbolted it. Rusty hinges squeaked as the door swung open.

"This way!" the girl said.

Riese heard the Huntsmen crashing through the bakery behind them. The faceless magister urged them on. "Stop the heretics! They're getting away!"

The two women darted out into a narrow alleyway behind the store. Heaps of garbage had been left to rot. The sour stench assailed Riese's nostrils. An underfed mongrel, gnawing at a bone, growled at the interruption. They veered away from the dog, but it barked at them anyway. Fenrir had much better manners.

So much for a stealthy exit, Riese thought.

Thankfully the Huntsmen had not thought to post men

out back. She and Usla fled the alley before their pursuers could investigate the barking. They ran out into a slightly wider avenue lined with shuttered shops and town houses. Riese let Usla lead the way. The girl knew these streets. Riese didn't. But was there any refuge to be found inside the walled town?

It didn't seem so. Desperate to escape the Huntsmen, Usla pounded on the doors of her neighbors. "Please! It's me, Usla! Let me in!"

Her frantic cries went unanswered. Riese thought she spotted worried faces peeking out through the window curtains, but the doors stayed shut against the fugitives. Candles were blown out to make it seem as though no one were at home. Valgard had learned its lesson well. None of Usla's former neighbors wanted to end up like her parents.

"It's no use," Riese said. She grabbed Usla by the shoulder and dragged her away from a door. "They're not going to help you. Not anymore."

The Huntsmen emerged from the alley. Riese and Usla dashed down the streets with the brutal mercenaries hot on their tails. Night had fallen, but nobody had bothered to light the streetlamps yet. Riese hoped the darkness would help them elude the Huntsmen but feared that was wishful thinking. She looked about for someplace to hide.

"Is there anywhere we can go?" she asked Usla urgently.

"I don't know," the girl said. "I used to think I knew this town, these people. They were neighbors. But now?"

They zigzagged through a maze of back alleys. An abandoned pottery shop beckoned, and they scrambled through a broken window. Riese briefly considered hiding in the murky ruin until the Huntsmen had gone, but then a shattered ceramic shard crunched beneath her feet, startling a colony of bats roosting in the rafters. The creatures squeaked angrily and flew out the window in a flurry of leathery wings. A stray cat screeched at the ruckus.

"Over there!" a voice shouted outside.

"Hel's spit," Riese cursed. The wretched bats had exposed them.

Abandoning stealth, they raced across the shop and darted out the front door, which opened onto a small square. They dashed into the square, where Riese found herself face-to-face with her past.

A statue of the empress Amara posed atop a weathered stone pedestal that appeared much older than the statue itself. Her cruel, imperious features were instantly recognizable. The sculptor had done an excellent job of capturing Amara in all her ill-gotten grandeur. Riese wished there were time to smash the marble face to pieces.

Ten years had passed since the Sect had placed Amara on the throne of Eleysia, after overthrowing the rightful king and queen on the very eve of Riese's coronation. The princess alone had survived the coup, although few, if any, knew that. The secrets of that horrible night were still lost in a haze of blood and fire.

Not a day went by that Riese didn't wish that Amara had never been born.

She glared at the statue, wondering whose figure had formerly stood there. Ulric? Kara? One of their honored ancestors? Riese wouldn't put it past Amara to supplant any one of Eleysia's legendary heroes or heroines. She clenched her fists.

One day you will pay for your perfidy, Cousin.

But first Riese had to survive. Her goggles captured the dying light as her eyes searched the square. Which way held their best chance of escaping the Sect?

The tower she had spied before loomed at the far end of the square. Unlike the surrounding structures, it was solidly built of stone and mortar. Coarse gray walls rose a full story higher than any other building in Valgard. A glass dome, ringed by a wrought-iron balcony, crowned the tower, whose cylindrical dimensions contrasted with the right angles of the other buildings. Riese wondered briefly what purpose the tower served. An armory, perhaps, or a prison? It resembled a lighthouse in a way, although the nearest coast was at least two provinces away.

Usla slowed as they reached the center of the square. She looked around uncertainly. At least three streets diverged ahead.

"Which way?" Riese asked.

"I'm not sure," the girl admitted. "This isn't the Valgard I knew. I don't know what's safe anymore."

Riese understood. She felt the same way about all of Eleysia.

"Over here!" a strident voice shouted from an upstairs window. One of Usla's former neighbors, informing on her. "In the square!"

Riese cursed under her breath. The Huntsmen would be here any minute. She knew that she couldn't hesitate any longer, and was about to choose a street at random when, unexpectedly, a different voice called out.

"In here! Quickly!"

A door opened at the base of the tower. A lanky figure was silhouetted in the lighted doorway. He beckoned to the women.

"Hurry!"

Riese feared a trap, but what choice did they have? She turned to Usla. "Who?"

"Horst, the astrologer." The girl looked baffled. "Just a crazy old man . . ."

How crazy? Riese wondered.

The Huntsmen poured into the square behind them, making up Riese's mind for her. A crossbow bolt whistled past her head.

"We're coming!" she shouted at the open doorway. The women put on a fresh burst of speed and rushed into the tower. The stranger stepped aside to let them pass, then slammed a heavy oak door behind them. It thudded into place.

"About time," he grumbled. "Took you long enough."

Riese skidded to a halt. She turned toward their rescuer and got a hasty impression of a skinny old man in rumpled attire. "Thank you," she said, gasping, "but why—"

"Not now," he said curtly. "We need to secure the door."

Shaped like a headstone, the massive door was large enough to allow at least two people to pass through side by side. Thick planks of weathered oak were reinforced by riveted steel bands. A sliding timber beam further barred the door against the intruders. Easily half a dozen locks and dead bolts guarded the door, including four vertical steel rods the old man lowered into drill holes in the floor. Not until all the locks and bolts were engaged did the man— Horst?—turn to regard his new guests.

"Done!" he announced with satisfaction. "That should hold off those devils for the time being."

Riese was impressed. She had seen treasure vaults less fortified.

What was this place?

She took a moment to look around. The interior of the tower was filled with metal scaffolding that stretched all the way up to the domed chamber above, which housed a large mounted telescope. Spiral stairways climbed the walls like ivy, connecting a series of catwalks and gantries around the circumference of the vast open space, while an elaborate clockwork apparatus occupied the ground floor of the tower. More than half a dozen bronze globes of various sizes were mounted atop vertical steel rods that rose at right angles from longer horizontal bars that radiated like clock hands from the base of a raised metal platform at the center of the room. Interlocking gears beneath the platform indicated that the spheres could set to orbit each other in complicated patterns. The largest globe, the size of a boulder, was perched atop a rod at the very center of the display. Gilded spikes radiated from the orb like beams of light. A smaller globe, off to one side, was etched with the outlines of familiar continents and oceans. Yet another sphere, no larger than a fist, had a metallic sliver sheen. Darkened craters created the illusion of a face, one Riese recognized from the night sky.

The moon, she realized. *And the world and the sun.*

The tower was an observatory, complete with an orrery— a mechanical model of the sun, moons, and planets. When set in motion by gears and counterweights, the orrery would cause the globes to mimic the orbits of diverse celestial bodies around the sun. Riese recalled Mimir striving patiently to teach her the paths of each star and planet using a much smaller orrery back at the palace, not that she had ever paid much attention to such things. Arkin had always been the better student.

Arkin . . .

She glanced down at her feet. Mosaic tiles formed constellations upon the scuffed floor surrounding the orrery, with glittering flecks of crystal representing the stars. Riese spotted the Lovers, the Kraken, the Raven, the Anchor, the Wolf, and other astrological signs. Long-forgotten lessons surfaced from her memory.

"The Celestial Menagerie." She lifted her gaze to the device in the center of the room. "And the largest orrery I've seen."

"Ah," the old man said approvingly. "A scholar."

"No," Riese said. "Not really."

Tearing her gaze away from the artificial cosmos, she inspected their rescuer more closely. He was a tall, scrawny scarecrow of a man, with a scraggly white beard that looked like it hadn't seen a comb since last winter. Bushy black eyebrows bristled above unclouded gray eyes. A ratty velvet cap covered his pate. A pale complexion suggested that he didn't see the sun much, while he looked like he could use a good meal as well. His rumpled shirt and trousers were clean but threadbare, giving an impression of faded gentility. White linen sleeves were rolled up to his elbows. A pocket watch peeked from a vest pocket. The patches on his knees did not match the original fabric. Riese gathered that the astrologer received little business these days.

"Your name is Horst?"

"At your service." Cultured tones betrayed an advanced education. He examined her in turn. "You are not from these parts, as the stars foretold." He turned his attention to Usla, who clung nervously to Riese's side. "But you . . . I've seen you before." A high brow furrowed as he searched his memory. "Usla, isn't it?"

She nodded.

"I thought as much." He gazed at her sadly. His voice grew somber. "What the Sect did to your family was an atrocity. You have my most profound sympathies."

Grief caught up with Usla again. She collapsed against Riese, burying her face against the other woman's shoulder. Sobs rocked her body. Riese awkwardly hugged her back. She wished there were some way to ease the girl's sorrow, but how did you comfort someone who had just found their only family murdered? Riese knew from experience that there was no cure but time . . . and revenge.

"Open up!"

Fists pounded on the door, intruding on the poignant moment. Riese recognized the imperious voice of the magister. Usla shuddered and held Riese tighter.

"Open in the name of the empress!"

Horst glared at the door. "Go to Hades."

Riese regarded him with respect and curiosity. "You have no fear of the Sect?"

"I prefer to despise them," he declared. "And I assure you the feeling is entirely mutual." He gestured grandly at the room-size orrery. "The Sect have little tolerance for teachings that run counter to their own vaunted prophecies.

They regard astrology as heresy, and have banned me from practicing my own profession." A scowl slyly shifted into a smirk. "But they can't stop me from watching the stars, which move regardless of their decrees."

They can try, she thought, frankly surprised that the Sect had not razed this tower already, as they had any number of libraries, museums, and temples that did not conform to their strictures. She could only assume that the cult was still consolidating its power in this remote region. Given time, they would doubtless do more than simply deprive the old astrologer of his livelihood: they would demand that he recant his "heretical" beliefs, or suffer the consequences.

"Granted," Horst added, "I've managed to avoid provoking them—until now."

The Huntsmen threw their shoulders against the door, which shuddered but did not yield. The magister shouted over the efforts of his agents to force their way in. His accented voice rang with righteous fury.

"Hear me! Know that you are sheltering a heretic, which means that you are also defying the will of the empress, who has entrusted the Sect with the spiritual welfare of her people. Unbar the door, or declare yourself an outlaw and an apostate!"

"Eh?" Horst feigned deafness. "What's that? I can't hear you?"

The magister raised his voice. "The girl belongs to us! See for yourself. She bears our mark!"

Horst gently took hold of Usla's arm and inspected her wrist. "Was this of your choice?"

She lifted her face from Riese's shoulder. Her eyes were

red and wet, but she shook her head emphatically. "You know it was not!"

"Then you are welcome here, as expected."

Riese was puzzled by his remark. "Expected?"

Hadn't he said something about their arrival being "foretold" before?

"In a moment," he said, deflecting her question. He eyed the door with concern. The Huntsmen were nothing if not persistent. For the first time Riese detected a trace of anxiety behind the astrologer's bushy whiskers. "I've been adding locks for years now, ever since Eleysia's golden age grew tarnished, so the door should hold. Still . . ."

Overstuffed bookcases, their shelves sagging beneath piled scrolls and tomes, were squeezed into the spaces between the metal scaffolding. Horst shuffled over to a stained wooden bookcase by the door and leaned his paltry weight against it. "If you fit young ladies could assist me?" He coughed hoarsely. "I fear these old bones are not as strong as they once were."

Nothing is, Riese thought. *Except maybe the Sect.*

She and Usla hurried to assist him. Adding their own vigor to his, they shoved against the heavy bookcase, which stubbornly refused to budge. Emptying the shelves would lighten the load, but Riese doubted that the Huntsmen would wait patiently while the three inside carted away the accumulated volumes. Instead she redoubled her efforts, straining every sinew.

"On my count," she grunted. "Three . . . two . . . one!"

The bookcase toppled over onto its side, blocking the doorway. Books and scrolls spilled onto the floor. A star chart depicting the winter sky unfurled atop the tiles. The overturned bookcase had become a barricade.

"Much better." Horst wiped the dust from his hands. "My thanks for your assistance. That should ensure us a bit of privacy, at least for the time being."

But how long could they truly hope to keep out the Sect? Riese pondered their options. She spotted a few interior doorways and closets. Was there an escape route somewhere? Perhaps a secret door or tunnel?

She hoped so.

Usla had another question on her mind. "You said you were expecting us?"

"Indeed. I've been watching for you for days now." He turned his back on the barricade and beckoned for them to follow him. "Come. Let me show you."

The elevated globes and metal rods formed something of an obstacle course as they crossed the tower. They had to duck and weave to avoid bumping into the mock moon and planets. Horst moved effortlessly through the maze, knowing the route well, but Usla briefly caught her cloak on one of the sun's spikes. The astrologer led them up a rickety metal staircase to the observation deck of the tower, high above the ground floor. Riese stepped cautiously onto the platform, but it felt sturdy enough. Gaps in the metal grille permitted a clear view of the model solar system below.

Like the orrery, Horst's telescope was the largest she had ever seen. Burnished brass knobs and levers were fixed to a hollow wooden cylinder that was easily as long as the bookcase they had just toppled. An eyepiece was installed into one side of the telescope, which was mounted atop a large brass ball bearing, allowing the telescope to be rotated and tilted at will. At the moment it was pointed out at the night sky, which was clearly visible through the glass dome. Stars glittered like ice in the dark purple firmament.

"Behold my pride and joy." Horst gave the telescope an affectionate pat. "With these powerful lenses I can probe the heavens, whether the Sect likes it or not." He tilted the telescope downward toward the town. "And, not incidentally, I could keep watch over the town gates as I awaited your arrival."

Riese was dubious. "But how did you know we were coming?"

"The stars," he replied. "They predicted your coming."

She wasn't sure she believed that. More likely the old man had heard of Usla's escape from the convent and knew that the Huntsmen were lying in wait for her. Still, she was grateful to be granted sanctuary, regardless of the reason.

Any port in a storm . . .

They could still hear the Huntsmen pounding on the door below. Axes hacked away at the steel-ribbed door. The magister bellowed above the din.

"Surrender, heretics! Every moment you defy us condemns you all. Give us the girl before you are all damned for eternity!"

Horst scowled. "Excuse me for a moment."

A sliding glass panel led out onto the iron balcony surrounding the dome. Riese and Usla followed him onto the gallery. A cold night wind chilled Riese and made her long for her cloak. From their lofty vantage point they were able to gaze down at the Huntsmen laying siege to the tower.

The mercenaries and magister looked like dolls, but not the sort any sane child would ever want to play with. Riese was very glad that the observatory was built of stone and not timber. At least the Huntsmen could not readily set the tower on fire.

"Bloody-minded fanatics," Horst muttered. "Bring their bullying to my door, will they?"

Tin pots and buckets were lined up along the balcony. He hefted one and leaned out over the railing. Broken glass and rusty nails rattled in the pail.

"Look out below!" he shouted before dumping the contents of the bucket onto the Huntsmen. They scattered, covering their heads, as the nails and glass fragments rained down on them. Horst laughed uproariously at their inglorious retreat. "That's right! Run, you cowardly miscreants! There's more where that came from!"

The magister and his minions withdrew beyond the range of Horst's armaments. The Huntsmen shook the jagged shards from their clothes. From this height it was hard to tell how badly any of the men might have been injured. Riese guessed that their wide-brimmed hats and heavy coats had shielded them from serious harm, but they seemed to be in no hurry to tempt Horst's wrath again. They conferred with the magister.

"Citizens of the Empire!" The magister shook his fist at the tower. "I will give you until dawn to reconsider your misguided defense of the heretic. Surrender her to us tomorrow morning, and you may still escape the dire consequences of your treason!"

The Huntsmen fanned out around the observatory. Torches were lit to combat the darkness. Clearly the mercenaries intended to stand watch throughout the night, just in case Usla and the others attempted to slip away before dawn. The magister himself exited the square. Was he merely retiring for the night, or going in search of reinforcements? Riese wished she knew.

"Dawn?" Usla gazed down at her pursuers. "I don't understand. What are they waiting for?"

"They're hoping we'll give you up without a fight," Riese explained, "if they give us time enough to worry about our own safety." Her resolute tone made it clear that this wasn't going to happen. "They're also not certain what other surprises our friend here may have in store. Safer to attack by day when there's more light. In the dark it's too easy to run into hidden traps and pitfalls."

Horst snorted. "They're just used to dealing with cowards, like the rest of this spineless town. They're not prepared to deal with people who won't tremble at their scare tactics."

"I'm old enough to remember when things were better," the astrologer said, "and I'm not about to renounce my life's work just because that witch of an empress has given the Sect free rein in Eleysia." He let out a weary sign. "Besides, it's not as though I have all that many years left to worry about anyway. Unlike you young people."

Usla backed away from Riese and Horst. "Maybe you should listen to them," she suggested. "Why sacrifice yourselves for my sake? Let them have me." Her red-rimmed eyes brimmed with tears. "I have nothing left anyway."

"You have your child," Riese reminded her. "Do you want him or her to be raised by the Sect, to become one of their creatures? That's not what your parents would have wanted . . . for either of you."

Her words appeared to hit home. Usla's hand went protectively to her belly. Horst's eyes narrowed as he grasped that more than their own lives was at stake. He had the decency not to probe deeper.

"But what can we do?" Usla asked. She gazed down at the torches surrounding the tower. "They have us trapped."

"A valid question." Horst peered up at the sky. A stray cloud drifted above the tower. "Alas, the stars are worryingly silent on this point."

"Is there another way out of here?" Riese asked. Memories of her midnight trysts with Micah brought a pang to her heart. "A secret passage or tunnel?"

He chuckled sadly. "This is an observatory, my dear, not a royal fortress. It was built to allow the study of the celestial canopy, not to withstand a siege." He led them back inside the observation dome, away from the biting winds. "I have my own modest chambers in an addition at the rear of the tower, but the back door is clearly visible. Our enemies are bound to be watching it."

"Perhaps they'll give up and go away?" Usla said.

Riese knew better. "The Sect never gives up. They can be patient, if it serves their purposes, but they always get what they want."

Like Eleysia and the throne.

"Just so," Horst agreed. "You sound as though you have clashed with them before."

Riese let out a bitter laugh. She lifted her goggles.

"You could say that."

CHAPTER SIXTEEN

Then

RIESE BARGED INTO THE PARLOR.

"Herrick!" she demanded. "We need to talk."

A helpful servant had alerted her to the Sect's return to the palace. She found the emissary and his young acolyte in conference with Amara. The baroness scowled at the interruption.

"Riese!" she protested. "Where are your manners? The magister and I were just discussing the Sect's missionary efforts in Hariasa."

Riese didn't care. "This doesn't concern you, Amara." She stalked across the room to confront Herrick, clutching a small leather bag, drawn shut at the top. Metal rattled inside the bag. She shot Amara a warning look. "Your business with the Sect will have to wait."

The acolyte—Randolf, wasn't it?—flinched, but Herrick appeared unconcerned by the irate princess. He turned toward her slowly. His dark cowl and goggles concealed his true feelings, assuming he had any. "Is there a problem, Your Highness?"

"A big one," she declared. "Who gave you permission to scare my little brother with your horror stories?"

"Horror stories?"

"You know," she accused him. "Ragnarok. The end of the world. War and flames and purification."

"Ah." He nodded in understanding. "You speak of the prophecies of Sonne."

"Prophecies?" She snorted in derision. "More like scare tactics, unsuitable for children."

Randolf spoke up. "Our apologies, Princess. We meant no harm."

"Indeed." Herrick cut off the acolyte with a curt gesture. "I merely wished to prepare the young prince for the perilous times ahead." He stepped toward Riese, who fought an urge to retreat from his intimidating presence. "Perhaps you would also care to learn more of our teachings?"

"Hardly," she scoffed. The chilly emissary made her skin crawl, but she held her ground. "Nothing about your so-called Sect interests me." She stared at him defiantly. "In fact, I'm afraid I must return your generous gift. It doesn't seem to work anymore."

She untied the bag and dumped its contents onto the carpet. Shattered pieces of the music box landed at his feet. Riese smirked, recalling the satisfying crunch the mechanism had made when she had stomped on it. Broken gears, springs, and pins littered the floor. Amara gasped out loud.

"I see," Herrick said coolly. "A most unfortunate . . . accident."

She shrugged. "I never liked the tune anyway." Her face hardened as she looked the magister right in the goggles. "Stay away from my brother."

"Surely," he said, "that is for the queen to decide."

Riese couldn't believe his arrogance. "You are guests in

this kingdom," she reminded him. "We don't need you here."

"Are you quite sure of that, Princess?" He loomed over her. "The time may come, and soon, when Eleysia will be grateful for our assistance."

Was that a threat? How much did Herrick know about the slaughter in Geffion?

Probably everything, she guessed. A defeat of such magnitude could not be kept quiet. Riese had already heard the servants whispering anxiously among themselves. Everyone was frightened. Except Herrick, perhaps. Riese wasn't sure he was even capable of feeling fear—or any other human emotion.

Was that the Sect's idea of purification?

"Really, Riese," Amara chided her. "Your rudeness is quite unacceptable." She rose from her chair to placate the emissaries. "I must apologize for my young cousin's behavior. The current troubles have us all on edge."

"I understand," Herrick said. "Know that Eleysia can rely on the Sect in these difficult times."

"That is good to know," Amara told him. "I am sure I speak for the queen when I say your friendship is greatly appreciated."

Riese had heard enough. It disgusted her to hear Amara fawning over the Sect, and on her mother's behalf, no less. "Just stay away from Arkin," she repeated. "Don't make me tell you again."

She stormed out of the room.

"Tell me," Riese asked Mimir, "what do you know of the Sect?"

The aged scholar sat across from her at a desk in the library. He was supposed to be helping her memorize her lineage, but she had more pressing matters on her mind.

Despite her insistence earlier that she had no interest in the Sect and its teachings, she realized she needed to know more about them. For Arkin's sake if nothing else.

Mimir looked uneasy. "Perhaps we should concentrate on your studies instead."

"Please." She leaned across the table, which was covered with yellowed scrolls and chronicles. "They're worming their way into Eleysia and the palace more and more every day. I need to know who I'm dealing with."

"Well . . ." He glanced at the door to make sure it was closed. As far as Riese knew, Arkin was playing with his toy soldier outside in the garden; they had the library to themselves. "I *have* been making some inquiries of my own."

That's more like it, Riese thought. *I knew he wouldn't let me down.*

"And?" she prompted.

He sighed and put aside a thick leather-bound tome. "As nearly as I can determine, the Sect worship a goddess named Sonne, who is locked in conflict with her treacherous brother, Lune, who was born of the evils of the world. Their sacred prophecies speak of Ragnarok, a final battle at the end of time that will decide the fate of creation. Acolytes, rejecting the corruption and imperfections of the world, seek to 'purify' themselves by affixing sacred relics to their bodies—and replacing their flawed mortal flesh with finely crafted mechanisms." A look of distaste flickered across his face. "In this way they hope to achieve enlightenment."

"How awful!" Riese exclaimed, recoiling at the thought. No wonder Arkin was having nightmares. "Where did they get such a gruesome idea?"

"The Sect was founded by a mysterious individual named Ritter, about whom I have been able to learn little." He shook his head wearily. "Not even if he is alive or dead."

"Well, if he's anything like Herrick," she said, "let's hope he's long gone."

"Now, now," Mimir chided her gently. "We must be tolerant of the beliefs of others. There are many ways to the truth. Only a barbarian believes his way is the only way."

"Maybe," Riese said grudgingly. She was in no mood to give the Sect the benefit of the doubt. "But what do you *really* think of them?"

He glanced again at the door and thought long and hard before speaking again. "I confess," he said finally, "that I find certain aspects of their teachings . . . disturbing. Perhaps I am simply getting old and set in my ways, but I am troubled by the way they reject their own humanity—and make a sacrament of self-mutilation. Nor do I entirely approve of this whole Ragnarok business. History teaches us that doomsday prophecies risk becoming self-fulfilling." He spoke gravely, peering over the tops of his spectacles to make sure she was paying attention. "Beware any cult, Your Highness, that looks forward too eagerly to the end of all things. Such people have little to lose—and will often stop at nothing to win their holy war."

Riese nodded. She appreciated Mimir's talking to her like she was an adult, even if his warnings sent a chill down her spine. First the Nixians and now the Sect. Why couldn't the rest of the world just leave Eleysia alone?

"But what of my mother?" she asked. "Will she accept the Sect's help?"

"She may have no choice," he said grimly.

CHAPTER SEVENTEEN

"BLESS YOU FOR YOUR SACRIFICE," the queen told the dying soldier. "Go to your ancestors with honor."

The tent was filled with wounded. Row after row of cots held the refuse of battle: burned, maimed, scarred. Because there were too many casualties for the army hospitals, large tents had been set up on the plains outside the city walls. The makeshift infirmary reeked of blood, waste, and infection. Doctors and nurses in starched white uniforms wearily tended to the injured men and women, many of whom had lost eyes, ears, or limbs. The chorus of groans and sobs pained Riese. Her mother had felt obliged to pay her respects to the soldiers, who had fought so hard in Eleysia's defense. Riese had insisted on joining her. It was her duty, after all.

"Thank you, Your Majesty," the soldier rasped. Bandages covered one side of his face. His right arm was missing. Although a surgeon had amputated the limb in hopes of saving him, the infection had already spread to his chest. He was not expected to last the night.

"Be brave," Riese said gently. Like her mother she wore

simple traveling clothes—a dark wool cloak over a plain linen dress. Now was no time for pomp and regalia. "What is your name?"

"Lars, Your Highness." He was only a few years older than she. Recognition dawned in his remaining eye. "You were there, weren't you? At Geffion?"

She was surprised that he had even noticed her in that chaos. She wished she remembered him. "Yes. I was."

"Then you know what it was like." Anger contorted the unburned half of his face. "Don't let those Nixian butchers get away with this." A solitary fist clenched at his side. "Send them back to the slaughterhouse where they belong."

"Be at peace." Kara stroked his head to calm him. "Rest assured that you will be avenged."

Riese wished she could be so sure of that. Her mother's words seemed to soothe the man, but Riese had her doubts. As he had said, she'd been at Geffion. She had seen the pride of Eleysia sent running. Lars had not been the only one to fall there.

Where had the Nixians found such dreadful new weapons? Nobody seemed to know.

"Sleep well," the queen told Lars before she and Riese moved on to the next cot, and the cot after that. The sight of so much suffering made it hard to maintain a brave face. Riese was glad that Arkin had stayed behind at the palace. He'd wanted to come, but she and her mother had both judged that this call would be too disturbing for him. Amara was back at the castle as well. Although the overly helpful baroness was usually eager to assist the queen as much as possible, she had stayed behind this time, supposedly to look after Arkin, but Riese suspected that, in fact, Amara simply did not wish to be confronted with the ugly reality of war. She imagined Amara wrinkling her nose at the grisly surroundings.

Not nearly sweet and smiley enough for her, Riese thought, *or am I being unkind?*

A doctor met them at the end of the row. His dark coffee-colored face showed obvious signs of fatigue. Dried brown stains speckled his white jacket, which looked like it hadn't been washed in days. "Thank you for coming, Your Majesty, Your Highness," he addressed them both. "I'm sure these poor souls appreciate it."

"How are you faring, Doctor?" Kara asked. "Do you have everything you need?"

"I wish!" He laughed bitterly. "More patients are being shipped to us every day. We're simply not equipped to deal with this many casualties. We're running low on bandages, medicines, food." He shook his head. "And that's not even taking into account the civilian refugees."

Riese knew what he meant. She had spotted the refugee camps on the way here. They clustered around the army outpost in hopes of protection. From looters and bandits as well as Nixians.

"I understand," the queen said. "I'll see what can be done."

"Thank you." He bowed his head. "We'll be grateful for whatever you send us. Potions, powders, linens, herbs."

Riese wondered what had become of the medicines she and Micah had tried to deliver to the front. The last she had seen, they'd been being carried away by a runaway cart. Had

Micah gotten away safely? Was he still assisting that apothecary? In truth she had been keeping one eye out for him this entire visit, just in case he was delivering more remedies or, worse yet, was among the wounded. She didn't know whether to be relieved or disappointed that she hadn't spotted him yet.

Probably just as well, she mused. She wanted to see him again, and know that he was well, but how would she explain "Valka" touring the hospital with the queen? *I don't want him to find out who I really am. That would change everything.*

She realized that they had finished their rounds. The doctor held open a flap as they stepped outside for some much needed fresh air.

A depressing vista greeted their eyes. Beyond the military encampment the refugee camps extended for acres in every direction. Ragged tents and shelters, of less durable fabric than the army tents, housed hundreds of dispossessed Eleysians, driven from their homes by the war. Smoke rose from countless small cooking fires and funeral pyres. Empty fields had been stripped clean of crops. The sky was gray and overcast. Storm clouds gathered on the horizon.

"So many," the queen observed in dismay. "So very many."

"And more arriving every day," the doctor said. "Their homes lost to the invaders."

Farther up the road high stone walls defended the city near the palace. Sentries manned the battlements. "Can't they take shelter in the city?" Riese asked.

The doctor shook his head. "There's no more room. The city is already overwhelmed with refugees. The gates have been barred to keep the rest from flooding in. Guards have been needed to drive them back."

"How has it come to this?" Kara said, appalled. "That Eleysia's capital must turn away its own people in their time of need?" She gazed out at the dismal camps. "I must go among them. Let them know that their queen has not forgotten them."

An honor guard of soldiers from the palace stood by outside the tents.

"I'm not sure that is wise, Your Majesty," the captain of the guard stated. Egil was his name. He wore a plumed helmet and had his sword sheathed at his side. He gestured toward the royal carriage, which waited nearby. "Perhaps you and the princess should return to the palace."

"No." Kara's mind was made up. "I must see for myself what my people are enduring, and do what I can to comfort them." She turned toward Riese. "Wait for me in the carriage."

"Not a chance," Riese said. "I'm going with you."

Her mother smiled proudly at her. "Yes. Perhaps you should." She took Riese's hand. "You *are* Eleysia's future. The people need to see you."

Just as long Micah doesn't, Riese thought. *Let me keep that for myself.*

"Please lead the way, Captain," Kara instructed. "My people await."

"As you wish, Your Majesty," he agreed, sounding none too happy about it. The honor guard, which comprised six armed men and women, escorted them beyond the neatly organized army camp into the sprawling disorder all around them. Sentries patrolled the border between the army camp and the civilians. A graveyard, marked by crude stone cairns, was already being filled.

"Stay sharp," the captain ordered. "These are desperate people."

As bad as the hospital tent was, the refugee camp was worse. Riese was confronted by heartbreaking scenes of want and suffering. Tattered rags hung upon impoverished men, women, and children who seemed to have escaped the Nixians with little more than the filthy clothes on their backs. Gaunt faces, lean with hunger, stared bleakly at the ground. Moles, pigeons, and squirrels roasted on spits above burning heaps of dung. Riese saw families fighting over a single scrawny rodent. An almost palpable sense of despair hung over the camps, along with the stench from an open latrine. Many families appeared to be sleeping out in the open with no cover at all. Riese heard no singing, no laughing; not even the children had stirred themselves to play. Unhappy babies bawled shrilly, the sound scraping at Riese's nerves. She could scarcely believe that such squalor actually existed in Eleysia, let alone in the very shadow of the capital. At least it was still summer, she reflected while nervously eyeing the approaching storm. How would these huddled masses cope once the weather turned colder?

She wished she could take them all back to the palace with her.

Their impromptu tour attracted attention. The defeated people looked up from the dirt. They cried out in surprise. "Is that the queen?" A crowd surged toward them. "The queen! The queen is here!"

The guards formed a protective ring around the royals,

but Kara would not be kept from her subjects. She pushed past the captain.

"My poor people!" She raised her voice to be heard over the growing hubbub. She held out her arms. "It pains me deeply—"

Riese wasn't sure what her mother could possibly say that might relieve the refugees' suffering, but it turned out not to matter. A cacophony of agitated voices drowned out the queen's words. People shouted and pleaded, frantic to be heard.

"Please, Your Majesty! Help us!"

"Make them open the gates! Let us into the city!"

"My children are starving! We need food!"

"The enemy razed our home! We have nothing!"

"Take my baby, I beg you! She's not safe here!"

Most of the voices sounded merely desperate or frightened, but Riese heard anger as well:

"The king has failed us! He was not strong enough!"

"Why didn't you protect us?"

Kara winced. The accusations clearly struck her like a blow to the face. "Please!" she cried out, trying in vain to make herself heard. She waved her arms in the air. "You must be patient! Eleysia will prevail—"

"Your Majesty, take care!" Captain Egil rushed between the queen and the increasingly feral mob. His soldiers tightened their ring around the royals as they struggled to hold back the crazed refugees attempting to reach Kara. "Keep back!" he bellowed, drawing his sword from its sheath. "No one touches the queen!"

The other guards followed suit, drawing their own weapons as well.

"Captain, no!" Kara gasped. "Stay your hand!" Her face was pale with shock; she had never needed to be protected from her own subjects before. "These are Eleysians! They would never hurt me!"

Riese wasn't sure that was true anymore. The crowd needed someone to blame and was getting uglier by the moment. People glared at them with wild eyes and muttered sourly, not caring who heard them. Riese felt like a target. If only she had thought to bring her expandable baton!

The danger was not lost on the captain. "My queen! It is not safe here!" He struck a burly ruffian in the face with the hilt of his sword, breaking the man's nose. Angry curses erupted from the crowd. "We must get you and the princess away from this place!"

But was that even possible? Riese looked around. The mob had them both surrounded and outnumbered. Only six guards stood between them and a multitude of furious rioters. She couldn't even see the carriage through the crowd blocking their escape. It might as well have been on the other side of the mountains.

This may have been a mistake.

Strident voices assailed them:

"The queen has forsaken us!"

"Don't let her get away!"

"You can't leave us here! Not like this!"

A rock struck the captain's helmet. He reeled backward, his sword arm drooping. Riese spotted a dagger at his hip. She darted forward and snatched it from its sheath.

"Excuse me, Captain," she apologized. "Mind if I borrow your knife?"

She felt slightly better with a weapon in her hand.

Her mother, on the other hand, still appeared unable to grasp what was happening. "Please, my people! Do not forget who you are!" she exhorted them. "We are not animals! We are Eleysians!"

More rocks followed the first, along with bones, rotting vegetables, and clods of dirt. Trash pelted Riese, who tried her best to shield her mother. She tugged on the queen's arm, pulling her deeper within the shrinking ring of guards. "It's no good!" Riese shouted, hoping to get her mother to face the truth. "They're not listening to you! They've lost too much!"

"Get her!" A pack of rioters broke through the guards' ranks. "Don't let her abandon us again!"

"Stay back!" Riese leapt to her mother's defense. She slashed at the air with the borrowed knife. A wolfish snarl escaped her lips. "I'll cut you if I have to!"

"Riese!" The queen stared at her daughter like she barely recognized her.

Sorry, Mother, Riese thought. *Now is no time to play the pretty princess.*

Her flashing blade held the front line of refugees at bay but she knew she was only buying time. Maddened by grief and hunger, the irate mob threatened to wash over them like a tidal wave. Riese feared that she would never see Arkin again.

Take care of my brother, Amara, she silently entreated. *Prove that you truly value our family above all else.*

Then, just when all seemed lost, horns blared above the tumult. Wolves growled close behind Riese and the others.

Fresh troops came crashing through the mob, striking out at the rioters as the soldiers fought their way toward the imperiled royals. A pack of full-grown wolves led the charge, snapping and snarling at the terrified refugees, who scrambled over one another to escape the fearsome beasts. Soldiers on horseback savagely wielded clubs and maces against the mob. The ragged citizens went down with cracked skulls and broken teeth. Panicked refugees trampled over the fallen. The riot turned into a rout.

"No, no!" the queen cried out in anguish, more alarmed over the bloodbath than for her own safety. "Stop it! You're hurting them!"

"Your Majesty!" a mounted officer called out. Her long hair blew in the wind. "Praise the Fates we got to you in time." Wolves and soldiers surrounded Riese and Kara, who were yanked onto horses and rushed back toward the army camp. Within moments they were practically thrown into the waiting carriage. A door bearing the royal seal slammed shut. "Get them back to the palace!" the officer yelled at the coachman. Her upraised saber dripped crimson. "Now, by all you hold dear!"

The driver cracked his whip. The coach took off with a sudden lurch that threw Riese back against the plush velvet seats. Pounding hooves belonging to a team of six white stallions raced up the road toward the palace.

We made it, Riese realized. *We're going home.*

Her mother trembled beside her. "Merciful ancestors," she murmured, clearly shaken by what had just transpired. Wide, anxious eyes found her daughter. She clutched Riese's hand. "Are you all right, sweetheart? They didn't hurt you?"

"I'm fine, Mother. Don't worry about me."

Riese had never seen her mother like this before. The queen of Eleysia had always been a tower of strength, forever in command of every situation. Seeing her mother so troubled and uncertain was almost more frightening than the madness they had just escaped.

No, she reconsidered, it was *definitely* more disturbing.

"This can't be happening," her mother said, uncomprehending. Tremors rocked her frame. Her face was ashen. "This is Eleysia."

Riese wasn't sure what that meant anymore. This was not the stable, orderly kingdom she had always known. The whole world was changing, and not for the better. Was the Sect right? Was the final battle truly upon them?

She realized she was still gripping the captain's knife.

More bad news awaited them back at the palace.

"The situation is dire, Your Majesty," Mimir informed the queen. Shaken by the riot, she had demanded an immediate report on the state of the kingdom. Mimir was her oldest and most trusted adviser. He would not hesitate to tell her the unvarnished truth, no matter how unwelcome. The aged scholar leaned upon his cane as he addressed her. "That much is clear."

The queen braced herself behind her desk in the library. This was not a discussion to be had in the throne room before the entire court. Riese stood behind her mother, alongside Amara. As usual the baroness had managed to insinuate herself into the middle of things, supposedly to provide counsel and support for her royal cousin. More and more Riese thought Amara traded too much on her blood ties to the throne, as well as the memory of her revered mother. Alas, the queen still treated her as part of the family, and did not refuse her advice.

"Tell me," Kara said.

"Our attempts to broker a diplomatic solution to the crisis have proved an utter failure. The Nixians have expelled our ambassador, minus his head." Amara gasped, having apparently not yet heard this news. "And the war goes badly. The king's army has been unable to stop the Nixians from advancing on Asgard. Geffion is lost. Gleipnir and Vanaheimer will soon fall to the invaders."

A map, laid out atop the desk, illustrated the extent of the enemy's progress through the neighboring provinces. The Nixians had bypassed the mountains defending Asgard to the north and had split their forces, flanking the capital from the east and west. Asgard looked like a nut caught between a pair of pincers.

"It is only a matter of time," he stated, "before the war comes to our very door."

Kara stared at the map in disbelief. "But surely we are prepared to withstand any attack on the palace itself?"

"Your Majesty, I fear we must face the unthinkable: Asgard may fall to the enemy." He let his words sink in for a moment before hesitantly broaching another subject. "Perhaps you and your family would be safer elsewhere? Maybe Hariasa?"

"Of course." Amara leaned forward. "You and the children would be most welcome at my palace, humble as it is compared to your own."

Riese cringed. Prudent though Mimir's suggestion

might be, she hated the idea of relying on Amara's suffocating hospitality. *I just know she'd lord it over us.*

"No," her mother said firmly. "Never in recorded history has the queen of Eleysia fled Asgard. I shall not leave, no matter the risk." Her steely tone and expression made it clear that she would not be persuaded otherwise. Then she softened as she turned toward Riese. "But perhaps you and your brother should be sent away until the danger has passed."

"Don't even think about it," Riese declared. "I'm not going anywhere."

Her mother took her hand. "But—"

"I'm staying," Riese insisted. "This is my home too."

Kara smiled sadly. "Spoken like a true princess. Your father would be proud of you."

Riese squeezed her mother's hand. Despite her bravado, however, she felt sick inside. The very fact that they were discussing fleeing Asgard showed just how bad things had changed for the worse. Not so long ago she could not have even imagined Eleysia falling, or that the royal line would not continue as it always had. Indeed, the inevitability of her coronation had seemed more like a burden than a blessing. She had chafed at the way her future had seemed set in stone.

But not anymore.

Nothing's certain now, she thought. *I can't count on anything.*

Not even her parents.

CHAPTER EIGHTEEN

ONCE AGAIN SLEEP ELUDED HER. Riese lay beneath the covers, staring up at the ceiling. Every time she closed her eyes, images of the riot, the refugees, and the maimed soldiers erupted from her memory. She was almost afraid to fall asleep for fear of the nightmares awaiting her.

It was tempting to slip away to the falls and see if Micah was waiting for her, but what if her mother found her missing? The distraught queen would surely panic. Riese couldn't risk doing that to her mother, not after their close call at the riot today.

Maybe a few nights from now, she thought. *After Mother has had a chance to recover.*

She closed her eyes, determined to get some sleep. It was after midnight and the palace was quiet aside from the usual nighttime noises. A summer breeze rustled the window curtains. Sentries paced upon the battlements. A wolf howled in the distance. She sank into her pillow and tried to let the familiar sounds lull her into slumber.

Skitter. Clatter. Whirr.

A peculiar noise intruded on her rest. A faint metallic

clicking. She couldn't be sure, but did the noise sound . . . mechanical?

"Arkin?" she called out softly.

Was he playing with that stupid windup soldier again? At this hour?

No, she decided. The noise did not seem to be coming from her brother's room. Riese listened carefully, trying to place the clattering sound. The noise grew louder—and closer. With a start she realized it was coming from the foot of her bed!

She yanked back her feet and groped for the oil lamp on the bed stand. A turn of a screw caused a flint to strike, igniting the wick. A lambent glow lit up the room.

"Hel!" Riese exclaimed.

A shiny brass scorpion reflected the lantern's light. Clockwork machinery whirred inside its segmented thorax. Articulated metal legs skittered toward her. Vicious-looking pincers clicked at the end of its claws. A stinger poised atop the forward curve of its tail. The stinger glistened wetly.

Poison?

Riese didn't want to find out. Tossing the covers aside, she sprang from the bed and landed on the floor in her bare feet. Clad only in her nightdress, she reached beneath her pillow and snatched out her trusty baton. With everything going on, she slept better knowing it was there.

But she had never expected anything like this!

The scorpion's crystalline eyes rotated atop its head. Tracking her movements somehow, it changed course and twisted toward her. It flexed its eight legs and sprang off the bed. It flew at her face, snapping its pincers.

"Get away from me!"

She swung the baton and batted it across the room. The bizarre automaton bounced off a wall and onto the floor, where it swiftly righted itself. Its brass carapace was barely dented.

"Riese?" Arkin appeared in the doorway, drawn by the commotion. He rubbed his eyes. "What's happening?"

"Don't move!" Riese feared for his safety. What if the scorpion went after him instead? She yanked open the window curtains to let the moonlight in. "Stay right where you are!"

Arkin spotted the mechanical creature. He screamed in fright.

The scorpion hesitated, torn between Riese and Arkin. It swung back and forth upon the floor, uncertain which direction to proceed. Taking advantage of its indecision, Riese pressed the stud on her baton, which instantly expanded to twice its length. She leapt forward and swung the metal staff with all her strength.

"Got you!"

She smashed the staff against the scorpion's thorax. Jointed metal segments came apart, breaking its back, but Riese kept pounding the device, striking it again and again as though trying to squash an actual scorpion. Its polished shell broke apart, exposing intricate copper gears, springs, and filaments. Damaged mechanisms ground noisily as the scorpion's tail, and pincers jerked spasmodically. Riese smashed them to pieces.

"Riese! Arkin!" The bedroom door slammed open and their mother rushed into the room from the hallway outside, followed quickly by a brace of guards and Amara. Panic filled the queen's face. Her fur-trimmed dressing gown trailed across the floor. "What is it? Why did you scream?"

"It's all right, Mother," Riese said, breathing hard. She hit the battered scorpion one last time, then kicked the debris across the room. "I killed it."

"But . . ." The queen stared in shock at the scattered pieces. "What . . . ?"

Riese leaned upon the staff. Her pulse was still racing. "Some kind of clockwork scorpion," she explained. "I found it in my bed."

"By my ancestors!" Kara clutched her chest. She raced to her children. "Are you hurt? Did it attack you?"

"We're fine," Riese assured her. She crossed the room to Arkin. He clung to her for comfort. "I'm not even scratched. And it was after me, not Arkin."

"Thank the Fates! If anything had happened to either of you . . ." Her face hardened as her fear gave way to anger. "The Nixians! This is their doing. One of their spies must have planted that device in the palace. This is one of their terrible new weapons."

"Yes," Amara agreed. "Who else could be responsible?"

"Those monsters!" The queen clenched her fists. Riese had never seen her mother so furious. "Is it not enough that they ravage our lands and turn the people against us? Now they send their cowardly toys to kill my children?"

Arkin whimpered, alarmed by their mother's blunt words. Riese covered his ears.

"But I don't understand," Riese said. "Why me?"

"You are heir to the throne of Eleysia," Amara reminded

her. She hung back, safely away from the shattered pieces of the scorpion. "Of course they would want to eliminate you." She shuddered at the thought. "You would be a threat to them for as long as you lived."

Riese supposed she was right, and yet . . . "Why so outlandish a murder weapon?" She recalled the clicking and clattering that had alerted her to the scorpion's approach. Why send such a noisy mechanism to sneak up on a sleeping person? Now that she thought of it, another possibility crossed her mind. "Maybe it wasn't meant to kill me, just scare me. Or all of us."

"Nonsense." Her mother crushed the scorpion's stinger beneath her heel. "I know an assassination attempt when I see one. Amara is right. The Nixians were striking at the throne itself."

"Precisely," Amara agreed. "Why go to such trouble just to scare us?"

"I don't know," Riese admitted. But something about this didn't feel right.

Who could have planted the scorpion in the palace in the first place?

"This was indeed a Nixian assassination tool," Herrick declared. What remained of the brass scorpion was spread out atop the desk in the library. He held a serrated metal pincher up before his goggles for closer inspection. "The princess is lucky to be alive."

Riese huffed. "I can take care of myself."

"That remains to be seen," Amara said. She peered over Herrick's shoulder at the shattered automaton. "You have seen such devices before?"

He nodded. "The Sect finds it wise to stay abreast of such matters." Well-oiled gears clicked with his every movement. "Nixe is only the tip of the iceberg. New devices and inventions are spreading like a poison throughout this corrupted world, proof that the final days are upon us. The Sect has been forced to respond to this evil by studying the new sciences and adapting them to our purposes. There is no other choice. When the ultimate battle of Ragnarok comes, machines will decide the outcome, not crude muscle and sinew. We would be foolish to deny or ignore that."

Riese wanted to disagree, but Geffion had proved the limits of old-fashioned valor and warcraft. The Nixians had clearly proved themselves adept at forging fearsome new weapons of destruction.

Including the clockwork scorpion?

"Thank you again for responding so quickly to our summons, Magister." The queen presided over the conference from her chair. At Amara's suggestion she had sent for Herrick shortly after the apparent attack on Riese. "Your expertise is greatly appreciated. I confess I have never laid eyes on such a monstrous device before."

"Nor have I," Mimir admitted. He had made a partial attempt to reconstruct the scorpion, but had eventually conceded defeat. Loose gears and wires lay beside the bulk of the device. "A most ingenious, if diabolical, mechanism."

"The world is a tainted and imperfect place," Herrick said gravely. "Until the prophecies are fulfilled and creation purified, we must all be on our guard against the heretics." He bowed his head toward the queen. "Our order is resolved to master the new technologies before they master all of us.

It is our privilege to lend you whatever assistance you may require."

"Listen to him, Cousin," Amara urged the queen. "The Sect may be our only hope. We cannot afford to decline their assistance. Not when Asgard itself is in jeopardy."

Riese's stomach twisted at the idea of Eleysia allying itself with the Sect. Their disturbing teachings still unsettled her. Unfortunately, she couldn't think of a better idea.

"Perhaps you are right," her mother agreed. "This heinous assault on my children, along with the chaos encroaching on our doorstep, proves that something must be done." She reached for a pen and parchment. "I will write at once to my husband, urging him to return to Asgard to confer with you, Magister Herrick. The king and I rule Eleysia together, but, since he is commander of our army, it is best that he take part in any discussion regarding the war."

"Of course, Your Majesty." He stepped back from the desk. "We are at your disposal."

Amara looked on approvingly. "You're making the right decision, my queen. You will not regret this."

Riese hoped not.

CHAPTER NINETEEN

"Micah?"

The standing stones remained as imposing as ever. Riese rushed onto the ledge overlooking the falls. Ominous clouds threatened rain, but she didn't care. More than a week had passed since she'd lost sight of Micah at the battle, and she couldn't wait any longer. She needed to know that he had survived. Her eyes searched their secret spot but could not find him. She called out anxiously. "Micah?"

"Valka!"

She had not been looking high enough. He jumped down from atop a tall granite monolith and rushed toward her. Sheer joy and relief was written all over his face.

"Praise the Fates you're still alive." He hugged her tightly. "I didn't mean to leave you. I tried to turn the cart around."

"I know, I know." She cut off his apologies. "I don't blame you. The world went mad that day. There was nothing you could have done." She squeezed him back, as hard as she could. "I was worried about you, too."

"I've been coming here every night, looking for you."

He let go of her and stepped back to get a better look. "Are you all right? Were you injured?"

His obvious concern brought a lump to her throat.

"I'm fine," she insisted. "I wanted to come earlier, but . . ." She hesitated, wishing she could tell him about the riot and the brass scorpion and everything else, but that might reveal who she really was. "The palace has been in an uproar. There's never been a good time to slip away . . . until now."

"I can imagine," he said. "Are the royals safe? I heard something about a disturbance in the camps."

"They escaped, barely." She shivered at the memory. As usual, she looked for a way to change the subject. Her eyes glanced up at the looming monolith. "What were you doing all the way up there?" She spied the outline of his notebook beneath his vest. "Sketching again?"

"You know me too well," he said, chuckling. "I was tired of the same old view."

She held out her hand. "Show me."

"Nice try, but, no." He shook his head. "I'm still not good enough yet."

"Really?" She felt oddly hurt by his refusal to show her his drawings. "After all we've been through?"

Granted, she was still hiding her real name from him.

"Sorry. I'm just not ready." He must have seen the disappointment on her face, since he hastily spoke again. "I've got a better idea. Suppose I sketch you instead?"

"Me?" She hadn't been expecting that. "You want to draw me?"

"Why not?" He flashed her a winning smile. "I can't think of a more lovely model."

"Well, when you put it that way . . ." Blushing, she couldn't help being flattered by the notion. "Just don't think I'm taking my clothes off. I'm not posing for *that* kind of portrait."

"Spoilsport," he said, grinning. He took her by the shoulders and guided her over to the benchlike slab beside the standing stones. "Sit right there. The starlight suits you."

Riese tried to strike an attractive pose, and recalled sitting for that family portrait weeks ago. So much had happened since then. She wondered if she even looked like the same person anymore.

Maybe Micah would let her peek at her portrait when he was done?

The weather, alas, had other ideas. The wind whipped up suddenly, blowing leaves and pine needles about. Her hair refused to stay in one place, despite her best efforts to bat it away from her face. Storm clouds rolled toward them with alarming speed. A sudden chill raised goose bumps on her arms.

"Uh-oh," Micah glanced up at the darkening sky. He put away his pencil and sketchbook. "Looks like we ought to get out of here."

But they were already too late. The storm came upon them like an ambush. Driving sheets of rain and hail pelted them and drove them to seek cover behind the nearest upright monolith. Jagged streaks of lightning lit up the sky. Thunder boomed overhead.

The standing stones provided little protection. "I need to get back to the palace," she realized. What if the storm woke Arkin and he noticed she wasn't there? She pulled the hood of her cloak over her head and started toward the path "I'll see you soon!"

"Wait!" Micah called out. "It's not safe!"

The storm raged above them, as though the Sect's warring gods were fighting it out in the heavens. A blinding flash directly overhead was accompanied by an earth-shaking crack of thunder. Lightning struck the slope behind the ledge, triggering a rock slide. An avalanche of boulders crashed into the standing stones. Bits of rock and mud went flying. An unlucky monolith was jarred from its foundations. The huge slab of granite wobbled precariously, then fell toward Riese.

"Valka! Watch out!"

Micah tackled her, knocking her out of the way. The slab crashed to earth just where she had been standing before, even as the rock slide sent stones of varying sizes bouncing across the ledge. Micah lay atop Riese, shielding her with his body, as boulders rolled past them and over the falls. Rubble rained down on the crags below. Riese closed her eyes and waited for the rumbling to be over.

"Aaah!"

A rock cracked against Micah's skull. He grunted in pain, then collapsed atop her.

"Micah?"

He didn't answer. His body was limp. Dead weight.

"Micah!" Fear gripped her heart. She crawled out from under him. The worst of the rock slide appeared to be over, and she rolled him onto his back. An ugly wound on his temple bled onto the muddy ledge. She tried to rouse him, but he seemed to be out cold. "Micah! Can you hear me?"

He stirred slightly. "V-Valka?" He tried to lift himself, but lacked the strength. He sounded like he was on the verge of passing out again. "My head hurts."

She wanted to scream. Memories of her father lying bleeding upon the battlefield flashed through her mind. This was Geffion all over again, only this time there was no convenient steed to spirit them to safety. She was on her own.

The storm was already blowing past them, but the damage had been done. Micah lay wounded and only semiconscious. He needed help, she realized, and there was only one place to go.

The palace.

Grunting with effort, she hauled him up from the ground. She half-carried, half-dragged him down the hill. Micah drifted in and out, barely able to walk. The path was muddy and slippery beneath her feet, and more than once she had to stop to catch her breath. It seemed like forever before she finally reached the cleft beneath the castle walls.

"Where are we?" he murmured. "What is this place?"

"There's a tunnel," she explained. It felt odd to reveal her secret passage, but what choice did she have? Besides, if she couldn't trust Micah, who could she trust? "Help is waiting on the other side."

He chuckled weakly. "You're just full of surprises."

"Shush," she told him. "Save your strength."

The darkened drainpipe stretched before her. How was she going to manage to drag Micah through the tunnel and hold her lantern at the same time?

She couldn't, so she had to try something else.

"Excuse me," she whispered as she borrowed his goggles. The cleverly crafted lenses allowed her to see faint glimmers of light at the other end of the tunnel. She crawled backward through the slimy tunnel, pulling him after her. Rudely awakened bats squeaked in protest as she hauled him through the underground cistern to the hidden staircase. The prospect of carrying him up six flights of stairs to her bedroom was a daunting one, but she couldn't exactly ask a guard to assist her.

"This would be easier if you could walk more," she muttered.

"Sorry," he groaned. "Just a little dizzy."

Riese took a deep breath and started up the stairs. She held tightly to his arms, which were draped over her shoulders, while her back supported the bulk of his weight. His feet dragged upon the stairs behind her. Riese counted the steps off as she slowly climbed them, one by one. Every muscle ached. She couldn't remember ever doing anything so hard.

By the time she finally arrived at the top of the stairs, she was soaked with sweat and on the verge of passing out herself. A concealed lever opened the hidden door behind the fireplace.

"We did it," she said, panting. "We're here."

He didn't reply.

"Micah?"

The climb had been too much for him. He collapsed atop the hearth, unconscious once more. Riese crawled into the bedroom and tossed the goggles onto a dresser. She realized she needed help.

"Arkin!"

She stumbled into the adjoining room and shook her brother. "Wake up," she whispered. "I need your help."

"Riese?" He awoke groggily. "What's the matter?" His face went pale. "Another scorpion?"

"No, no," she assured him. "Nothing like that." She gestured toward her room. "Come with me. A friend of mine's been hurt."

Arkin followed her through the connecting doorway. He spotted Micah sprawled across the hearth. His eyes widened.

"Who is he? What's he doing here?"

"There's no time to explain," she said urgently. "Help me get him onto my bed."

"All right." Arkin said. Together they lugged Micah's limp body from the fireplace and lifted him onto Riese's bed. The hidden door clicked shut. A trail of mud stretched from the hearth to the bed. Riese made a mental note to clean it up before anyone else saw it. Arkin stared at the ugly wound on Micah's head. It had stopped bleeding but still looked bad. A swollen purple bruise surrounded the scab. "What happened to him?"

"There was an accident," she said tersely. "Go get Mimir, but be quiet about it. Nobody else must know about this." She knelt and looked him in the eyes. "I'm serious. Can I trust you to keep my secret?"

"You can count on me!" He dashed toward the door. "I'll be right back!"

"Quietly!" she reminded him. She locked the door after him.

Mimir's quarters were on the other side of the palace. Riese figured she had a few minutes before Arkin returned with help. She quickly wiped away the trail of mud with a rag, then glanced down at her own soiled attire, which was soaked and bloodied. She quickly changed into a plain linen dress. How on earth, she wondered, was she going to explain this to Mimir?

She waited tensely until she heard a knock at the door. She unbolted it to admit Arkin and Mimir. The old man hobbled into the room. Confusion showed upon his wizened face. "What is it?" he asked. "Arkin says there's an emergency." He froze at the sight of Micah stretched out atop the covers. "Who—"

"A friend," she said. "He's been hurt."

This hardly answered all the questions that were surely racing through his brain. "But I don't understand," he protested. "Who is he? What is he doing here?" He glanced at the door. "Does the queen know of this?"

"No, and she mustn't find out," Riese stated. "Please, Mimir, swear to me that you won't tell anyone."

"I don't know." He rubbed his forehead, trying to think. "A strange boy in your room? This is most improper."

"I had no choice," she insisted. "He's been hurt. You need to help him!"

The aged tutor was not actually a physician, but he was known for his wisdom and discretion. He had kept the counsel of the king and queen for decades. Riese trusted him more than any nosy nurse or sawbones.

"Please, Mimir! Help him, for his sake."

Her appeal to his compassion had its effect. "Very well,"

he grumbled, clearly not happy about the situation. "We will speak of this later, Your Highness, but first let us see to this boy." He examined Micah by the light of the oil lamp. "Fetch me some water and clean linens."

She and Arkin hurried to comply. She watched anxiously, in an agony of suspense, as Mimir cleaned and bandaged the wound, then lifted Micah's eyelids to inspect his pupils. He placed his fingers against Micah's throat. The old man's somber expression betrayed little.

"How is he?" she asked. Arkin stood beside her, holding her hand. "Is he going to be all right?"

Mimir completed his examination. "I believe the young man will recover. His skull is not broken, and his pulse is strong. He may have a slight concussion, but nothing he can't survive. However, I would not advise that he be moved tonight." He stepped away from the bed. "Now, then, Your Highness. Perhaps you can explain how we come to find ourselves in these unusual circumstances?"

Careful what you say, she warned herself.

"There is little to say," she answered, determined to brazen it out. "He is a friend. That's all." Although profoundly grateful for Mimir's help, she saw no reason to divulge everything, let alone the existence of the secret passageway. "There was an accident. He . . . fell and hit his head."

"I see," he said skeptically, clearly suspecting that there was more to the story. "This is a most serious matter, Your Highness. I confess that I am not at all comfortable with what I have seen here tonight."

She couldn't blame him. She was asking much of him.

"Please," she begged. "I know how bad this looks, but

I just wanted to spend some time with a boy my own age. It was a harmless flirtation at worst." She took his arm and squeezed it. "You can't tell anyone about this. Promise me you won't!"

He sighed wearily. "You are a princess of Asgard and heir to the throne. It would not do for there to be idle gossip about you, particularly in these perilous times. Your noble parents have troubles enough without a scandal at home."

"So you'll keep quiet?"

A rare smile cracked his dour features. "As difficult as it may be to believe, Princess, I was young once myself, and I am not so old that I don't recall my own adolescent adventures . . . and embarrassments." He assumed a sterner tone and wagged a finger at her. "But you need to be more careful. You are the future queen. You cannot make a habit of hiding young men in your room."

"Just until the morning, I promise!" She thanked him profusely. "I'll smuggle him out of the palace tomorrow."

"See that you do," he admonished her. "Until then you should keep watch over him tonight—and summon me at once if he takes a turn for the worse."

"I will, and thank you again. I truly appreciate this." She turned toward her brother. "Arkin, you should go back to your room now. I think you've had enough excitement."

"What?" Arkin looked at her in dismay. "That's no fair! I want to stay."

"I'm afraid not." She couldn't face the many questions he would surely throw at her once Mimir was gone. More important, he needed to be away from here before Micah woke up. She didn't want to have to explain why "Valka" was so close to the prince. "I'm going to be busy looking after my friend tonight. I don't have time for you right now."

"But I can help!" Arkin insisted. "Let me stay. Please."

Mimir took his hand. "Your sister is right. The patient needs his rest, as do you." He led Arkin back toward his room. "Come along, young prince. You've done your part tonight."

"Thank you, Arkin," Riese said. "We'll talk in the morning."

Muttering under his breath, her brother conceded defeat. She breathed a sigh of relief as Arkin and Mimir disappeared into the room next door, leaving her alone with Micah. She closed and bolted the door between their chambers, then pulled a chair over to his bedside and settled in for a long vigil. Despite Mimir's reassuring words, she watched over Micah with anxious eyes, hoping for some sign that he was getting better.

"Please wake up," she whispered. "Let me know you'll be all right."

She wondered how she would explain this to him if and when he did regain consciousness. Was there any way she could still pretend to be Valka?

Maybe if I tell him that the princess is away . . .

He stirred restlessly atop the covers. She loosened his collar to make him more comfortable. Perhaps she should try to get his wet clothes off? She tugged gently on his vest, and her fingers felt the outline of his sketchbook, which was still lodged in an inside pocket. Unable to resist, she reached beneath his vest.

Just a quick peek, she promised herself. She was dying to

see the portrait he had sketched of her. *I think I deserve a look after dragging him all the way here!*

She slid the book from his pocket. It was damp but appeared undamaged by the storm. She flipped it open.

The first thing she saw was indeed a pencil drawing of her posing on the bench. Her face was turned upward toward the sky. Micah seemed to have concentrated on capturing her eyes, lips, and hair. She was flattered by his efforts.

Is that truly how he sees me?

A smile lifted her lips. She glanced over at Micah, who appeared to be sleeping soundly. Pleased by her portrait, she lingered over it for several moments before finally turning the page. "Let's see what else you have here."

Her smile vanished in an instant.

"No!" she gasped. "It can't be."

She flipped frantically through the sketchbook. Instead of the nature drawings and scenic landscapes she had expected, the pages were full of detailed diagrams of the palace's fortifications, as viewed from the city streets as well as the falls. Meticulous notes charted the movements of the castle guards, their shifts and rotations and so on. Deliveries of arms and food had also been noted, along with every medicine shipped to the front.

He's been spying on us all along, she realized. *No wonder he was always so curious about what went on at the palace!*

Riese felt like a fool. How could she not have seen this? She staggered away from the bed, feeling as though she had just been run over by a chariot. Once precious memories of stolen moments together now seemed to mock her. She felt sick to her stomach. Her first romance . . . and it had all been a lie!

Now what was she supposed to do?

"Valka?"

Micah had been awakened by her gasps. He sat up abruptly, clutching his head. His eyes widened as he spotted her with his notebook. "What are you doing?" he cried out. "Give me that!"

He lunged for the book, but Riese refused to surrender it. Clutching it to her chest, she leapt to her feet and bolted for the door. He sprang from the bed and grabbed on to her from behind. She struggled to break free, kicking and squirming. "Let go of that!" he blurted. "Give it back!"

"Unhand me!" An elbow to his gut released his grip on her. She dashed to the door and fumbled with the bolt. "Keep away from me!"

"No! Wait!" Desperate to keep her from getting away, he seized the collar of her dress, which tore away from her shoulder. Fabric ripped, exposing her bare skin.

"What in—" He froze in shock. "That mark!"

Oh, no, Riese thought. *Not that, not now.*

She glanced back over her shoulder, the same shoulder that Micah was now staring at in stunned disbelief. She knew what he was looking at—the wolf's-head brand that forever marked her as a member of the royal family of Asgard.

The significance of the brand was not lost on him.

"You!" he exclaimed, putting the pieces together. He backed away from her in surprise. "You're the princess! Riese!"

"And you're a spy!" She spun around to confront him.

She tugged on the shoulder of her dress, but the torn linen refused to stay in place. She lowered her voice to keep from being overheard. "You've been lying to me this whole time."

"I had no choice! My sister depended on it!"

"Shut up!" She could barely stand to look at him. "I don't want to hear it."

"You have to!" He took hold of her shoulders. "Please, Valka. You have to listen to me!"

"Don't touch me!" She slapped his hands away. "And my name is Riese!" Angry tears burst from her eyes. "Was it all just a ruse? Were you just using me?"

She glanced in dismay at the fireplace. Her heart sank as she realized that she had just revealed the secret passage to an enemy spy!

But how could she have known what he really was?

"No! I never meant to meet you," he insisted. "That was just an accident." He stared glumly at the notebook in her hands. "The spying, my mission, that had nothing to do with us. But my sister . . . our leaders have her. They promised to release her if I did what they said."

Could he be telling the truth? She wanted to believe him, but she couldn't be certain of anything, not anymore. "How do I even know you have a sister?"

"You know I do." He pleaded with her. "I didn't lie to you, not about that." A hint of a Nixian accent crept into his voice. She wondered that she had never noticed it before. "You have a little brother, don't you? What would you do if he were being held hostage?"

Arkin's face flashed before her eyes. She remembered how angry she'd been when the Sect had frightened him.

Could it be that Micah had a point? Perhaps the world was not as black and white as she had believed. *If Arkin were in danger, I'd stop at nothing to protect him.*

Maybe Micah felt the same way about his sister?

"That doesn't change anything." She glared at him coldly, her arms crossed atop her chest. "You're still a spy . . . and an enemy of my people."

She knew she should scream for the guards, expose Micah for the spy he was, but how would she explain that to her mother? She stared in horror at the fireplace. How could she let him leave now that he already knew about the secret passage? But if he stayed here, he was almost certain to be put to death as a spy. Despite everything, she could not face the thought of watching him die.

He has saved my life twice, she remembered. *At the falls and during the rock slide. I owe him my life.*

She agonized over her decision. "How can I trust you not to reveal my secret passage to your masters?"

"I won't," he promised. "I swear it on my life. And my sister's."

She had no choice but to trust him. It was that or condemn him to death.

I'll have the passage sealed up afterward, she decided. *I'll tell Mother that Arkin and I just discovered it.*

She crossed the room and reopened the passage behind the fireplace.

"Leave." She held on to his notebook. "Before I come to my senses and have you thrown into the dungeon. Go and never come back."

He nodded. "Thank you for my freedom . . . and my life.

I swear I won't betray you." He staggered toward the waiting portal, looking slightly unsteady on his feet. Mimir had advised against moving him tonight, she recalled, but she couldn't worry about that now. Everything had changed.

"I'm so sorry, Valka." He caught himself. "I mean, Princess."

She shrugged, trying not to let her broken heart show. "I was never really that girl," she stated mournfully. "And you're not the boy I thought you were." Her throat tightened. "I never want to see you again."

He looked like he wanted to say more but thought better of it. Turning his back on her, he disappeared into the secret passageway. The hidden door swung shut behind him.

Riese threw herself atop her bed, sobbing.

It wasn't until he was long gone that she noticed that he had left his goggles behind. The borrowed lenses sat atop her dresser, reminding her of all she had lost.

She angrily tossed them into a closet.

CHAPTER TWENTY

"THANK YOU FOR GRANTING US THIS AUDIENCE, Your Majesties. You will not regret it."

Herrick faced the king and queen. The library doors were bolted to ensure the privacy of the meeting. Ulric and Kara sat behind the desk, while Riese and Amara stood off to the side. Several days had passed since Riese had banished Micah, and she still felt numb inside. The secret passage had been blocked at both ends. She wondered if she had done the right thing.

"Be quick about it," Ulric said gruffly. "I must return to the front."

Her father's face was more haggard than Riese remembered. His manner was brusque and less comforting too. She barely recognized him.

"Of course," Herrick said. "The war goes badly, I take it?"

The king paused before answering. He silently questioned his wife, who nodded in encouragement. "If the Sect is to be our ally, and this meeting fruitful," she said, "we cannot leave Magister Herrick in the dark. It is best that you speak freely."

He grunted in assent. "It is no secret, I suppose. Anyone with eyes can see what the Nixians are up to. The twin prongs of their invasion have joined up south of Asgard. Their combined forces are now marching on the capital. My army and I must make our last stand in the plains beyond the city walls." His finger stabbed at a map spread out atop the desk. "We will fight to the last man and woman, but I fear that the palace will soon be under siege." He turned to Kara once more. "If I fall, it will be up to you to defend the palace for as long as you are able."

It disturbed Riese to discuss strategy in front of Herrick, but, as her father had said, none of this was truly secret. That the war was at their doorstep, and that the final battle to defend Asgard drew near, was known to all.

"Perhaps it will not come to that," Herrick said. "The Sect is prepared to lend you its assistance in this crucial struggle."

"So I am informed," Ulric said skeptically. "How is it that a religious order knows of war and weaponry?"

"The coming battle between darkness and the light is the cornerstone of our faith, Sire. We would be remiss in our duty to our Goddess if we did not prepare to wage war against the evils of the world with every resource at our disposal. And in these dark days, when ingenuity and invention have been corrupted to create ever newer and more deadly weapons of destruction, we have had no choice but to counter this threat with mechanical creations of our own."

"I see," Ulric said. "I suppose I cannot fault your desire to fight back against this unholy new world. Very well, then. What have you to offer?"

"Technology to combat Nixe's insidious new tactics."

Herrick beckoned to Randolf, who stepped forward bearing a sealed wooden chest. The acolyte placed the chest upon the desk before Kara and Ulric. "For example . . ."

Herrick lifted the lid. Inside the chest was a supply of brass and leather masks. Goggles covered the eyeholes, while some sort of metal filter was positioned over the mouth and nose. The filters appeared to be filled with charcoal.

"These masks," he explained, "will protect your troops from the noxious gases the enemy has employed against you."

Riese recalled the soldiers at Geffion choking on the poisonous fumes. Her own eyes burned in memory.

"Interesting." The king examined the masks, holding one up to his face before putting it back into the chest. "I can see where these might be useful, provided they work as you claim."

"You may count on it, Sire," Herrick said. "And there are many more where these came from. We can provide your troops with these masks in quantity."

"How marvelous!" Amara clapped her hands. "You do not disappoint, Magister."

Riese shot her a dirty look. It was indeed possible that Eleysia needed to ally itself with the Sect, but there was no reason to be so jubilant about it. Riese still found Herrick and his apocalyptic prophecies unsettling.

"Is there more?" Kara asked.

"Indeed, Your Majesty," he answered. "Even now the Sect's finest minds are developing new inventions to serve the Goddess. With your permission, I shall appeal to the high priestess herself. She may choose to share our latest advances with Eleysia."

Riese wondered what these "advances" entailed. The Sect had too many secrets for her taste.

"In addition," Herrick continued, "we have taken the liberty of hiring a large contingent of mercenaries who can be placed at your disposal. Our Huntsmen will add numbers to your depleted troops."

Huntsmen? Riese thought. The ruthless mercenaries had long infested the kingdom. They were nothing more than bounty hunters and hired blades, selling their services to whomever offered them enough gold. What had possessed the Sect to employ such scum? Huntsmen were hardly fit to fight beside her father's troops.

"And in exchange?" Ulric asked.

"We seek only the gratitude of Eleysia," Herrick said, "and perhaps your blessing to spread our doctrines once the present storm has passed."

Riese frowned. She didn't like the sound of that.

"Mother, Father," she said cautiously, "perhaps we should think this over before doing anything rash."

Amara disagreed. "There is no time for indecision. The enemy is practically at our door. We must act now if we hope to save Eleysia."

"This is true," Ulric admitted. He shared his thoughts with the queen. "The Nixians' new weapons give them a decisive edge. We need an advantage of our own." He took her hand. "I wish I could promise you that our army will repel the foe before it lays siege to the palace, but I fear those would be naught but empty words."

"Very well." Kara made up her mind. "We accept your generous offer, Magister Herrick. Our fate is in your hands."

"A wise choice, Your Majesties." He turned to Randolf. "Ride at once to the high priestess. Tell her that Eleysia requires all that the Sect can provide."

"Yes, Magister." The young acolyte bowed his head toward the king and queen. "Your Majesties, if I may be excused?"

"Go." Kara dismissed him. "And give my thanks to your priestess."

The acolyte quickly exited the library. The Dullahan Monastery, where the high priestess Cacilia was said to reside, was at least three days' ride to the west.

"I shall remain behind," Herrick explained, "to offer whatever counsel might prove useful."

Ulric nodded. "I only hope that our trust in you is not misplaced."

"You have made the right decision," Amara assured the king and queen. "I feel safer already."

I'm glad somebody does, Riese thought.

Why didn't she feel the same?

"Smile," Amara says. "You look perfect."

Riese is confused. Her family is posing for a portrait again, but why are they all wearing gas masks? Herrick stands behind the easel, painting them with cool, meticulous strokes while Amara looks on over his shoulder. Kara and Ulric stand proudly behind their children, their faces hidden behind the grotesque leather masks. Arkin gazes up at her. Tinted goggles conceal his eyes. The sign of the Sect is emblazoned on his forehead.

Toxic fumes swirl about the parlor. Riese can't breathe; the mask is suffocating her. She tries to pull it off, but the straps bind-

*ing it to her head are too tight. She can't get them loose. Her fingers
tear frantically at the mask. Amara smiles blandly . . .*

"Princess! Riese!" A voice whispered urgently in her ear.
"Wake up."

She awoke with a start, finding herself back in her bedroom. A hand clamped over her mouth.

Riese's heart pounded. She seemed to have woken from
one nightmare into another.

"Don't be scared," the hushed voice said. "It's me.
Micah."

Micah? She didn't understand. What was he doing here?
She turned instinctively toward the fireplace. *It's not possible,*
she thought. *The passage had been sealed with a heavy steel door
bolted from the inside!*

"Don't scream," he urged her. "I need to talk to you."

He took his hand away from her mouth, freeing her.
She threw back the covers and scrambled out of bed on
the other side from where he was standing in the dark. She
reached beneath her pillow and yanked out her baton. The
bed formed a barrier between them. She resolved to keep it
that way.

She hurriedly closed the door leading to Arkin's room.
Her brother appeared to be sleeping through this midnight
confrontation. *Good,* she thought. This was between her and
Micah.

"Are you insane?" she accused him, keeping her voice
low to avoid waking Arkin. "I told you never to come back
here."

"I know." He was disguised as an Eleysian sentry, with a
steel helmet and a surcoat bearing the wolf's-head emblem of

the royal guard. Was that how he had slipped inside the castle? Or had he bribed someone? He held up his hands to show that he was unarmed. His head was no longer bandaged, she noticed. "But you need to listen to me. You're in danger."

"You think I don't know that?"

Micah's unexpected return was the last thing she needed right now. Her father, in the dubious company of Herrick, had gone to make his final stand against the Nixians, even as the castle prepared for a long siege in case the enemy could not be turned back. Food and water were already being rationed, while the smiths were working around the clock to manufacture fresh arms and armor. Gates were being reinforced. Heavy boulders and cauldrons of oil waited atop the battlements.

"We're all in danger," she said angrily. "Thanks to you and your Nixian masters!"

He flinched at her harsh words. "But you don't understand. The danger's not where you think it is. Your army has fallen for a deception."

"What deception?" Her heart sank in anticipation. "What do you mean?"

"The assault from the south is a feint, a distraction. Those forces are mostly composed of conscripts drafted into our army after we conquered their lands. They're just fodder. Our best soldiers, the cream of the Nixian military, are hiding in the mountains to the north, waiting to launch a sneak attack on this very palace."

"The north?" Her jaw dropped in surprise. The rocky peaks looming behind the palace had always been regarded as impassable, at least by any sizable force. "That's impossible."

"No, just difficult." He chuckled bitterly. "That's the problem with your glorious kingdom, Princess. You've been unchallenged for so long that you can't even imagine what a determined foe is capable of. You've been coasting on past triumphs for generations, convinced that you're invulnerable." He glanced down at his sentry disguise. "Look at how I managed to fake my way into this castle. Not that it was easy, mind you."

She couldn't deny his accusation. According to her history books Eleysia had not faced a serious threat since the Storm Rider rebellion many ages ago. And that historic battle had been waged far to the south. The fighting had never come close to Asgard. *Small wonder that we simply assumed the mountains would protect us. They always have before.*

"Where are they hiding?" she asked. "Tell me."

"In a secluded canyon on the other side of the peaks." He spoke confidently, as though he had seen the lurking invaders with his own eyes. "They're just waiting until they hear that your father's army is fully engaged elsewhere. Then they'll come pouring down onto this place like an avalanche."

Riese could all too easily imagine what that would be like. Catapults and ballistae would fire upon the palace from the hills. Flaming missiles, giant arrows, and poison gas would rain down upon her home, followed by hordes of bloodthirsty raiders. The enemy would overrun the castle, striking down all who opposed them and maybe even those who did not. There would be flames and bloodshed, screams and shouting. What would become of Arkin? Of her mother?

She shook her head, trying to clear the ghastly images

from her mind. "How do I know you're telling the truth?" She kept a tight grip on her baton. "You've lied to me before."

"You have to trust me," he pleaded. "I'm risking my life just coming here. Doesn't that count for anything?"

"What about your sister?" she challenged him. "Won't your masters punish her for your betrayal?"

"They don't know I'm here, and if we're lucky, they never will. Aliza will be safe as long they don't know I warned you." He sounded like he was trying to convince himself. "I just want to save you both!"

She still wasn't sure she believed him. "But you're betraying your own country. What about your loyalty to Nixe?"

"To blazes with Nixe!" he said bitterly. "What did Nixe— and our glorious leaders—ever do for me except imprison my sister and blackmail me into serving them? After they let us starve in the streets. What do I care who wins this stupid war?" He shook his head. "That's the difference between us, Princess. You have a duty to your kingdom. My only loyalty is to the people I care about . . . like my sister and you."

Riese searched his face, looking for any hint of betrayal. She felt torn between her doubts and the times they had spent together. How well did she know him, truly? In the end, she could only trust her gut—and her heart.

"I believe you."

He sighed in relief. "You need to flee with your family . . . before it's too late."

"No." She shook her head. "My mother will never abandon Asgard, no matter what. There has to be another way." A low chest of drawers sat by her bed. She pulled open a drawer and took out a pencil and a loose scroll. Genealogy notes were scribbled on one side of the parchment. She flipped it over and handed him the blank side. "Show me where that canyon is—exactly."

"Why?" he balked. "What good will that do?"

His hesitation stoked her suspicions. Despite his protestations, was he truly willing to side with Eleysia against his own country?

"You're the artist," she challenged him. "Draw."

"Fine," he agreed impatiently. "Just so you know I'm on your side." He flattened the scroll atop the bed and quickly sketched out a crude map. He handed it back to her. "Here. Now do you trust me?"

She stepped over to the window to examine the map by starlight. It looked usable. She would just have to hope it was accurate as well, and that this whole thing wasn't some elaborate deception. "Maybe," she answered cautiously. "We'll see."

"What are you going to do now?" he asked.

"Warn my father. What else?" She rolled up the map and thrust it into the bodice of her nightdress for safekeeping. "You had better leave. You don't want to be here when my mother finds out about this."

That was an understatement. Riese was not looking forward to telling her parents about Micah, and how she had let him go earlier, but it had to be done for Eleysia's sake. Her secrets were nothing compared to the safety of the kingdom—and her family.

"You're probably right." He headed toward the door, then turned to look back at her. His anguished expression matched the pain in her own heart. "I'm so sorry things turned out this way. You . . . you'll always be Valka to me."

She believed him. That was the worst part.

"Just go." She lowered her baton. "Quickly now. I can't afford to give you much of a head start."

"I don't blame you," he said sadly. "Good-bye, Riese."

She held herself together while he crept out into the hallway. Chances were, she would never see him again.

Good-bye.

Dabbing a tear from her eye, she put away her baton and came up with a plan. She hurried to Arkin's room, where she found him still lost in slumber. He clutched his windup soldier in his arms, letting it guard him against nightmares.

I could have used one of those.

"Arkin." She gently nudged him awake. "Get up. I need you."

"Again?" He sat up and glanced around, as though expecting to find another unconscious boy passed out on the floor. He gave her a puzzled look. "What now?"

"Listen to me." She lit the lamp by his bed so he could see how serious she was. "I need you to tell Mother something right away. It's important."

He yawned. "Why can't you tell her?"

She dragged him back to her own room and started changing into her riding gear. Thinking ahead, she snatched Micah's goggles from a drawer.

"Because I need to tell Father."

CHAPTER TWENTY-ONE

RIESE GALLOPED THROUGH THE NIGHT.

The sky was cloudy, dark, and moonless; without Micah's goggles she wasn't sure how she would have found her way. Her horse's hooves tore up the lonely dirt road beneath her. Time was running out. She had to get to her father before he wasted his remaining forces on the Nixian diversion, leaving the palace undefended from a sneak attack. The fate of Asgard—and perhaps all of Eleysia—depended on her.

Assuming Micah was telling the truth, that is.

The good news was that she did not have far to ride. The bad news was that this only proved just how close to home the war had come. She rode past empty fields and abandoned refugee camps; those unable to find shelter behind the city walls had fled elsewhere in anticipation of the enemy's advance. Muddy fields, plundered of crops, were littered by debris left behind by the homeless masses. Riese spotted a broken cooking pot lying in a ditch, beside an unburied corpse. Vultures had stripped every last bit of meat from the bones.

At least she hoped it had been vultures.

Torches and lanterns soon glowed ahead of her, at the end of the road. What was left of the once proud Eleysian army had taken up a position to the north of a wide river, where the water was shallower and easier to ford than elsewhere along the river's length. It was expected that the enemy would attempt to cross here, making it the ideal spot to make one last stand against the invaders. Bridges and ferry docks had been burned to slow the invaders' progress.

"Halt!" Armed guards rushed to block her. "Who goes there?"

Pikes pointed in her direction. Riese pulled back on the reins, bringing her courser to a stop. She threw back her hood and lifted her goggles.

"Riese! Princess of Asgard!" She remained astride her horse, whose flanks were lathered in sweat. "I bring urgent news for my father. Make way!"

A guard stepped forward, holding aloft a torch. His chain mail looked rusty and worse for wear. She knew him as a sentry from the palace, recently redeployed to the front. With any luck she wouldn't have to bare her brand to prove who she was, although she was fully prepared to do so if necessary.

"Your Highness?"

Recognition shone in his eyes. He stepped aside and called out to the other sentries.

"Make way for the princess!"

The pikes withdrew, and she rode unobstructed into the camp, which appeared much less grand than the one she had beheld in Geffion, before the slaughter. The tents were more threadbare, the troops more ragged and worn down.

Ill-fitting cloaks and armor hung on baby-faced youngsters and gray-haired veterans, many of whom appeared barely fit to serve, as well as upon various unsavory-looking individuals who might once have been judged unworthy to fight alongside the pride of Eleysia. So desperate was the army for fresh blood that convicts and criminals had been pardoned to fight for their country, assuming they didn't desert at the first sign of danger. Riese was disturbed to see Huntsmen, recognizable by their brimmed hats and long coats, mingling among the troops. Had her father truly been reduced to relying upon mercenaries, bounty hunters, and cutthroats?

So it seemed.

Her father's tattered standard flew above his tent. Shouting guards heralded her approach. Ulric burst from his tent, followed by Herrick. Riese assumed that Herrick had been conferring with her father on military matters. She was not happy to see him. She would have preferred to speak to her father alone.

"Riese?" The king scowled unhappily, clearly not pleased by this unexpected visit. "You don't belong here. You should be with your mother!"

Not exactly the warm welcome she was accustomed to, but she tried not to take his short temper personally. No doubt the coming battle weighed heavily on his mind. And just wait until he heard what she had to confess!

"I'm sorry, Father." She dismounted and handed over the reins to a nearby sentry. "But I have vital news. The enemy is even now preparing to attack the palace from the north. They have lured you away with a diversion."

"A diversion?" He stared at her in confusion. "What are you saying?"

She quickly shared what Micah had told her, omitting for now the source of her intelligence. She withdrew his map from her boot and handed it to her father. "The Nixians are massing in the mountains as we speak."

"An intriguing scenario," Herrick said coolly. He sounded neither surprised nor alarmed by her report. His gloved hand claimed the map, which he studied with interest. "And how is it that you come to know this?"

Riese swallowed hard. She had known this question would arise, and that she would have to answer it honestly. She could not hide the truth from her father, not if she expected him to believe her. Her eyes glanced around the torch-lit camp. She was not comfortable having this conversation out in the open. There were too many ears around.

"That is best explained in private." She nodded toward the tent. "Perhaps inside?"

Her father gave her a quizzical look. He appeared puzzled, and worried, by her reticence. "Very well." He held open the flap that led into the tent. "Briskly now. I want to know what this is about."

They stepped inside. The tent's stuffy interior was rough compared to the luxury of the palace. Muddy tracks covered the carpet. A long wooden table was covered with charts and reports, as well as plates of fruit and smoked meats that had gone largely untouched. Her father's fur-covered cot looked as though it had not been slept in for some time. A hanging oil lamp sputtered overhead, and candles were burning low.

A half dozen generals and captains surrounded the table. Many sported fresh scars, eye patches, slings, and other painful souvenirs of combat. They bowed their heads as the king rejoined them. Surprised expressions greeted Riese's entrance.

"Princess?"

"Leave us," Ulric commanded. "And see that we are not disturbed."

The other men and women hastily departed the tent, but Herrick remained. He seemed in no hurry to leave. Riese looked pointedly at the door.

"Well?" she asked impatiently.

Herrick stayed right where he was. "I have pledged to advise your father to the best of my ability. I cannot do so without full knowledge of the facts."

She frowned. "Father?"

"Let him stay," Ulric declared. He crossed his arms and stared expectantly at her. "Now tell me where you heard this."

Fine, Riese thought. She turned away from Herrick, speaking only to her father. She took a deep breath before answering.

"There is . . . a boy . . . I have been meeting with, secretly."

"A boy?" Ulric echoed. His expression darkened. A vein began to pulse at his temple. "What boy? How long has this been going on?"

"His name doesn't matter," she said. "I didn't know it, but he was a Nixian . . . and a spy." She hurried to finish before her father erupted. "He was scouting Asgard for the invaders. He warned me of the sneak attack."

Ulric stared at her in shock, momentarily speechless.

"And why would he do that?" Herrick asked. "If indeed he was a Nixian spy?"

"For my sake," she said. "He . . . liked me, I suppose, and wanted me to flee the castle before it was too late. With Mother and Arkin." She approached her father, anxious to make him understand. "He may have been of Nixe, but he didn't want any harm to come to me."

The certainty in her own voice surprised her. Not until she'd said it out loud had she realized that she truly believed everything Micah had told her.

But would her father?

"My own daughter?" the king roared. "Consorting with the enemy?" His face turned purple with fury. He raised his hand, and for a moment she feared he might actually strike her, but instead he turned away in disgust and collapsed into a folding wooden chair. He buried his face in his hands, unable to even look at her. "How could you do this to your family? To Eleysia?"

His words stung worse than any blow, but she did not flinch. There would be time enough to accept the consequences of her actions later, if they all lived to see another day.

"You don't need to forgive me, Father, but you *must* listen to me. Asgard is in peril. Mother and Arkin are in danger."

"The princess is right," Herrick said, unexpectedly taking her side. "Her errors, no matter how regrettable, are not our most pressing concern at the moment. If what she says is true, then we must act accordingly . . . and without delay."

That Herrick was agreeing with her took Riese by surprise. The irony was not lost on her.

Ulric nodded. He rose slowly from his chair and stalked across the tent to confront Riese. Cold, unforgiving eyes regarded her. His voice was stern and demanding. He spoke as a king, not as a father. "And do you believe what this . . . boy . . . told you?"

"Yes, Father. With all my heart."

"I see." He turned his back on her and strode over to the cluttered table. His arm angrily swept the piled maps and papers onto the carpet. A goblet and plate of food crashed to the ground as well. "So . . . now what are we to do?"

Herrick joined him at the cleared table. "If I may say so, Your Majesty, the princess's revelation may present us with a unique opportunity." He spread Micah's map out before them and pointed at the location of the secluded canyon. "We know now where the main force of the Nixian army is hiding. If we move quickly, we may be able to turn this situation to our advantage—and strike a fatal blow against the enemy."

"I don't see how," Ulric said. "Those mountains are many miles to the north, beyond the city and the palace. Even if we mobilize our troops at once, we would never be able to dispatch a force into the hills without alerting the enemy." He shot a scornful look at Riese. "There are, I am told, far too many Nixian spies and informers at large. How on earth could we catch the enemy unawares?"

A thin smile lifted Herrick's lips, possibly for the first time.

"Leave that to me, Your Majesty."

CHAPTER TWENTY-TWO

THE AIRSHIP DESCENDED FROM THE NIGHT SKY.

Brilliant lights mounted to its keel flooded the desolate fields north of the camp. A steam-powered propeller at its stern allowed the immense craft to fly against the wind. It was held aloft by a ribbed inflatable balloon many times the size of the wood-paneled gondola suspended beneath it. The balloon was shaped like a pumpkin seed with its point aimed at the bow, while the gondola itself resembled the royal yacht, complete with polished brass rails and portholes. A painted oculus adorned its hull, while a rudder guided its flight. The sign of the Sect was emblazoned upon the balloon. The ship blotted out the sky.

Riese had never seen anything like it.

"Behold the *Eye of Sonne*." Herrick gestured at the astounding craft. "The flagship of what will soon be an airborne armada such as this world has never witnessed before."

"By my ancestors!" Ulric, along with everyone else for acres around, gaped at the descending airship. His bearded head craned back to take in the sight. "A flying warship?"

"At your disposal," Herrick stated. "Dispatched by the high priestess to defend Eleysia."

The aircraft seemed only to grow in size as it lowered itself toward the earth. Rings of soldiers backed away, giving it a wide berth. Only Herrick took the ship's arrival in stride. He stood by calmly, his arms clasped behind his back.

More details came into view. A wooden figurehead in the likeness of the Goddess Sonne led the prow. Black smoke gushed from exhaust pipes at the stern. A line of brass spouts ran the length of the hull. Riese wondered at their purpose.

"Ho there! Look out below!"

Randolf appeared upon the deck of the ship, accompanied by a crew of similarly masked acolytes. He leaned out over the bulwark to hail the crowd below. Thick ropes were hurled over the rails. Huntsmen on the ground ran forward to capture the dangling cables and moor them to the earth, so that the gondola was held fast less than six feet overhead. The airship floated above them, straining at its bonds.

All right, Riese conceded. *Consider me impressed.*

"You asked how we might surprise our enemies in the hills," Herrick reminded the king. "See my answer."

Ulric could not look away from the massive airship. He stroked his beard.

"Tell me more."

Before Herrick could elaborate, his acolyte slid down a taut cable to join them on the ground. "Your Majesty. Magister," Randolf greeted them. His eyes widened behind his mask as he belatedly noticed Riese. "Princess? I did not expect to find you here."

"She shall not be here much longer." Ulric scowled at Riese. "Return to the palace at once. Tell your mother how you have disgraced us." His tone was ominous. "We will speak again . . . later."

Of that Riese was sure, but first she needed to know if there was still any future to worry about. "Please, Father. Let me come with you." The prospect of riding the magnificent airship into battle thrilled her. "I'm already here. Let me see this to the end."

"You've done enough already," he declared. "It's time you learned to stay where you belong." He threw out his arm, pointing back the way she had come. "Leave us."

"But, Father—"

"Silence, Daughter. For once do as you are told." Turning his back on her, he walked away with Herrick. "Let us plan our attack," the king said. "What else is this remarkable craft capable of? What weapons does it carry?"

Randolf was courteous enough to bow his head before taking his leave of her as well. "Take care, Your Highness. May you have a safe journey."

He hurried to catch up with Herrick and her father. Riese found herself alone and abandoned.

Good, she thought. A sly smile lifted her lips. Her father had made a tactical blunder. Distracted by the amazing airship, and the possibility of finally striking back at the invaders, he had neglected to assign any soldiers to escort her back to the palace. She was on her own. *I can work with that.*

Under no circumstances was her father leaving in the airship without her. Never mind the chance to actually fly among the clouds; she needed to watch his back as well.

The airship was breathtaking, she would give the Sect that, but she was not about to let them carry her father off into the sky unless she came along too. The princess of Eleysia had to protect her king, whether he liked it or not. She racked her brain as she explored the camp. There had to be some way to sneak aboard the airship, but how?

Her questing eyes fell upon a solitary warrior woman sharpening her sword by a campfire. A suit of chain mail protected her torso. A steel helmet, complete with nose guard, concealed her features. In size and shape she was not unlike Riese.

"Pardon me, soldier." She approached the woman. "Do you know me?"

The soldier looked up from her sword. She jumped to her feet. "Princess!"

Riese was not surprised to be recognized. She guessed that news of her arrival had already circulated around the camp.

"I have a favor to ask of you," Riese said. "Might I borrow your mail and helmet?"

"Gladly, Your Highness." Without hesitation she removed the armor and handed it to Riese. She held out her sword as well. "Do you require my blade?"

Riese was moved by the soldier's eagerness to serve. "No, thank you." She offered the woman her own cloak in return. "Keep your sword. You may need it."

Riese quickly pulled the mail coat over her tunic, then placed the helmet on her head. Both fit snugly. Micah's goggles hung from her belt, hidden beneath the skirt of the mail shirt. She wished she could inspect herself in a mirror, but those were likely to be in short supply at an army camp. She would just have to keep her head low and hope for the best.

"Will that be all, Your Highness?" the soldier asked.

"I think so." Riese contemplated the other woman, who appeared only a few years older than her. Auburn hair was cut short. A scar added character to her cheek. "What is your name, warrior?"

"Valka," the woman replied.

Riese didn't know whether to laugh or cry. The Fates, she decided, had a puckish sense of humor.

"Many thanks, Valka. I go to end this war. Pray that our ancestors are with us."

She left the loyal soldier behind and hurried back to the landing field, where she spotted her father still conferring with the Sect. She crept closer while pretending to be simply admiring the looming airship.

"I must lead the attack myself," the king insisted. "For the honor of Eleysia."

"Of course," Herrick agreed readily. "I wouldn't dream of suggesting otherwise." He turned toward Randolf. "How soon may we depart? It is imperative that we strike before dawn."

"The firebox is being refueled as we speak," the acolyte reported. "And the crew is conducting a safety check of all vital components." He consulted a pocket watch. "We should be able to set out within minutes."

He glanced around to make sure that all was in order upon the ground. His gaze fell upon Riese, who was standing several paces away, doing her best to be inconspicuous. His eyes widened behind his mask. She couldn't be sure if he recognized her or not, but was that a hint of an amused smile on his face? She waited tensely to see if he would expose her, yet he simply looked away and continued reporting on the airship's status. Riese was grateful for his silence, if he actually did know it was her.

I always thought he seemed more . . . human . . . than Herrick.

A rope ladder was lowered from the gondola. "After you, Sire." Herrick gestured toward the ladder. "Your ship awaits."

Ulric looked back at his warriors. "What of my personal guards?"

"A small escort can be accommodated, of course," Herrick assured him. "But perhaps only a half dozen warriors? It is a matter of weight. But you may be confident that our crew will be more than sufficient to carry the fight to the enemy."

Riese didn't like the idea of her father being separated from the bulk of his army. More than ever she felt determined to accompany him aboard the ship.

"Very well," Ulric said. "Let us depart."

His guards preceded him onto the airship. After they pronounced it safe, he bravely boarded the craft. Herrick and Randolf followed after him, and the ladder was drawn up again. The ship's steam engine chugged into gear, and its propeller began to spin. Huntsmen released the mooring cables, setting the airship loose. Riese ran forward and grabbed on to one of the dangling ropes before it rose out of reach. She clenched it tightly with her hand, knees, and feet.

The cable lifted her up into the air, faster than she

would have preferred. *Don't look down,* she told herself as she started to shimmy up the cable toward the gondola above, but she couldn't resist taking a peek.

She instantly regretted it.

The comforting solidity of the earth fell away with alarming speed. Within minutes she was hanging many hundreds of feet above the ground, where only birds and kites were meant to be. The dive from the rock ring was nothing compared to the terrifying drop beneath her now, and this time there was no welcoming lake to break her fall. Nothing mortal could survive such a plunge.

Angry shouts, coming from above, reached her ears. She looked up to see a masked acolyte peering over the rail at her. He called out to his fellow crew members.

"We have a stowaway!"

Hel, she cursed silently. She had hoped to board the ship unnoticed, but apparently that had been wishful thinking. Her heart sank as the alert airman drew a knife from his belt and began to hack away at the cable supporting her. Riese climbed faster, hoping to reach the rail before the rope was completely severed, but she feared that was overly optimistic as well. A vivid image of her fragile form plummeting to the earth popped unwanted into her brain.

"Don't!" she shouted, abandoning any attempt at stealth. "I'm with the king!"

At first the acolyte ignored her pleas. His blade sawed at the cable that had become her lifeline. But then her cries attracted a more attentive ear.

"Belay that!" Randolf ordered, intervening just in time. He raced across the deck of the gondola and snatched the knife from the other acolyte's hand. He leaned over the bulwark. "Bring her aboard. Now!"

Airmen pulled on the fraying cable, speeding her ascent. Strong hands pulled her roughly over the railing onto the deck. She gasped in relief as she felt solid wooden planks beneath her feet. Maybe she wasn't going to fall to her death after all, or at least not right away.

Now I just need to avoid being thrown overboard!

The commotion did not escape her father's notice. "What's going on there?" he demanded from the open bow of the ship, where he and Herrick stood atop a raised observation deck. He glared fiercely at the disturbance. "Who is that intruder?"

She was dragged forward, past the enclosed cabin and bridge, to the bow. Her father and Herrick gazed down on her. An acolyte removed her helmet.

"Riese?" Her father's eyes bulged from their sockets. He looked more startled than upset, although that was likely to change. A telltale vein throbbed at his temple. "I told you to go back to your mother!"

"I'm sorry, Father, but this is my war too. You can't deny me the chance to fight for my kingdom." She boldly met his gaze with her own. "You and Mother always say that I'm the future of Eleysia. In that case, I think I deserve to see that future decided, one way or another."

Her words gave him pause. He gazed down at her sternly.

"It would be difficult to turn back," Randolf pointed out. "Returning the princess to the camp would cost us precious time."

"Very well," Ulric said grudgingly. "You've come this far. You might as well join us."

"Thank you, Father." She had been afraid that she might be confined to a brig or storage hold for the duration of the voyage. She imagined she heard a note of pride in his voice, but perhaps she was just fooling herself. "I promise not to get in the way."

He grunted. "I'll believe that when I see it."

"Clearly the princess's persistence is not to be under-estimated," Herrick observed. She wasn't sure if that was intended as a compliment or not. "I shall have to remember that."

"Do," she advised him.

Now safely aboard, and apparently not going any-where, she took a moment to survey her surroundings. The wooden gondola boasted a central cabin surrounded by an open deck. Brass rails topped the polished mahogany bul-warks. The steam engine thrummed beneath her feet, but otherwise the aircraft flew through the sky without the noisy clatter of, say, a team of horses. The massive balloon bil-lowed overhead, its shape defined by taut wooden ribs and wire. Riese remained awed by the incredible craft. She was familiar with the concept of hot air balloons, but what the Sect had achieved was far more impressive—and intimidating—than any floating basket.

What other innovations might they be capable of?

The *Eye of Sonne* soared over the nocturnal countryside, faster than any earthbound carriage or steed. Not confined by gravity or terrain, the airship traveled as the crow flew, bypassing the hills and rivers below. Riese peered over the rail. The world beneath her resembled a miniature model. Tiny buildings and barns reminded her of a toy farm she had played with as a child. Roads and pathways looked likes lines on a map. The occasional traveler was no larger than an insect. Riese could see where the *Eye of Sonne* had gotten its name. The view from the gondola was like gazing down from heaven.

"The wind is with us," Ulric noted, as though sailing the sea. "A good omen."

"Indeed, Sire," Herrick agreed. "We are making good time."

The lights of the capital could be seen up ahead. The royal palace reigned proudly in the foothills above the city. Riese wondered how her mother and Arkin were faring. Her brother had surely warned the queen of the Nixians' deception by now. How had her mother reacted?

"We should alter our course to avoid passing directly over the city," Herrick instructed Randolf. "No need to attract undue attention." He waited to see if the king had any objections before continuing. "And douse the hull lights. Stealth is our strategy now."

Ulric nodded in agreement.

"Yes, Magister." Randolf crossed the deck to the forward wall of the cabin, where a rubber tube with a brass mouthpiece hung upon a hook. He spoke into the tube, relaying Herrick's instructions to the bridge. "Go to midnight flying."

The floodlights upon the hull went dark, throwing the landscape below into shadow. Randolf opened a cabinet attached to a bulwark and handed out goggles not unlike the ones worn by Micah. "These lenses will allow us to navigate by night," he explained.

"Yes." She plucked her own goggles from her belt. "I know."

Her father eyed her suspiciously.

"They are often employed by miners," she elaborated. "Or so I am told."

Ulric snorted. "You still have much to explain, Daughter."

"In due time, Father."

The airship banked away from the capital, detouring around both the city and the palace, then climbed to match the rising terrain below. At first the mountains appeared to block their path, but the *Eye of Sonne* simply rose higher, so that they soared above the southern slopes. Gazing down through her goggles, Riese spied the rock ring atop the falls. Her throat tightened. Where was Micah now, she wondered, and why did she still care?

They climbed above the tree line. Rocky peaks and narrow mountain passes rolled by beneath them. The air grew thinner and she began to feel slightly light-headed. She held on to a rail to steady herself until the dizziness passed.

Careful, she thought. *I need to keep my wits about me.*

They crossed the tops of the mountains. Herrick employed a spyglass to scout the terrain on the northern slopes. "We should be coming within sight of the enemy encampment soon," he announced, "assuming it actually exists."

"It's there," Riese said. *It has to be.*

She prayed that Micah had not lied to her . . . again.

"We shall see." Herrick lowered his voice. "Order the crew to maintain silence. I don't want to hear a cough or dropped hammer until we have engaged the enemy. Is that understood?"

"Perfectly, Magister." Randolf spoke into the voice tube. "Rig for silent running."

Riese leaned over the rail, looking anxiously for some proof of her claims. Distant flickers of light caught her eyes.

"There it is!" she whispered, pointing ahead. "Down there!"

Relief flooded her. She—and Micah—had been vindicated. He had not deceived her.

Just as he had warned, a sizable force had amassed in a canyon bordered by steep granite walls. Tents and campfires filled the gorge. Catapults and ballistae sat in various stages of assembly; Riese assumed that they had been carted piecemeal up the slopes. At least three divisions of Nixian soldiers waited to lay siege to the palace on the other side of the mountains—not that Riese intended to give them the chance.

"It appears the princess's intelligence was correct," Herrick observed. "The danger she spoke of is quite real."

"Indeed," her father conceded. He gave her an approving nod. His tone warmed somewhat. "You may have done Eleysia a great service, Daughter, despite your recent transgressions."

Riese welcomed his praise. It was good to know that he had not completely disowned her. "I could not stand by while our land was in danger. No matter what."

"As you have proved," Herrick noted. "The Sect shall not forget that."

A chill ran down Riese's spine. Was that flattery—or a threat?

Coming from Herrick, it was hard to tell.

The airship came upon the canyon under cover of dark, gliding silently upon the winds like a pendulous gray cloud. The Nixians slept unsuspecting in its shadow.

"We are in position, Sire," Herrick said. "Shall we commence the attack?"

Ulric nodded. He glared down at the hidden camp. Long weeks of losing ground and lives to the enemy could be seen in his furious expression. His finger traced the wound on his brow. He raised his fist.

"Rain destruction upon them!"

"As you command, Sire."

Herrick gestured to Randolf, who relayed the command to the bridge. "Open the tanks!"

The *Eye of Sonne* dipped low over the camp, startling Nixian sentries who spotted the craft too late for their own good. They shouted in fear and surprise.

"Look out! Up above us!"

The brass nozzles opened along the undercarriage of the ship. Boiling oil sprayed onto the camp below like black rain. Tents, flags, and warriors burned beneath the deluge. Canvas and clothing caught fire. Screaming figures, slick with oil, ran about frantically before collapsing onto the ground. Officers burst from flaming tents only to be caught in the searing downpour. Their death agonies were terrible to behold.

Remember Geffion, Riese thought, horrified by the awful spectacle. She forced herself to recall all the fear and suffering Nixe had inflicted on Eleysia and its innocent neighbors. *Think of the dying soldiers in the hospital tent, and the refugee camps.*

The dreadful memories steeled her to keep watching, even as she couldn't help looking for Micah. She dreaded spotting him down below, amidst the chaos.

He's a spy, she reminded herself, *not a soldier.*

With any luck he was far from here.

The element of surprise being long gone, the ship's landing lights reignited, exposing the slaughter below in greater detail. Riese raised her goggles, as did her father. Herrick's eyes remained hidden behind his tinted goggles. Riese was tempted to avert her own eyes.

Pandemonium consumed the camp, but the braver of the Nixians attempted to mount a defense. Crossbows and fire throwers fired up at the airship, but the attacks fell far short of their target. Flaming arrows dropped back down onto the camp, adding to the carnage and confusion. At the same time, Sect airmen lined up along the bulwarks, picking off the survivors with spears and arrows. The missiles struck home repeatedly. Fleeing soldiers dropped in their tracks.

"Arm me!" Ulric growled. Not content to let his new allies fight his battles for him, and eager to exact his own vengeance on the invaders, he seized a spear from a nearby acolyte and hurled it down at the camp with all his might. The lance impaled a Nixian officer, pinning him to the ground like a butterfly mounted for display. "Feel the wrath of Eleysia!"

He claimed another spear from an airman and thrust it at Riese.

"Me?" she asked, gazing uncertainly at the weapon.

"You have earned the right to strike a blow against the enemy." He handed the spear to Riese. "Teach them to fear the future queen!"

Riese swallowed hard. Her mouth went dry.

Was this a test? Hunting a boar was one thing, but she had never actually killed a human being before. Her heart quailed at the prospect, but she knew she could not disappoint her father, not after failing him before.

"So I shall."

Accepting the spear, she leaned over the rail. Her nervous gaze fell upon a terrified Nixian soldier running for cover. Thankfully they were too far up to make out his face.

Think of Geffion.

She flung the spear, which flew straight and true. Part of her secretly hoped that she would miss, but instead it struck him squarely in the back. He toppled face-first onto the ground. Riese's gorge rose. She clenched her jaws to keep from throwing up.

"Well done!" Her father slapped her on the back. "That's the daughter I remember!"

She swallowed a mouthful of bile. It seemed that she had bought her father's forgiveness with blood.

"An excellent throw!" he said proudly. "Well done!"

A sudden jolt rocked the deck. Thrown off balance, she grabbed on to a rail to keep from falling. "What—"

Peering over the bulwark, she saw that the Nixians had managed to get a catapult and a couple of ballistae into operation. A gigantic steel arrow had pierced the hull of the gondola. Hot oil streamed from the gap.

"We've been hit!" Ulric exclaimed. "The bastards are shooting back at us!"

Riese glanced up. What if a missile punctured the great balloon holding them aloft?

"Higher!" Randolf obviously had the same thought. He shouted into the speaking tube. "More altitude! Rise! Rise!"

The steam engine labored, pumping more hot air into the balloon. The airship rose swiftly, but would it be fast enough? Herrick yanked open a wooden cabinet and hastily handed out gas masks to Riese and Ulric.

"Simply as a precaution," he stated before placing a mask over his own hooded face. The overlapping masks hid every last trace of his humanity, so that he resembled a creature of brass and leather. The filter distorted his voice. "It is best to be prepared."

His timing could not have been faulted. Riese was still fumbling with the straps of her own mask when a glass sphere arced over the rail. It shattered upon the deck, releasing a cloud of sulfurous yellow fumes only a few yards away from Riese. Her eyes watered. Her throat burned.

She tugged the mask into place. It was heavy and claustrophobic, but what choice did she have? Her eyes stopped stinging. She took a cautious breath and found that the filter seemed to be working. The air no longer made her choke.

"Riese?" Her father checked on her with obvious concern. His own mask made him look less like her father and more like some unsettling mechanical apparition. Her nightmare of hours ago rushed back into her thoughts. She hugged herself to keep from shivering. "Are you all right, Daughter?"

"Yes, Father. I'm fine. Don't worry."

The airship rose rapidly. Another gas bomb crashed against the hull but failed to reach the deck. A giant arrow, shot from a ballistae, fell short of the keel. It plunged back toward the canyon.

"That is high enough," Herrick decided. "Empty the remaining tanks."

A second wave of hot oil jetted from the nozzles. Boiling death rained down on the Nixians, who shrieked and ran from the canyon. The last of the defenders abandoned their posts and deserted the camp. Their ranks came apart as they fled madly into the hills and down the slopes, trampling over one another in their frenzied exodus. Diving spears and arrows struck random stragglers in the back. Within minutes of the attack the hidden base had been reduced to an empty ruin. Nothing remained but burning wreckage and bodies. No further missiles slammed against the ship. The *Eye of Sonne* gazed down on its victims.

"Victory is ours!" Ulric roared. He peeled off his gas mask, exposing his jubilant visage. He clasped Riese in a powerful bear hug, his earlier anger seemingly washed away by a rush of triumph and relief. "Look at them! See the vermin run like the cowardly rats they are!"

Riese took off her own mask. The mountain air smelled only of smoke.

"Is it really over?" she asked. "Is the palace safe?"

"Asgard stands!" her father proclaimed. "As it always shall!"

Cheers erupted aboard the airship. Even Herrick allowed himself a slight smile.

"Indeed, Your Majesty. The Nixians will not soon forget this night."

"Nor shall I," the king declared. He let go of Riese and offered Herrick his hand. "You have my deepest gratitude, Magister. Know that the Sect will be welcome in Eleysia for as long as I live!"

"No thanks are necessary, Your Majesty." Herrick took Ulric's hand. "We sought only to preserve the safety of your noble kingdom . . . as the Goddess wills."

Riese looked on with mixed feelings. Herrick still made her skin crawl, but she had to admit that the Sect had proved a valuable ally. Their help had undeniably turned the tide of battle, and perhaps saved all of Eleysia from destruction.

But what exactly did the Sect get out of it?

Does it matter? she asked herself. Such doubts seemed rather churlish at the moment, and perhaps unworthy of her. Following her father's example, she approached Randolf. "You have my thanks as well," she told the young acolyte. "We could not have won this victory without you."

He bowed his head. "Your Highness does me a great honor."

"You deserve it," she said. "I mean it."

Ulric turned away from the rail. He scratched his beard. "Now, then, what of the remaining armies? To the south?" He patted the walls of the airship. "Can we rain havoc on them as well?"

"We will need to refuel and rearm," Randolf reported, "but after that—"

"We will send them running back to Nixe, if not their graves!" Ulric grinned wolfishly. For the first time in weeks, he looked like the proud and confident king Riese remembered. "They will think the heavens themselves are wreaking vengeance upon them, and they will be right!"

Riese hugged her father once more. Even after witnessing the Nixians' retreat with her own eyes, she could scarcely believe how quickly their fortunes had reversed themselves. For weeks it had seemed that hope was lost, yet now at long last the war had turned in their favor and ultimate victory was in sight.

"Is it truly over?" she asked again. "Eleysia will not fall? We're safe again?"

"Yes," her father promised her. "Thanks to you . . . and the Sect."

Riese supposed she could live with that.

CHAPTER TWENTY-THREE

THE FLAG OF NIXE STILL FLEW ABOVE THE FORTRESS.

But not for much longer.

Count Alexander Borgos, onetime ambassador to Eleysia, gaped in horror from the roof of a high watchtower overlooking the battlements below. Armed guards stood by stoically but did little to ease his mind. The view from the turret offered a breathtaking view of the surrounding territory—and of the approaching army. Clouds of dust on the horizon warned of troops on the move. Vast airships, of the sort that had so recently brought the Nixian military to ruin, flew in advance of the dust. Borgos saw his own doom drawing nearer.

Numerous towns and fiefdoms had already surrendered to the Eleysians. Rumor had it that the ruling generals and the entire high command had already fled into exile, or else committed suicide, rather than stand trial as war criminals. Only this solitary fortress, the count's own private refuge, had not yet fallen to Ulric and his army.

But that was only a matter of time.

"You lied to us!" He wheeled away from the dismal vista

to rail at his coconspirator. "You promised us an empire!"

Cacilia, high priestess of the Sect, was unshaken by his accusations. She was a tall, regal woman with flowing red hair, whose immaculate white robe proclaimed the purity of her convictions. She stood by calmly, her hands steepled before her. She wore a gilded mask, consisting of two crossed metal bars, that was fitted over the lower half of her face like a bridle, leaving her dark eyes exposed. The shape of the mask evoked the sign of the Sect.

"You may have misinterpreted the prophecies," she said evenly. "It was never meant that Nixe supplant Eleysia, only that you provide a doorway through which the Sect might enter that greatest of all kingdoms. The throne of Eleysia awaits the Anointed One many years hence." She gazed out over the world, as though seeing the future stretch out before her. "Such is the will of the Goddess."

In truth, events were unfolding exactly as foreseen. The Sect had been working patiently to fulfill the prophecies for many years now. She looked back with pride on all that they had accomplished so far.

First they had readied the Nixians by covertly despoiling their lands. Wells had been poisoned, crops blighted, forests and orchards torched, dams made to flood, all to the end of driving the hungry Nixians to the point of desperation. Then had the Sect quietly provided the ambitious generals with tempting new weapons and incited them to wage war on their neighbors, even as the Sect retained the means to foil their ambitions later.

The war had served its purpose, allowing the Sect to infiltrate Eleysia and prove themselves invaluable to the royal family. Now the Sect could commence the real work of conquering the kingdom from within, just as the sacred prophecies foretold.

A pity Count Borgos could not appreciate that.

"Prophecies?" he snarled. "What do I care for your prophecies?" Once crisp and military in his bearing, the former ambassador was now sweaty and disheveled. His face flushed with anger. Stubble carpeted his jaw. His uniform was rumpled and soiled. "At your urging we invaded the wolf's lair—and now its jaws are at our door. What are we to do now?"

"That is not my concern," she replied. The Nixians had been useful pawns, but the time had come to clear them from the board. "I can only advise that you accept your fate with what little dignity remains to you."

"You scheming witch!" He shook his fist at her. Spittle flew from his lips. "Ulric will be here soon, but I'll see you burned at the stake first!"

For a second she thought he might lunge at her himself, but instead he called out to his guards.

"Seize her!"

She made no effort to flee. She only nodded at the guards, who converged on Borgos instead. They grabbed on to him roughly, much to his surprise.

"Wait! What are you doing?" He struggled helplessly in the men's grip. "Unhand me at once! I command you!"

His confusion was pathetic. He was clearly in need of illumination.

"Your authority has passed," she explained. "Nixe has outlived its usefulness . . . as have you."

She gestured at the low stone wall girding the rooftop. The guards dragged him toward the edge. His face drained of color as he realized what was to come.

"No!" he said hoarsely. "You can't do this!"

"Farewell, Count. The Goddess thanks you for your service."

Without further ado the men lifted Borgos off his feet and heaved him over the wall. His final scream trailed away before terminating in a sudden impact many stories below. She did not bother looking over the wall to view his crumpled remains. Nothing could have survived such a fall.

"Let it be known that the count has taken his own life," she informed the guards. "You have done well."

The captain of the guards approached her. The mark of the Sect was tattooed upon his wrist. He bowed his head in respect.

"Ulric's army draws closer, High Priestess," he reminded her. "We need to escort you from this doomed place."

"Soon," she promised. "Our work here is almost done."

All that remained was to eliminate any evidence linking the Sect to Nixe. It would not do, after all, for the hand of the Goddess to be seen too soon. Much work, and many years, remained before the Anointed One would be ready to take his place upon the throne. But the Sect was one day closer to ensuring that ultimate victory.

"Burn everything," she commanded. "Kill everyone. Let no trace of our presence remain."

As the Goddess willed.

CHAPTER TWENTY-FOUR

"The war is over," Queen Kara proclaimed. "Let all of Eleysia rejoice!"

The royal family, bedecked in finery, greeted their subjects in the throne room, which now hosted a lavish victory celebration. Festive banners and streamers hung from the ceiling, and rose petals carpeted the floor. A brass band triumphantly played the national anthem, while a pack of wolves, sporting studded velvet collars, howled in harmony. Giddy courtiers and honored guests cheered. Fenrir curled at Riese's feet, chewing a bone.

Riese waved dutifully from the dais. Her gown was rather too frilly for her taste, and the lacy collar itched, but she couldn't complain, not after coming so close to losing everything. A little pomp and circumstance was a small price to pay for knowing that Eleysia—and her family—was safe at last.

"See?" Arkin whispered to her. He held up his toy soldier, which he had insisted on bringing to the celebration. "I told you my warrior would beat the Nixians. He chased them all away!"

"So he did," she replied, indulging him. "Good work."

The queen waited for the cheers, howls, and music to die down before speaking again. She and the king stood before their thrones. The pelts of fallen wolves were draped over the thrones in honor. As usual the rest of the royal family sat one tier below them.

"My heart swells with pride," Kara said. "Once more Eleysia has shown that its honor and courage can withstand any challenge, no matter how terrible. We are grateful to every loyal citizen and soldier for their bravery, but there are a few whom we wish to thank personally at this moment." She held out her arms. "Will the emissaries of the Sect please come forward?"

The crowd parted, and Herrick approached the throne, shadowed as ever by Randolf. Polite applause greeted them. Riese suspected that many longtime advisers to the throne were leery of the Sect's newfound influence at court. She saw Mimir watching pensively from the sidelines. Fenrir started to growl, but Riese quickly hushed him.

She forced herself to keep smiling.

"Magister Herrick," the queen said warmly. "On behalf of all of Eleysia, the king and I wish to express our profound gratitude to the Sect for aiding us in the late war. We owe our victory, and our very survival, in large part to your timely assistance. Know that your loyalty and friendship will never be forgotten, and please accept this token of our esteem."

She beckoned to Amara, who stepped forward to present Herrick with an engraved silver chalice. Runes upon the cup chronicled the airship's defense of Eleysia. Amara flashed a radiant smile, no doubt enjoying being the center of attention.

"Hariasa thanks you as well," she purred, "and looks forward to a long and prosperous alliance."

Herrick accepted the chalice. "The Sect is honored by your generosity, and is pleased to have played some small part in Eleysia's salvation." He handed the cup to Randolf. "And we wish to return your beneficence with a gift of our own."

What now? Riese wondered. *Another music box? A miniature airship?*

Startled gasps came from the rear of the chamber. The other guests backed away in shock as two masked acolytes marched into the room, dragging a prisoner between them. Iron manacles bound the captive's wrists and ankles. He sagged between the acolytes as though unable to stand under his own power. His bare feet dragged across the floor, clearing a path through the rose petals. His head drooped toward the floor, hiding his face, but Riese recognized his sandy brown hair and leather vest at once.

Micah!

She clasped a hand over her mouth, but not before a horrified gasp betrayed her. The gasp did not go unnoticed by her father, who scowled behind his beard. His eyes narrowed in suspicion. "What is this?" he demanded. "Who is this boy?"

"A spy, Your Majesty," Herrick explained. "Our Huntsmen caught him attempting to cross the border." He reached beneath his dark green jacket and drew out a handful of maps and sketches. "Incriminating maps and notes were found on his person."

The crowd reacted with shock and anger. Hostile eyes

glared at the prisoner. Surly muttering quickly escalated into heated outbursts.

"Traitor!"

"Nixian filth!"

"Hanging is too good for him!"

"Silence!" The queen held up her hand to quiet the room. She peered gravely at Herrick and his prisoner. "Is this true, Magister? Is the boy's guilt certain?"

"Beyond a doubt." Herrick seized a handful of Micah's hair and yanked his head up so that his face could be seen. "He confessed all when put to the question."

Of course he did, Riese thought, sickened. Micah's battered face bore witness to a brutal interrogation. A black eye was swollen shut. His lip was split. Purple bruises discolored his jaw. Dried brown stains caked his clothing. She bit down on her knuckles to keep from crying out. Memories of Micah's handsome face, grinning at her beneath the waterfall, tore at her heart. *What have they done to you?*

His one good eye found her, then quickly looked away. He stared bleakly at the floor, unwilling or unable to speak in his own defense.

"Justice demands that he be put to death," Herrick suggested. "But that privilege belongs to you, Your Majesties."

Death?

Riese bit her tongue. Once perhaps she would have spoken out immediately, no matter who was listening, but she had learned that a princess could not always act without thinking. Although she could not bear to see Micah in chains like this, she somehow kept from crying out in protest.

Instead she looked up at her parents and whispered

to them, too quietly for anyone beyond the dais to hear. "Mother, Father, please. I must to speak to you in private. This is wrong."

Ulric eyed the prisoner suspiciously. Kara looked concerned.

"Perhaps we should discuss this later," the queen replied in a low voice. "Now is not the time."

"Please, Mother." Riese could not risk letting Micah out of her sight. Who knew what might happen to him before she could stop it. "Don't let them take him away. Not before you hear me."

Perhaps it was the urgency of her tone, or simply the fact that Riese was behaving like a princess by being properly discreet, but her mother granted her petition. "Very well," Kara said before raising her voice to address the assemblage. "Friends and loyal subjects, let not this ugly business intrude on your celebrations. Please enjoy yourselves while the king and I deal with this matter. We will return shortly."

Ulric barked at his guards. "Bring the prisoner."

Riese glimpsed Mimir looking on as the royal family exited the dais. He appeared troubled. Had he recognized Micah from that night in her room?

Probably.

They retreated to a private chamber adjoining the throne room. The guards dragged Micah roughly into the room. He put up no resistance. Herrick stood watch over his prisoner, while Ulric dismissed the guards. "Stand by outside," the king instructed them. "I will call you if this beaten cur misbehaves."

As usual Amara took the liberty of accompanying the

royals. "What now, Cousin?" she asked Riese, sounding both scandalized and disappointed. "Is there no end to your surprises?"

"Must she be here?" Riese protested. "This does not concern her."

"Amara is a trusted member of this family," the queen said, "who stood by us staunchly during the late crisis. She has never abused our trust . . . unlike others I could name."

Riese resented the way Amara had wormed her way into their family circle, practically replacing Riese in her mother's affections, but decided now was not the time to fight that battle. This was about Micah, not Amara. *I need to stay focused,* she thought. *This will be hard enough without raising a whole other issue.*

She was on shaky ground as it was.

"What is this about, Riese?" her mother asked.

"I'm sorry, Mother, Father, but I had to talk to you." She pointed at Micah. "You can't execute him. It isn't right."

Micah lifted his head.

"Valka," he whispered hoarsely. "I'm so sorry . . . "

She longed to go to him but thought better of it. She needed to make her parents see reason first.

"This is him, isn't it?" Ulric growled. "The boy you spoke of?" He glared at Micah, contempt dripping from his voice. "The spy."

"His name is Micah," she said. "And he's the one who warned us of the sneak attack on the palace, remember? He saved us all!"

"Only after spying on your defenses in the first place," Herrick pointed out. "That he later admitted his perfidy does not excuse the fact that he placed all of Asgard in danger, and had the audacity to involve the princess herself in his espionage."

"That wasn't his fault!" Riese protested. "He didn't even know who I was. Not at first."

This was not the first time she had tried to explain how she had come to know Micah. After returning from the war, she had been obliged to give her parents a carefully edited account of her secret friendship with Micah, leaving Arkin and Mimir out of the story, and omitting certain embarrassing details. As expected, she had endured many a stern lecture, but her role in saving Asgard had gone a long way toward mitigating her parents' disapproval, as had the general jubilation over the end of the war. Indeed, everyone had seemed eager to put the events of this dreadful summer behind them.

Until now.

"That matters not," Ulric said coldly. The scar on his forehead stood out against his flushed complexion. "We have seen too much evil and suffering, lost too many loyal warriors and comrades, to ever forgive a creature of Nixe, let alone one who trifled with my daughter's affections." His face and voice were as hard as granite. "Do not forget. We offered Nixe charity before . . . and were repaid in blood!"

Riese's heart sank. War had hardened her father, even more than she had realized before.

"The Nixians must never again confuse your mercy with weakness," Herrick advised, feeding the king's righteous ire. "They must suffer the consequences of their crimes. Without exception."

Riese saw there was no tenderness to be found in her father, not where the enemy was concerned. "Please, Mother," she pleaded. "Micah is an orphan, with a sister who depends on him. He was forced to spy on us. Banish him from the kingdom if you must, but spare his life . . . for my sake."

Kara shook her head. "I am sorry, Riese, but you saw how the court demanded justice before. Our people expect us to punish our enemies, not pardon those who took part in the recent atrocities." She clearly believed she was doing the right thing for Eleysia, if not for her daughter. "Sacrifices must be made for the greater good. Someday, when you sit upon my throne, you will understand."

"Never!" Riese said bitterly. She could not believe that her own mother could be so heartless and unforgiving. Hot tears streamed down her cheeks. "No throne is worth this!"

"It pains me that you feel that way," Kara said, "but the boy's fate is sealed." She summoned the palace guards. "Take the prisoner away. He is to be beheaded at dawn."

Micah slumped between his captors. He did not protest his sentence.

"A hard choice, Your Majesty." Herrick released Micah's hair, letting his chin drop onto his chest. His acolytes turned the captive over to the guards. "But a wise one. Let this corrupted youth serve as an example to any who might plot against Eleysia again."

"So be it," her father said harshly. "Death to the spy."

Riese ran weeping from the room.

CHAPTER TWENTY-FIVE

Riese had never visited the dungeons before.

She descended a narrow spiral staircase whose rough stone walls were devoid of plaster or ornamentation. The dungeons were located deep beneath the castle, below even the cellars and storerooms. Water trickled down the walls. Was it just her nerves, or did the very air seem to grow colder and clammier with every step? Dawn was still hours away, and torches sputtered in their sconces.

Micah had only a few hours left to live.

"Halt!" a gruff voice called out as she reached the bottom of the stairs. "Who goes there?"

To her relief only a solitary jailor guarded the dungeons at this late hour. The war had severely depleted the palace guard, causing them to be stretched thin. Clad in furs, the guard sat at a low table before a long dimly lit corridor of cells. He lurched to his feet at the sound of her footsteps. He seized the pike.

"Name yourself!"

"The princess Riese," she answered, stepping into the candlelight. "Come to visit the prisoner." She held out a flagon of wine for the guard's inspection. "I bring refreshment to ease his final hours."

She moved to enter the corridor, but the guard blocked her path. "Forgive me, Your Highness, but I cannot allow you to pass. The king and queen expressly forbid it."

Riese had feared as much. "I am your future queen," she reminded him. "I command you to step aside."

"I am sorry, Your Highness." The man shifted uncomfortably but did not get out of the way. Keys jangled on his belt. "But I have my orders."

She regretted putting him in this spot, but Micah's life was more important. "Please, I won't tell anyone. I swear it."

"I will give the prisoner the drink," he volunteered, hoping to placate her. "But you cannot go farther." He rested the end of his pike upon the floor. "Perhaps if you speak with your noble parents . . ."

Riese did not surrender the flagon. "Wait!" she said abruptly. "Do you hear that?"

A clattering noise came from the top of the stairs, beyond the bend of the wall. The whirring of metal gears echoed off the damp stones.

"No!" She backed away fearfully. "The Nixians! They're trying to kill me again!"

"Keep back, Princess!" The jailor rushed past her, pike in hand. He had doubtless heard of the clockwork scorpion that had invaded her bedchamber weeks before. "No cowardly mechanism will harm you!"

He charged up the steps, leaving her alone for the moment. Her frightened expression was replaced by a smirk.

Thank you, Arkin, she thought, grateful for the distraction. *That was perfect timing.*

Wasting no time, she hurried past the guard station into the murky corridor beyond. Rows of empty cells lined the hallway on both sides. Rusty metal bars waited to cage any prisoners. There were no torches upon the walls. The only light came from the jailor's candle.

"Micah!" she whispered urgently. Her eyes searched one cell after another. "It's me! Where are you?"

"Valka?" Someone stirred in a cell up ahead. "Riese?"

She raced down the hall and peered through the bars. Micah scrambled to his feet, wincing from injuries. His cell was even worse than she had imagined. Mold coated the unyielding stone walls. Dirty straw, strewn upon the floor, was all he had to sleep on. Cobwebs hung from the corners. A bucket of waste offended her nostrils.

Micah gripped the bars, his bruised face only inches away from her. Darkness concealed the worst of his injuries. In the gloomy shadows he looked slightly better than he had in the throne room, which wasn't saying much. "What are you doing here?" he asked. "Is this wise?"

"Not in the slightest." She put down the flagon and tried the door, only to find that it required a key to unlock it. She withdrew from her sleeve the dagger she had "borrowed" from Captain Egil during the riot. She slipped it between the bars to Micah. "Listen quickly. Here's what we need to do. . . ."

She had barely finished explaining her plan when the jailor came stomping back down the stairs. Arkin's windup soldier was clutched in one hand. Finding Riese missing, he rushed anxiously down the corridor. "Princess?" he called out anxiously. "You shouldn't be here!"

He froze in shock, silhouetted within the arched

entrance to the hallway. The tin soldier slipped from his fingers. His eyes bulged at the sight of the princess being held hostage by his prisoner. Reaching through the bars, Micah had one arm around Riese's waist and a knife at her throat. Her back was pressed tight against the bars.

"I'm so sorry," she whimpered, sounding scared and contrite. With any luck the guard would be too alarmed to wonder where the dagger had come from. "I should have listened to you, but—"

"Shut up!" Micah sneered at the jailor. "Drop the pike . . . or Eleysia will need a new heir."

The weapon clattered to the floor.

"Good," Micah said. "Now unlock the door."

"Nixian bastard," the guard cursed, but he did as he was told. Rusty hinges creaked as the door swung open. Still holding the knife to Riese's throat, Micah slid out into the hall.

"Give her the keys," he ordered, "then turn around and face the wall."

The guard hesitated, clearly unwilling to let the princess out of his sight.

"Do it!" Micah snarled.

Riese added a sob for emphasis.

Muttering darkly, the jailor handed the keys to Riese, who claimed them with trembling hands. It wasn't hard to be pretend to be frightened. Everything about what she was doing was terrifying—including the consequences if she and Micah were caught.

"The wall," Micah reminded the man.

The guard rotated away from them. Micah waited until the jailor's back was turned before letting go of Riese. She snatched the flagon from the ground and cracked it over the guard's skull. He groaned and dropped to the floor.

"Sorry about that," she murmured. "But my friend's head is at stake."

"And I'd like to hang on to it," Micah added, "no matter how sore it is." Thrusting the dagger into his belt, he claimed the guard's pike as well. "Now what?"

"Follow me," she instructed.

Searching through the palace library, Arkin had found a shortcut to the secret tunnel. Taking Micah's hand, Riese guided him through a maze of dusty cellars to a locked oak door. She fumbled with the jailor's keys until she found the one that fit. The door creaked open, revealing the stairs to the cistern. A familiar dank odor wafted up from below.

Micah leaned upon the pike. He looked weak.

"Are you up for another hike?" she asked.

"To save my head? Count on it."

Despite his injuries from the brutal interrogation, he kept up with her as they made their way through the cistern until they reached the sturdy door that now sealed the passage. After some deliberation, her parents had installed the door so that the tunnel could still be used as an escape route during a siege. Straining, Riese and Micah lifted the heavy steel bolt holding the door shut from the inside and fled the castle. The sky was still dark when they emerged from the drainage pipe, muddy and covered with goo. Riese had stowed fresh clothes and supplies at the mouth of the tunnel. Micah turned his back as she quickly changed into her leather hunting gear and trousers. She reclaimed her baton and goggles.

Frantic shouts came from atop the palace's outer walls. A bell tolled. Horns sounded. Riese guessed that Micah's escape—and her "abduction"—had been discovered. Swarms of soldiers would soon be searching for them.

"We can't stay here," she said. "The entire kingdom will be looking for us."

"You don't have to come with me," he said. "You've already done enough. More than I deserve."

She wasn't ready to say good-bye yet. "You saved my life, remember? At least three times. I figure I still owe you a save or two. Besides," she added with a shrug, "you may still need a 'hostage' again before tonight is over."

"Can't argue with that. Although, you know, I'm not sure why everyone is so worked up about a mere serving girl."

His impish smile brought a flood of emotion. It seemed the Sect had not beaten the old Micah out of him. Trying not to let her feelings show, Riese punched him in the shoulder.

"Don't push your luck," she said. "Let's get going."

They couldn't risk heading down into the city, so they took the path up to the rock rings instead. If Micah could make it across the mountains, he might have a chance of slipping out of Asgard undetected. Riese wasn't sure how far she intended to go with him.

Maybe until she knew he was safe?

"This is good," he said as they approached the ledge. He used the stolen pike as a walking stick. "I used to have some provisions hidden here. Maybe they're still intact?"

"Maybe."

Riese's eyes grew moist. She had not been back to the rock ring since the night of the storm. So much had happened since then. Those idyllic nights under the moon would never come again. The world had changed too much.

She couldn't pretend she was just an ordinary girl anymore.

They followed the path onto the ledge. Two fallen monoliths now stretched below the standing stones. If not for Micah, she might have been crushed beneath one of them. Down below, burning lanterns and torches lit the palace. Distant horns still sounded the alarm. Bells tolled. Soldiers on horseback poured from the gates. Riese wondered if her mother and father were among them.

"That's far enough!" a harsh voice declared. "Give us the princess!"

Two Huntsmen stepped out from behind the rock ring. One held a hatchet, the other a hand scythe. "You were right," one congratulated his partner. "They did come back here."

Riese cursed herself for their carelessness. They should have realized the Sect would know all about this place, especially after interrogating Micah. Returning to the falls had been more sentimental than smart. *We should have known better.*

The mercenaries fanned out to block the paths leading away from the falls. "Shall we take him alive?" one asked.

"Too much trouble," the other declared. "They're just going to behead him anyway. We might as well save them the trouble."

The first man chuckled. "Maybe we should charge extra for the service."

Riese took their bloodthirsty banter seriously. Micah was in no shape, she realized, to fight the bounty hunters. She saw only one hope of saving him.

"Thank the Fates you found me!" Breaking away from Micah, she ran eagerly toward the Huntsmen. She kept her baton tucked against her arm, out of sight. "I was so frightened!"

"Don't worry, pretty princess," the nearest Huntsman said. "You'll be home soon enough."

The dark of night helped conceal her intentions. Riese pushed the button that caused her baton to snap to its full length. She swung it at the Huntsman's head, decking him before he even knew what she was up to. The other man was too far away to strike at, so she flung the staff like a spear instead. Startled, he ducked out of the way. The staff went flying over the falls and crashed loudly upon the rocks below.

"Backstabbing slut!" the Huntsman spat. "I'll take you back to your family in pieces!"

He charged at Riese, his axe held high. She looked around for some way to defend herself. Maybe the other Huntsman's scythe? Could she possibly grab it in time?

"Leave her alone!"

Micah slammed into the man, knocking him over the edge of the falls. The Huntsman shrieked in terror as he plummeted to his death. Riese heard his body smash upon the rocks. His brimmed hat drifted away on the wind.

"Micah!"

Momentum had carried him halfway over the falls as well. He tottered unsteadily on the brink, waving his arms to keep from losing his balance. He looked only seconds away from falling.

"Hold on!" Riese sprinted across the ledge. She grabbed

his arm and pulled him to safety. They collapsed together onto the ground. She hugged him tightly and kissed him.

That was too close! How many times did she have to almost lose him?

The kiss was not nearly long enough. She wished she could lie in his embrace forever, but it wasn't safe. The unconscious Huntsman would be waking soon, and only the Fates knew who else might come looking for them. She reluctantly pulled away from him.

"Are we even now?" he asked. "I've lost count."

"Me too," she admitted.

Rising to their feet, they hastily checked on the downed Huntsman, who was still out cold. She took a moment to bind his wrists with his belt, while Micah gagged the man with his own woolen scarf. This was going to be difficult to explain later, but she would have to ford those rapids when she came to them. If she was lucky, nobody would take the word of a hired cutthroat over that of a princess of the realm. Rank did have its advantages at times.

Micah, on the other hand, had no such protection.

"You need to run from here," she urged him, "before anyone else finds us." Her words caught in her throat. "This place isn't safe anymore."

Once the falls had been their private refuge. But those days were over.

"Come with me," he said. "I need to find my sister, but we can do that together."

Riese shook her head. It was tempting, but, no. "I'm not Valka, not really. I can't just run away."

Not long ago she would have liked nothing more than

to flee her royal duties and responsibilities for good, and simply let her parents rule Eleysia as they had always done. But her faith in their infallibility had been shaken by this turbulent summer. She still loved her parents, but she saw now that they had their own dangerous blind spots and weaknesses. She could not just abandon them. Somebody had to keep an eye on the Sect and look after Arkin.

Her family needed her. Eleysia needed her.

"You have your sister," she said sadly, "and I have my kingdom. That's who we are and why we can't be together."

He kicked angrily at the ground. "It's not fair."

"I know," she said. "But as long as I'm with you, they'll never stop looking for us. You'll be safer without me."

"But not happier."

The Huntsman stirred restlessly nearby. There was no time for a long good-bye.

"Go," she insisted. They both knew he could never return to Eleysia—on pain of death. "Find your sister." She took off her goggles. "Here, take these back. You may need them."

"Keep them," he told her. "To remember me by."

There was nothing more to say. She watched silently as he slipped away into the hills overlooking the ledge. Within minutes he had vanished into the wilderness.

"Good-bye," she whispered. "Forever."

She held the goggles close to her heart.

CHAPTER TWENTY-SIX

FOR GENERATIONS THE MARBLE SUNDIAL HAD adorned the garden outside the parlor. Riese recalled glancing at it after rushing home from her boar hunt so many weeks ago, before the war. But mere tradition had not protected the ancient timepiece from the winds of change sweeping over her kingdom. The sundial had been uprooted and banished to some musty cellar beneath the castle. In its place was the imposing mechanical clock Herrick had presented to the queen at their first meeting. Now that the war was over, it had finally found a home—right where the sundial used to be.

"You will find," Herrick said, "that this mechanism keeps much better time than the obsolete relic you had here before. And, of course, it will operate regardless of the weather or the time of day. Its hands will keep turning even in the dead of night."

A smattering of applause greeted his declaration. An assemblage of honored guests had gathered in the garden to witness the installation of the clock. Its conspicuous location testified to the Sect's growing influence at court. Riese gathered that her parents had deliberately chosen this spot to further honor the alliance that had saved the kingdom.

"Quite remarkable," the queen said. "The Sect's ingenuity never fails to impress."

"Very clever," Ulric agreed.

"Tick, tick," Arkin chimed in. "Tick, tick."

Riese didn't like it. Things were changing too fast. She couldn't help thinking that something precious was being lost.

Along with some people.

Her eyes scanned the faces admiring the clock. Conspicuously missing was Mimir, who had abruptly retired to a small library in a distant province. Although her parents would not admit it, she rather suspected that the Sect had played some part in putting the venerable scholar out to pasture; Mimir's uneasiness regarding the Sect may not have gone unnoticed by Herrick. Or perhaps Mimir simply wanted no part of this new alliance?

He was not the only one. Glancing around, Riese noted that some of the applause seemed halfhearted at best. She wondered how many nobles and generals had seen their own positions suffer relative to the Sect, or else feared defying Herrick. The enigmatic magister was a fixture at court now. He even had his own chambers in the palace.

The clock struck noon. A bell chimed twelve times. Hunter and wolf chased each other around the track beneath the clock faces.

"How marvelous!" Amara exclaimed, clapping more loudly than anyone else. The finest furs trimmed an elegant silk gown. Silver and platinum glittered on her hands, ears, and bosom. The war had filled her coffers, increasing her power and influence at the expense of the royal treasury. She laughed in delight. "Don't you think so, Riese?"

"I suppose," Riese allowed. To be honest the automata reminded her too much of that clockwork scorpion. "But I miss the sundial."

"Now, now," Amara chided her. "We mustn't cling to the past." She turned to the acolyte standing at her side. "Isn't that so, Trennan?"

The acolyte was a newcomer to the court. Unlike Herrick, he went unmasked save for a tinted brass monocle over one eye. Short blond hair covered his scalp. He had a bland, unassuming manner. "As you say, my lady."

"Have you met Trennan?" Amara asked Riese. "The Sect has assigned him to my service. He'll be accompanying me back to Hariasa. It seems the Sect has many intriguing ideas on how to improve the efficiency of our factories and workshops."

He bowed his head in deference. "I look forward to serving you, my lady."

"Oh, I'm certain you will prove quite indispensable," Amara said confidently. "The Sect's ingenuity can only make Hariasa all the more prosperous. And the rest of the Eleysia too, of course."

Riese didn't care what went on in Hariasa. Just as long as Amara was finally leaving.

Chances are, I won't see her again until my coronation, Riese thought. Thankfully that was still months away.

"Excuse me," Riese said, taking her leave of Amara. "I'll let you two confer in private. A pleasure to meet you, Trennan."

"Thank you, Your Highness. May the Goddess watch over you."

Not if I can help it, she thought.

The parlor doors called out to her. Had she made enough of an appearance at this event? Gazing across the garden, she saw that Arkin and her parents were still preoccupied with admiring the new clock. They didn't look like they needed her at the moment, and frankly she was in no mood to make small talk and coo over the Sect's latest intrusion. She quietly made her way toward the door.

"Leaving so soon, Your Highness?"

Herrick stepped between her and the parlor. *Hel,* Riese thought. She had hoped to escape unnoticed.

"I think so," she said politely. "I'm a bit weary."

"Small wonder after your recent ordeals." He made no move to let her by. "It is fortunate that you somehow escaped your captor unscathed. Surely the Goddess had you in her care."

"Perhaps," she said vaguely. "That whole night is a blur. All I remember is running for my life."

This was not a discussion she was eager to have with anyone, let alone Herrick of all people. To her surprise and considerable relief, the surviving Huntsman had kept silent about his defeat at her hands, perhaps not wanting to accuse the future queen of treason, but how much did Herrick know about what had truly happened? Was it possible the Huntsman had reported back to him?

"A pity the spy managed to escape," Herrick continued. "I remain puzzled as to how he managed to obtain the dagger he employed to capture you."

"Yes," she said tersely. "That *is* a mystery."

"One of my men is missing as well." Inscrutable lenses examined her. "I don't suppose you know what might have become of him?"

Riese stiffened. "I'm sure I have no idea."

"Of course not." His hood remained in place, but his skepticism was plain. "A word of advice, Princess. You should choose your allies more carefully."

They were beyond casual conversation now. She stared back at him, refusing to be intimidated. "And my battles?"

"Those especially." He leaned toward her, invading her space. His icy voice abandoned all but the slightest trace of diplomatic evasion. "It would be better for all concerned if you welcomed the Sect as your royal parents have. You don't want us as an enemy."

Too late, Riese thought. She could not forget how the Sect had tortured Micah and almost cost him his head. Her parents might be blind to the Sect's ambitions, but she could not afford to be. She was the future of Eleysia, after all.

Whether the Sect liked it or not.

"Do not forget," she warned him in turn, "you are still guests at this court."

"Perhaps, but I do not see us leaving soon."

"Nor am I." She pushed past him. "Take care, Magister. This is not over."

"No," he agreed. "It is not."

A cloud passed over the sun, and the temperature dropped in the garden. Riese shivered. The long, bloody summer was almost over, she realized.

Fall was coming.

CHAPTER TWENTY-SEVEN

Now

THE SUN ROSE ON VALGARD.

Despite his threat to attack at dawn, the magister waited until the streets were fully lit before returning to the besieged observatory. The day was clear and sunny, with nary a cloud in the sky. It would have been a glorious morning, Riese observed, if not for the ultimatum hanging over them all.

"Hear me!" the magister commanded from safely out of range of the balcony and its hazards. A brass megaphone amplified his voice. "This is your last chance. Turn over the girl Usla, and we may show mercy. Continue to defy us and you will surely share her fate!"

"As though I would stake my life on your promises!" Horst scoffed. Along with Riese and Usla, he glared down at their enemies from the balcony. "I'll take my chances here, thank you very much."

Riese shared his skepticism. She didn't believe the Sect's offer of leniency for a minute. Mercy was not in their scriptures.

She warmed her palms around a mug of hot tea. With

luck the spiced brew would help keep her alert. None of them had slept a wink last night. She peered at the trio of Huntsmen flanking the magister. If they were also weary from standing watch over the tower all night, they didn't show it. The scarfed mercenaries looked just as implacable as ever.

"I'm so sorry," Usla said. The borrowed cloak was still draped over her shoulders. She hugged herself to keep warm. "I never meant for anyone else to get hurt."

Riese wondered if the girl blamed herself for her parents' deaths as well. "It's not your fault," she told Usla firmly. "Blame the Sect. They're the ones who brought their evil to your home."

Usla nodded. Riese hoped she understood.

"My patience is at an end!" the magister declared. "What is your decision?"

Horst replied by taking a stinking chamber pot, practically overflowing with filth, and dumping it onto the cobblestones in front of the tower's barred entrance. The magister and his human hounds stood too far back to be splattered by the pot's fetid contents, but the astrologer's message was both clear and pungent.

"Very well." The Magister's leather mask hid any disgust he might have felt. "Let it be noted that the Sect, in its infinite compassion, offered you a chance to repent. But you have condemned yourselves."

He raised his arm as though to signal an attack. Riese expected the Huntsmen to cautiously approach the door with their hatchets, but instead they glanced behind them. Had the magister summoned reinforcements? Riese had feared as much. She waited to see what else was arrayed against them. Yet more Huntsmen, perhaps?

The rumble of wheels, rolling ponderously over the paving stones, reached her ears before she spied anything, but then an immense machine came into view. A thick wooden log, at least three yards long and a foot in diameter, rested atop a forged metal chassis. The head of the log was encased in iron, with the mark of the Sect embossed upon the metal. A brass steam engine was located above the rear axles, behind the log. Puffs of white vapor whistled from pipes and valves. Connecting rods and cylinders waited to transfer power from the boiler to the engine. Gauges and stopcocks adorned the apparatus. Straining townspeople, whom Riese assumed had been conscripted by the magister, pushed and pulled the massive construct across the square toward the observatory. Riese spotted Olav among them, gasping from his exertions. She had little sympathy for the aged guard. For all she knew, he was the one who had betrayed them to the Sect in the first place.

At the very least he could have warned us to stay out of Valgard.

"By the stars," Horst rasped. "That looks to be a most formidable machine."

Riese agreed. She knew a battering ram when she saw one.

And steam-powered to boot!

She wondered where it had come from. Had it been already here in Valgard, stored away in a stable or warehouse, or had the magister arranged to have it brought to the town overnight? Probably the latter, she guessed. No wonder he had waited until now to commence his assault on the observatory.

"Position the Hammer," he commanded. "Justice waits to be served."

The ram was rolled into place before the front door of the tower. Horst reached for another bucket of nails, but the magister had prepared for that tactic. Shield-bearers defended the ram and its operator from attacks from above. A Huntsman opened fired on the balcony with a crossbow, driving the tower's defenders back. A steel-tipped bolt smacked into the railing only inches from Riese's fingers. A second bolt left a hairline crack in the glass dome behind her.

"Inside!" she ordered as they were forced to abandon the balcony. Riese slid the glass door shut. Sunlight filled the observatory, making it almost uncomfortably warm. The light spilled through the grated observation deck onto the orrery below. Another bolt smacked against the glass.

The magister had planned his assault well.

But she had not been idle either.

A steam whistle hooted. Riese heard the Hammer chug to life. A moment later the tower shuddered as the ram slammed into the door with earthshaking force. The bang rattled the metal globes in the orrery below. Usla gasped and placed a hand over her belly.

"Well, I can't fault their engineering," Horst said dryly. "More's the pity."

The ram smashed into the door again and again, like an enormous piston. Riese could not see the machine from within the dome, but she could readily imagine the metal cylinders expanding and contracting as they fed the engine's power to the ram.

Well-named, the Hammer made short work of the observatory's defenses. The heavy door bulged inward, even as the myriad locks and bolts strained to withstand the repeated blows. Oak planks splintered. Iron bands buckled. The bookcase-turned-barricade quivered with every strike. Only a few more impacts, Riese guessed, and the tower would be breached.

"It's time." She glanced up at the sky, shading her eyes against the golden sunlight pouring through the glass dome. She lowered her goggles and nodded at her unlikely allies. "Places."

She headed for the stairs, only to feel Usla's hand upon her arm. The girl looked up at her anxiously. "Be careful."

"I always am," Riese assured her. The reckless princess, who had once taken for granted the peace and safety of her kingdom, had died along with the rest of her family. The woman she had become had learned how to survive in a far more dangerous world.

And when to fight back.

She rushed down the rickety metal stairs, which rattled beneath her rapid descent. Horst and Usla remained upon the observation deck, watching intently. Riese's heart was pounding. Fear and anticipation sharpened her senses, temporarily banishing fatigue. What matter that she hadn't slept all night? Her mind and body were primed for battle.

Danger was the most powerful stimulant of all.

Even taking the steps two at a time, she barely made it down in time. No sooner had she set foot on the ground floor of the tower than the head of the ram broke through the door, which split right down the middle. With a thunderous crack the main wooden bolt snapped in half. Flying splinters made Riese grateful for her goggles. A broken lock landed at her feet.

"They're coming!" she shouted to her comrades. A waste of breath, really. There was no way they could have missed it. "Get ready for company!"

She drew her dagger.

Only the overturned bookcase barred the way now. Shoved forward by the force of the ram, it scraped across the floor. The Hammer withdrew, then surged forward again, colliding violently with the obstruction. The bookcase skidded across the floor, away from the entrance, which now lay open to the invaders.

So much for their barricade.

Riese braced herself for the onslaught. She backed up against the wall, out of the door's line of sight. It felt strange to be going into battle without Fenrir beside her. If only he'd been here, she could have used his loyal fangs and claws right now.

She wondered if she would ever see the wolf again.

The Hammer itself blocked the doorway now. Forced labor pulled it backward, leaving behind an open gap, through which a volley of crossbow bolts invaded the observatory. Riese flattened herself against the wall as random quarrels ricocheted off the orrery's suspended bronze globes. Through sheerest chance a deflected bolt bounced toward her face. Riese spun to one side, so that the missile struck the curved stone wall behind her instead. It landed by her feet, and she snatched it up from the floor. She tested its point, which was still sharp enough to pierce skin.

Perhaps she could return it to its sender?

The salvo of missiles provided cover for the three Huntsmen, who charged silently into the observatory in search of their prey. Three ruthless killers versus an old man, a pregnant teenage girl, and a nameless vagrant. Any sensible person would have said that the odds were in the mercenaries' favor.

Unless Riese did something to remedy the situation.

"Now!" she shouted, exposing her position. "Show them the light!"

A blinding glare greeted the Huntsmen as they came through the doorway. Caught by surprise, they threw up their hands to protect their eyes from the brilliant light, which was brighter than a desert sun. They cried out as a sudden, searing pain burned the uncovered portions of their faces. Exposed flesh turned red and raw.

"That'll teach you," Horst chortled. "Never underestimate the fury of the heavens!"

Up on the observation deck, visible through the metal grille that supported them, he and Usla whooped triumphantly. Along with Riese they had toiled all night to reposition the mirrors and lenses in the giant telescope so that it could focus the daylight into a weapon, just as Riese had used her goggles to light her campfire only yesterday. Working together the old man and the girl swiveled the telescope, which was now an enormous magnifying glass, to keep the scorching beam concentrated on the dazzled Huntsmen, who recoiled from the light like unclean spirits.

Serves them right, Riese thought. *They're the ones who kept us waiting until dawn.*

But the trick with the telescope wasn't the only surprise in store for the invaders. Dashing forward, Riese tripped a lever on the orrery, releasing a spring that set the model planets and moons in motion around the sun. Well-oiled gears turned, their metal teeth engaging, as the bronze spheres began to sweep through the air in complicated elliptical orbits. Moons circled planets. Planets circled the sun. Riese had spent hours trying to memorize the pattern.

Now to find out if all that effort had been worth it.

With her knife in her right hand and the captured crossbow bolt in her left, she sprinted across the room toward the invaders. Rotating metal rods threatened to trip her, but she deftly hurdled them even as she wove between the moving globes. The moon arced toward her head, but she saw it coming and ducked in time. The fist-size satellite whooshed past her, continuing its intricate dance with the sun, world, and other planets.

Riese didn't watch it go. She kept her eyes on the disoriented Huntsmen, who were still reeling from the glare when she fell upon them. Filters on her goggles protected her own eyes, giving her what she hoped was a crucial advantage.

Whirling like a dancer, she drove the point of the captured bolt into one Huntsman's gut with all her strength, while slashing at another with her dagger. The quarrel sank deep into the blinded mercenary's stomach, and she let go of the shaft, confident that she had struck a mortal blow. Her knife attack was less effective, however. Aiming for the throat, she'd missed and merely sliced across a shoulder instead, drawing blood and an angry curse. A crossbow dropped from his wounded arm. Riese kicked it away. He staggered backward, clutching his shoulder. Only paces away the gut-stabbed mercenary grunted in pain. Although he tried to yank the bolt from his stomach, it was too late. He crumpled to the floor, his twitching body falling across the mosaic constellations. A crimson puddle drowned the Lovers and the Raven.

So far so good, Riese thought. *But this isn't over yet.*

The third Huntsman, realizing his danger, swung a hatchet blindly at the commotion. Riese somersaulted out of the way, then thrust out her leg to trip the man. He stumbled forward toward his wounded comrade.

With a sickening thud his axe lodged itself in the other Huntsman's neck. Blood soaked through the thick wool scarf masking the casualty's face. A muffled rattle escaped his throat before he dropped to the floor. His body joined the other Huntsman's. The altered telescope cast a radiant spotlight upon the corpses, as though a particularly bloody melodrama were being performed upon a stage. Riese hoped to make it to the last act.

I can't let the Sect win, she thought. *Not again.*

Grasping his mistake, the remaining Huntsman bent to yank his axe free. He lowered the brim of his hat to shield his eyes and cautiously circled Riese, trying to keep his back to the blinding glare. Upon the observation deck Horst swung the telescope around to keep the Huntsman targeted by the light. Riese attempted to get the light behind her as well, in order to hide in its radiance, but the crafty Huntsman moved to block her. He swung his bloody hatchet at her. It whooshed through the air.

"I'll have your head," he snarled. "And the old man's, too."

Armed only with her knife Riese retreated into the orbits of the orrery, while keeping a close eye on her adversary. Although the battle was now one against one, they were hardly evenly matched. He had a hatchet. She had only a knife. What's more, he was taller, with a longer reach, which gave him an advantage in close quarters. She considered throwing the knife at him but quickly rejected the notion. A miss would leave her empty-handed.

She couldn't take that chance.

Instead she sought shelter within the orrery, taking care to keep the moving globes between her and the Huntsman, who pursued her into the model, despite its many moving parts. The orrery forced him to step cautiously, but he did not abandon the duel. Glaring at Riese from beneath the brim of his hat, he appeared intent on avenging his fallen comrades—and perhaps claiming a bounty on Usla's head? They stalked each other throughout the miniature solar system, striding between the heavenly bodies like warring gods or giants. Interlocking gears ticked away in the background. According to Horst the orrery would operate for several minutes before winding down. Riese wondered how much time she had left.

Not nearly enough, she guessed.

An opening gave the Huntsman a shot at Riese. He lunged forward, swinging his hatchet, but the world itself came to her rescue. A metal globe emblazoned with familiar oceans and continents swung between the Huntsman and Riese, obstructing his attack. The hatchet struck the sphere instead, gouging a dent in the heart of "Asgard." The bitter symbolism did not escape Riese. This was hardly the first time the Sect had injured the world.

Frustrated, the Huntsman swore behind his scarf.

Better luck next time, Riese thought. She moved in rhythm with the globe, like a second moon, while the Huntsman chased her in turn like a comet of ill omen. His hate-filled eyes were fixed on her with murderous intent. This was the part, she reflected, where Fenrir ought to spring from nowhere to rip the mercenary's throat out. Alas, the wolf was stuck prowling the woods outside town. She was on her own.

Or was she?

The Huntsman stiffened abruptly, as though struck from behind. Bloodshot eyes bulged from their sockets, then glazed over. The hatchet slipped from his fingers, and he toppled face-first onto the floor.

Usla stood behind him, clutching a bloody hatchet.

"That's for my mother and father," she said coldly. "And for my baby."

"Usla?" Riese gaped. Caught up in her deadly game of cat and mouse, she had not even seen the girl come down the stairs, let alone wrest the hatchet from one of the fallen Huntsmen. That had never been part of the plan, yet Riese could hardly begrudge the girl the kill. Heavens knew Usla had her own score to settle with the Sect and its creatures.

"Thank you." Riese stepped out from behind the dented globe. "Your parents taught you courage."

Usla stared at the hatchet, looking sick to her stomach. She flung it away. Her face was pale and slightly green. She swallowed hard. Riese guessed that Usla had never killed a man before. She silently cursed the Sect for creating a world in which such brutal milestones were necessary. Once upon a time Usla might have lived her entire life without blood on her hands.

Just like me.

A cry from above shattered her reverie.

"Watch out!" Horst shouted frantically. "He's coming for—"

His warning was cut short by a crossbow bolt that penetrated the metal grille to strike the astrologer in the chest. Gasping, he sagged against the telescope, which spun away from him. Denied its support, he dropped to his knees upon the observation deck.

"So falls another heretic," the magister announced, lowering a crossbow. He stood only a few yards away, just outside the orrery. His clockwork relics clicked mechanically. Internal gears whirred and hummed. "His false science was no protection against the truth."

"Horst!" Usla ran for the stairs, desperate to attend to the old man, who had been the only soul to grant her sanctuary in her own hometown. Fearing for his life, she gave no thought to her own safety. "Hold on! I'm coming!"

Riese saw the danger even if the girl did not. "Usla! Wait!"

"Apostate!" The magister moved with machinelike speed and precision to intercept her. His arm lashed out, clubbing her in the side of the head with the solid wooden stock of his crossbow. "Faithless slattern!"

The blow knocked Usla off her feet. She tumbled to the floor and did not get back up again. Blood trickled from her scalp. Dazed, she whimpered almost too softly to be heard. The magister nudged her sprawled form with the toe of his boot, perhaps to ascertain if she was only feigning unconsciousness.

"Pray to your heathen ancestors," he admonished her, "that the child you carry has not been harmed by your recklessness. The Sect does not forgive any damage to its property."

Riese's blood boiled. "Leave her alone, you monster!"

Her outburst got the magister's attention. Lacking another bolt to fire, he discarded the useless crossbow and turned toward Riese. Gears whirred mechanically as he drew a hand scythe from his belt. The polished silver crescent gleamed in the sunlight. Soulless glass lenses contemplated Riese, who felt like a specimen under a microscope. The fiendish magister reminded her far too much of Herrick.

"I don't know who you are, stranger, but you should not have involved yourself in this matter. This was between the girl and the Sect. It did not concern you."

That he did not recognize her came as a relief to Riese. Granted, there was no real reason to expect that he would; as far as the world was concerned, the princess was long dead. But it was comforting to know that her secret was still safe.

Even if her life and freedom were not.

"What do you intend to do with her?" Riese challenged the magister. "Take her back to that prison you call a convent?"

"And let her infect the other novitiates with her heresy?"

He chuckled coldly, in a manner that chilled Riese's blood. "Hardly. She will be kept in seclusion until she bears us the child that is our due, who will be raised as an acolyte from birth. Only then, once she has discharged her duty to the Sect, will she be made to serve in another manner—as an example of what befalls those who defy us."

Riese glared accusingly. "Like her parents?"

"Indeed. But in an even more public fashion."

"We'll see about that." She didn't know what sort of barbaric spectacle the magister had in mind, nor did she want to. As far as she was concerned, it was never going to happen. She nodded at the bodies littering the floor. "Looks to me like you're all out of Huntsmen, and I doubt that those cowed townspeople outside are in a hurry to take me on, not after what I did to your men."

"Perhaps," he conceded. "Whipped dogs usually run from a wolf." He shrugged his shoulders. "But I can deal with one foolhardy meddler myself."

He might be able to at that. Riese grimly assessed the situation. Horst shot, Usla unconscious, Fenrir nowhere near. She had no more allies and no place to run.

So what else was new?

Her gaze darted from side to side, tracking the dance of the spheres. A desperate strategy popped into her mind.

"Give my regards to your Goddess."

She hurled her knife at the magister. It lodged itself hilt-deep into his chest. Riese waited to see if he would fall, but no blood leaked from the wound. Metal gears scraped against the blade somewhere deep inside him. He plucked the knife from his chest and tossed it aside.

"An excellent toss, stranger. It might well have killed me . . . were I still nothing more than mortal flesh."

Damn it, Riese thought. *What kind of creature are you?*

She stumbled backward, retreating deeper into the mock solar system. The gilded sun rotated atop its perch at the center of the orrery. She put the large spiked globe between her and the magister. He chuckled dryly.

"You cannot hide behind this toy forever," he declared. "You are nothing but flesh and blood. Weak, fragile, corrupted. I have been perfected. I will not tire or relent in my holy cause until your blood has been spilled in honor of the Goddess."

Keep him talking, Riese thought. "That's what you think."

"I do not think. *I know.* The final battle is coming. Only the Goddess, and those who follow her, will endure in the kingdom of the Anointed One. The Sect is eternal."

"No," she said. "The world is."

Intent on Riese, he had lost track of the heavens. The model planet, swinging low in its orbit, collided into him from behind, knocking him forward onto the sun. Gilded spikes, radiating from the great orb, impaled him.

But would that be enough to kill him?

Gears gnashed inside him, grinding against the metal spikes. Blood seeped from whatever fleshly organs he had been unable to do without. He jerked spasmodically upon the spikes like a malfunctioning machine. Springs snapped. His lungs labored like a leaky bellows. His chin drooped onto his chest. The straining gears ground to a halt.

"Magister?"

No answer came from the skewered figure. He spoke

no more of prophecies or purification. One magister, it seemed, would not live to see Ragnarok.

"Good riddance," Riese said.

Gasping for breath, she wove her way out of the orrery and hurried to check on Usla. The girl lay sprawled upon the floor where the magister had struck her. She stirred and sat up slowly, clutching her head. One hand went to her belly.

"Wha–what happened?"

Her eyes widened at the sight of the magister impaled upon the sun.

"We did it," she realized. She gazed in wonder at Riese. "You did it."

An agonized groan came from above.

"Horst!" Riese remembered.

She dashed up the scaffolding with Usla close behind her. They found the old man lying upon the deck, the crossbow bolt still buried deep in his gut. Riese saw at once that the wound was mortal.

"No, not you, too," Usla sobbed. She dropped to her knees beside the dying astrologer and took his hand. "I'm so sorry. This is all my fault."

"Hush," he croaked. "I have no regrets." He gazed up at the sky through the glass roof of his observatory, as though seeing past a bright blue curtain to the stars beyond. "The heavens foretold it."

"Thank you," Riese told him. "For all you've done."

Was the old man proof that there was still hope for Eleysia, she wondered, or was he simply the last of a dying breed?

Like me.

"Do not bother to bury me," he told them. "Leave me here where I can watch the stars forever." Ragged coughs racked his trembling frame. "Flee this place while you still have a chance."

"We will," she promised. "Your sacrifice will not go to waste."

He nodded, content. His eyes found hers.

"The stars spoke of you," he murmured weakly. "You have many trials ahead, many roads to wander and difficult choices to make. But in the end you must find your own destiny . . . and take back your name."

He said nothing more. His eyes closed and his breathing slowed. Riese and Usla sat by him until he slipped away, then laid him out as he had instructed, lying on his back with his face to the sky. Riese opened his eyes before she left.

His final words followed her out of the tower.

What did the stars really know of her future?

CHAPTER TWENTY-EIGHT

"THANK THE ANCESTORS YOU'RE SAFE! We thought we had lost you forever!"

Usla's grandparents lived on a remote farm in the hills of Aesir, far from what passed for civilization under Amara. The modest homestead appeared both isolated and self-sufficient. Sleeping fields waited for spring. A clear brook wound past a small but sturdy farmhouse. A plump bulldog dozed upon the porch, and chickens clucked in the henhouse.

Usla would be safe here, Riese judged, and her baby as well.

She and Fenrir watched from the edge of the farm as the older couple embraced Usla for perhaps the fiftieth time. Overjoyed to be reunited with their stolen granddaughter, they could not stop marveling at her miraculous return, and seemed eager to meet the child she carried, regardless of its origins.

Riese allowed herself a rare smile. Happy endings were scarce in Eleysia these days. You had to enjoy them while they lasted.

Fenrir brushed against her. She scratched his head. His

ears and tail were relaxed, and his tongue lolled between his jaws. He made a happy noise.

"I know," she agreed. "It's a good day."

Usla finally broke away from her family. Smiling broadly, her face aglow, she joined Riese and Fenrir over by the road. She wore a clean, neatly pressed dress that had once belonged to her mother. Her blond curls were already beginning to grow back.

She handed Riese back her cloak. "Thanks again for the loan."

"My pleasure."

"You know," she reminded Riese, "you still haven't told me your name."

"Trust me, it's safer if you don't know."

Usla pouted. She patted her stomach, which had grown in the time it had taken them to travel from Valgard to here. She was showing more now.

"But how will I know what to name my baby?"

Riese had a ready answer.

"After your father if it's a boy. After your mother if it's a girl."

Riese was touched that Usla would even think of naming her child after her, but better that she honor her own parents than curse the baby with the name of a fallen princess. Perhaps someday it would be safe to name a child after Riese or her martyred kin, but who knew when that might be?

"Must you go?" Usla pleaded. "My grandparents would be happy to let you stay for as long as you like." She began to choke up. "We owe you so much."

Riese shook her head. She was touched, and tempted,

by the heartfelt offer but knew better than to accept their hospitality any longer. She could not afford to stay in one place too long. Her past might catch up with her, which could put Usla and her family at risk.

She couldn't take that chance.

"Thank you," she said. "Truly. But I have to keep moving on."

Usla fought back tears. "But where will you go?"

Riese wasn't sure. South probably, away from Asgard and the center of Amara's empire. With any luck the Sect had not yet consolidated its control in some of the outer provinces yet.

Or so she hoped.

"Heimdall, perhaps. Or Vidar."

Were those distant realms far enough away from her past? Deep in her heart she doubted it. What had Horst said again? That she had many trials and journeys ahead?

Riese still wasn't sure she believed in astrology, but that was one prophecy she could believe in.

"Be well," she told Usla. "And take care of your baby."

"I will," the girl promised. "Thanks to you."

Riese put her well-worn cloak back on. She turned away from the farm. Fenrir trotted beside her. Fresh food and water hung upon her belt, thanks to her new friends' generosity. A dusty road stretched before her.

Perhaps someday she would find her own way home.

Riese's journey continues at Syfy.com.